CHRISTOPHER BUSH
THE CASE OF THE CORNER COTTAGE

CHRISTOPHER BUSH was born Charlie Christmas Bush in Norfolk in 1885. His father was a farm labourer and his mother a milliner. In the early years of his childhood he lived with his aunt and uncle in London before returning to Norfolk aged seven, later winning a scholarship to Thetford Grammar School.

As an adult, Bush worked as a schoolmaster for 27 years, pausing only to fight in World War One, until retiring aged 46 in 1931 to be a full-time novelist. His first novel featuring the eccentric Ludovic Travers was published in 1926, and was followed by 62 additional Travers mysteries. These are all to be republished by Dean Street Press.

Christopher Bush fought again in World War Two, and was elected a member of the prestigious Detection Club. He died in 1973.

CHRISTOPHER BUSH

THE CASE OF THE CORNER COTTAGE

With an introduction
by Curtis Evans

DEAN STREET PRESS

INTRODUCTION

LABOURING UNDER SUSPICION
CHRISTOPHER BUSH'S CRIME FICTION IN THE POSTWAR YEARS, 1946-1952

SEVEN YEARS after the end of the Second World War, Christopher Bush published, under his "Michael Home" pseudonym, *The Brackenford Story* (1952), a mainstream novel in which a onetime country house boots boy, having risen for some time now to the lofty position of butler, laments the passing of traditional English rural life in the new postwar order, as signified by the years in which the left-wing Labour party held sway in the United Kingdom (1945-51). The jacket description of the American edition of *The Brackenford Story* reads, in part:

> *The Brackenford Story* is the story of a changing England. William saw the political enemies of the Hall gradually successful, whittling away the privilege it stood for. He saw squire begin to sell his land, the taxes increase, the great Hall sold, the beautiful trees along the drive cut down. And then with a Second World War, nationalization, rationing, pre-fabricated houses and queuing. William recalled with gratitude the kindness of his masters and their sense of responsibility for others. He saw that the bad old days of Toryism were not so bad after all. And he never lost his sense of outrage at the loss of something he felt was worthy of preservation.

A few years earlier, in July 1949, Anthony Boucher, the postwar dean of American crime fiction reviewers and a highly socially conscious liberal (small "l"), wrote with genial bemusement of the conservatism of British crime writers like Christopher Bush, in his review of Bush's latest crime opus, *The Case of the Housekeeper's Hair* (1948), making topical mention of a certain anti-Utopian novel penned by a distinguished dying tubercular English writer, which had just been published in June. "However much George Orwell, in *Nineteen Eighty-Four*, may foresee the forcible suppression of 'crimethink' under 'Ingsoc,' English socialism in 1949 takes pleasure in exporting mystery novels which disapprove of the Government and everything about it," Boucher observed with wry irony. "Like most of his colleagues, Christopher Bush is tartly critical of the regime; and an understanding of his unreconstructed Tory attitude is necessary if you're to hope to understand the motivations of this novel."

In both the detective novels and mainstream fiction which Christopher Bush published between 1946 and 1952, Bush, like many other distinguished mystery writers of the Golden Age generation (including Agatha Christie, Dorothy L. Sayers, Georgette Heyer, John Dickson Carr, Edmund Crispin, E.R. Punshon, Henry Wade and John Street), indeed was critical of the Labor government and increasingly nostalgic about a past that grew ever more golden in blissful, if perhaps partially chimerical, remembrance. Yet keeping Bush's distinct anti-left bias in mind, fans of classic crime fiction will find between the covers of the author's crime novels from these years--*The Case of the Second Chance* (1946), *The Case of the Curious Client* (1947), *The Case of the Haven Hotel* (1948), *The Case of the Housekeeper's Hair* (1948), *The Case of the Seven Bells* (1949), *The Case of the Purloined Picture* (1949), *The Case of the Happy Warrior* (1950), *The Case of the Corner Cottage* (1951), *The Case of the Fourth Detective* (1951) and *The Case of the Happy Medium* (1952)--fascinating observation of postwar social malaise in the age of British imperial decay and domestic austerity, as well as details about the rise of rationing, restriction and regulation, the burgeoning black market and, withal, that ubiquitous flashily-dressed criminal figure from Forties and Fifties Britain: the spiv (dealer in illicit goods).

Puzzle-minded mystery readers also will find some corking good no-nonsense "fair play" mysteries. "Few writers can equal Christopher Bush in handling a complicated plot while giving the reader a fair chance to solve the riddle himself," avowed the American blurb to *The Case of the Corner Cottage*, while Anthony Boucher applauded Bush's belated return to the American fiction lists after the Second World War, declaring: "It's good to have Mr.

Bush back after too long an absence . . . he presents the simon-pure jigsaw-puzzle detective story with unobtrusive competence." Concurrently in the United Kingdom, author Rupert Croft-Cooke, who himself wrote fine detective fiction as "Leo Bruce," pointedly praised Bush's "urbane and intelligent way of dealing with mystery which makes his work much more attractive than the stampeding sensationalism of some of his rivals."

In the pages which follow this introduction by all means attempt, dear readers, to match your keen wits against those of that ever-percipient gentleman sleuth, Ludovic Travers. Frequently in tandem with his old friend Superintendent George Wharton and with occasional input from his smart and sophisticated wife Bernice Haire, the former classical dancer, Ludo continues to hunt, in his capacity as a sort of special consultant to Scotland Yard (or "unofficial expert," as he puts it), more not-quite-canny-enough crooks. Additionally Ludo, a confirmed fan of American crime films like *The Blue Dahlia* (1946) and *Call Northside 777* (1948), comes to find himself in ownership of the Broad Street Detective Agency, perhaps the finest firm of private inquiry agents in London. In these old and new capacities in the postwar world Ludo confronts his greatest cornucopia of daring and dastardly crimes yet.

THE CASE OF THE CORNER COTTAGE

CHRISTOPHER BUSH'S evident fondness for American private investigator crime fiction has already been noted several times in prior introductions to reissued volumes in the Ludovic Travers mystery saga, most notably in the introduction to *The Case of the Magic Mirror* (1943), where Bush even paraphrases Raymond Chandler's famous line likening his sleuth to a "shop-soiled Galahad." However, the Ludo Travers detective novel which arguably most apes the style of American hard-boiled icons Dashiell Hammett and Raymond Chandler and their many Forties and Fifties imitators is *The Case of the Corner Cottage*, a milestone in the Travers saga that was first published in the United Kingdom in 1951 and the United States the next year. As noted by blogger Nick

Fuller, who praised *Cottage* as a neatly-constructed mystery with "plenty of interest" and "a neat twist at the end," the novel bears considerable resemblance to Hammett's classic path breaking crime tale *The Maltese Falcon*, with Ludo recalling Hammett's tough private investigator Sam Spade in resolutely determining to avenge, in his own proper and gentlemanly fashion of course, a most underhanded murder of a trusted friend and colleague. There is further resemblance to Hammett's masterwork in Bush's novel as well, but I will the leave readers to discover the rest for themselves.

In the first few pages of *The Case of the Corner Cottage* Ludo Travers divulges to us that his friend Bill Ellice, head of the Broad Street Detective Agency in which Ludo has taken an interest since the war, has recently passed away, the victim in August 1948 not of foul play but rather a sudden massive heart attack. Ludo thereupon purchased the Agency from Ellice's daughter, with the hope that his friend Superintendent Wharton of the Yard will join him when Wharton finally takes his long postponed retirement. In the meantime Bush has hired Wharton's former right-hand man, ex-Chief Inspector Jack Norris, a veteran of previous Bush novels like *The Case of the Tudor Queen* (1938) and *The Case of the April Fools* (1933), in the latter of which Norris plays a leading investigative role. As the new owner of the Agency, Ludo in September finds himself called upon to deal with the shocking murder of his leading operative, the dashingly handsome Godfrey Prial, the late Bill Ellice's "white-headed handful of a boy," a graduate of Felsted School and of Cambridge (like Ludo Travers) lately returned to the PI routine after having done intelligence work in the war.

Godfrey Prial has been found shot dead in his room at a hotel in the village of Shireton (where he was vacationing), after having sent Ludo a cryptic missive suggesting that he might have been on the spot in East Anglia doing some sort of freelance gumshoeing, as it were. Did the perspicacious Prial pick up some knowledge of illicit goings-on, Ludo begins to wonder, which made it too dangerous for someone to allow Prial to go on living? Unimpressed with the efforts of the local head copper, who with cruel aptness is named Inspector Poorly, Ludo and his men at the Agency begin investigating Prial's death themselves. Their attention soon focuses on recent events at a lonely homestead known as Copley's Corner, located in the East Anglian village of Stadmore. The cottage's most recent tenant had been elderly James Monaghan, a pious but eccentric adherent of the Catholic faith. On the night of Valentine's Day, 1948, Monaghan had been viciously set upon by a person or persons unknown and his cottage ransacked, with the result that the now thoroughly demented old man had to be placed in a mental asylum, where he spends his days mumbling and mindlessly fingering his rosary.

How these events relate to Prial's murder remains to be determined, but it seems like the local vicar, Reverend Charles Comfort, a penurious and unprepossessing individual, might know something about it, as might London businessman Henry Laver, flashy owner of an Amusement Arcade and a Palais de Danse (dance hall) in the London commuter belt community of Hadenham Green. ("Don't imagine anything idyllic, by the way, about Hadenham Green. . . . a hundred years ago it was a Green; now it's well inside the outer ring of [London] suburbs and redolent of fried fish.") Over time Ludo uncovers a multitude of clues, such as Monaghan's whistling mug with a view of the coastal resort of Skegness and Prial's pornographic antique snuffbox. There might as well be a fatal female or two in the offing in this splendidly devised tale of murder and mystery, which is riddled with devious and deadly twists and turns that would have done justice to the master himself, Dashiell Hammet.

Curtis Evans

PHASE I
THE PRIAL CASE

CHAPTER I
GODFREY PRIAL

THIS IS my own, private Case. No academic exercise, as it were, on behalf of a vague thing known as Justice. No Scotland Yard comfortably in support: no anything, except me and Hallows. Working out our own salvation, so to speak, or should I say somebody else's damnation. But it comes to the same thing.

It's funny that after more than twenty years—But that's beginning at the wrong end. I ought to start off with Godfrey Prial. But I'm not so sure. Maybe it should be myself. Not that it matters again provided the ultimate set-up comes through perfectly clear, and that I don't take too long over it.

Take myself then, since we've got to begin somewhere. For over twenty years I've been working, as a colleague of Superintendent George Wharton, on murder cases in which the Yard was concerned, and I'm likely even at this very moment to be asked to resume the partnership, and in spite of my connection with the Broad Street Detective Agency. But George Wharton would never be called in to handle such cases unless they were pretty complex, and complex murder cases don't eventuate all that often, and it's obvious then that my job at the Yard is pretty spasmodic, with long intervals in which to go about my own private occasions.

Luckily I have money of my own. I also have a loathing of idleness, and that is why of recent years I filled in the intervals between Yard jobs by giving a hand to an old friend, Bill Ellice, of the aforesaid Broad Street Detective Agency. From time to time when Bill was short-handed, I did various odds and ends in a friendly and generally unpaid sort of way, and if he had to be absent, I took charge.

During the last few years Bill was always talking of disposing of the business and I was hoping to acquire it as a kind of permanent refuge in times of idleness. George Wharton was thinking of coming into partnership with me on retirement, but then the Powers-That-Be, as he calls them, induced him to stay on and that left me just where I was before. It was a partnership with George that I wanted, not something of my own. Then in the first week of August, 1948, Bill more or less settled the problem for me, with a heart attack in the office.

Well, I had to decide quickly one way or the other. I talked the matter over with Bernice, my wife, and I bought the business from Bill's daughter, and always with the hope that George would eventually join me. It was a sound and profitable concern with a first-class reputation. We had contract work with two Insurance Companies, and various Town or Provincial stores, in addition to the usual routine run of enquiries. Bill, but for his groggy heart, would undoubtedly have taken on more operatives and moved to bigger premises, but I didn't want expansion. I wanted to feel my feet and know as much about the ramifications of that business as Bill had done. And I hadn't the least intention of slaving myself into the same sort of early grave as Bill had dug for himself. That was why I at once looked round for a kind of managing director, and I was lucky to get Jack Norris, an ex-Chief Inspector with whom I'd worked more than once at the Yard. All August then, and into September, Norris and I were busy as squirrels rummaging into every corner of that business, and at the end of it he felt safe sitting in Bill's old chair and I felt happy about seeing him there.

All I had to do from then on was to keep a general eye on things or give a decision where he preferred to have my views alongside his own. That also left me free if the Yard should still need me. So much for myself, then, and the Broad Street Detective Agency. To the outward eye Jack Norris was now that Agency and it was his name that appeared as Managing Director on the firm's cards and paper.

And so to Godfrey Prial. He was one of our key operatives and, now you have had briefly the background against which he worked, it is essential to see the man himself. At once I must admit that the sketch must necessarily be inadequate and possibly misleading. But it shall be as complete as I can make it, and because a knowledge of the man is vital if certain of his actions are to be deduced and explained. There will be nothing else from which you will be able to extort a clue or initiate a theory. What I shall try to do is to give you every facet of the man and leave your mind's eye to form and retain its own composite picture.

Throughout the war the Agency had been short-handed and forced to replace some of its mobilised men with what I might call the ex-copper, stereotyped, none too imaginative, easily recognisable but reasonably reliable kind—for lack, that is, of something just the opposite. Then towards the end of 1945 some of the old hands began drifting back. I was in the office with Bill on the morning when Godfrey Prial turned up again.

From time to time Bill had told me various things about him, and it hadn't been hard to gather that he was Bill's white-headed handful of a boy. I slowly began to realise that Prial—viewed by Bill in even the romantic light of absence—had been somewhat complex: an *enfant terrible* who had made Bill's heart miss beats: an easy-goer whose unorthodoxy and serene indifference could both charm and infuriate, and altogether a breezy freshness in the stuffiness of routine. But the fact remains that when Bill told me of some chance that Prial had taken or some dangerous short-cut or even some deliberate and risky flouting of the law, there would always at the end of the yarn be a smile that somehow indicated a posthumous and secret approval. And from what I gathered, it was Godfrey Prial who had always had the, what I might call, off-the-record jobs, where a man has to stand on his own two legs and rely on his own wits to find just why two and two don't happen to be making four. And none of those jobs had ever been anything like a flop or Bill would have made no bones about telling me so.

As I said, I was in the office that morning when Godfrey Prial walked in. He had joined up in 1940 and, thanks to his French and Italian, had been drafted to Intelligence. He had been parachuted once into Italy and twice into France, and after surviving all that, had had the bad luck in the spring of 1945 to have an encounter with a booby-trap. Though he had recovered from a nasty wound in the belly, the savour, as he wrote to Bill, had gone out of things, and he was going to wangle release on medical grounds.

I forget what I was talking over with Bill, but Bertha Munney, receptionist-secretary, suddenly buzzed through. I couldn't make out any words, but her usually pleasant official sort of voice was queerly hysterical. Bill grinned and turned to me as he replaced the receiver.

"Godfrey's back!"

That's what he intended to say. All he got out was the first syllable, for the door was open and Prial was making for him, a grin on his face and his hand well out.

"Bill, you old war horse! How's things?"

"Can't grumble," Bill said, and fairly wrung his hand. "What about you, Godfrey? Feeling fit again?"

"Fit as a flea. Never better. But don't give it out to the Press."

I had moved to the background and his eyes and mind had been so much on Bill that he hadn't really taken me in. When he did look my way, the grin slowly went and the eyes slightly narrowed. I think he was placing me as a client, and a not too usual one at that. Six-foot three of leanness, a head of none too tidy badgering hair, and huge horn-rims on a somewhat predatory beak make up an ensemble that isn't crowding the pavements.

"Ah!" said Bill. "Godfrey, this is Mr. Travers—Ludovic Travers. I told you about him in one or two letters which you've never dam-well answered."

I had a friendly smile.

"Nice to see you, Mr. Travers. How's the old brigand been treating you?"

"Not too harshly," I said. "Glad to see you looking so fit."

He was about six foot, leanish, and the tan of a summer convalescent camp still on him. His hair was black and his eyes a warm brown, and in a virile, immensely attractive sort of way he was as good-looking a chap as I'd seen for a mighty long time. His voice was charming too.

"Sit down," Bill said. "When're you coming back?"

"Monday?"

"Fine," Bill said, and tried a leg-pull. "Just about give you time to finish off your gratuity."

"There's still a bit in the old oak chest," Prial told him amusedly. "But what about a little drink, just to celebrate. You for it, Mr. Travers?"

"It's a proposition," I said.

"Produce the necessary then, Bill."

"Dammit, Godfrey," Bill told him just a bit testily, "you know as well as I do there's nothing kept in here."

"What about that bottle that's kept for the customers? You know, Mr. Travers; the ones who faint when they hear Bill's terms."

"The same old Godfrey," Bill told him a bit wryly. "I was hoping the war would have sobered you up. Sit down and don't be so dam-restless. Tell us all about Intelligence. Picked up anything, have you, that might be useful here?"

Prial handed his cigarette case round and began talking most amusedly about Intelligence, which had been superlative, he said, provided you worked on the basis that it hadn't got any. Take a certain little assignment he'd been given throughout most of the autumn of 1944—a sort of liaison job between American and British forces in a certain sector. What with the Americans being induced to assume that at some particular time he was with the British, and the British assuming he was with the Americans, he had managed to keep clear of both for what he called some very restful periods.

"Did I have a time!" He chuckled at the thought of it. "But it didn't last, though. Not that they rumbled me. It's risky work suspecting a real live major. I just got bored. Sort of gave myself up."

He gave a reminiscent, regretful shake of the head. "The wages of sin, though, Bill. If I'd held down that job I'd never have got a hunk of iron in my belly. Still, there we are. Monday, back to the old treadmill. Which reminds me, Bill. Before then, oughtn't we to talk business? Not that I'm worrying."

"We shan't quarrel," Bill told him soberly.

"No," he said, and smiled. "But seriously, Bill, what about a quick one at the Prince of Wales? Dammit, we ought to have some sort of celebration."

"Can't be done," Bill said. "There's someone due in a few minutes. Some other time, Godfrey. Next time you're in."

"The damn fellow never would take time off," Prial told me with a shake of the head. "What about you, Mr. Travers?"

"Give me five minutes and I'll be with you."

"Fine," he said, and was on his feet. "I've got a little job to do myself. Be with you in the saloon bar in five minutes. Be seeing you, Bill."

A cheery wave and he was gone. I heard Bertha's excited voice and knew she must have waylaid him in the corridor. Bill was still smiling wryly.

"A nice chap, that," I said. "I like him."

"One of the best," Bill told me. "Wish to God, though, he wouldn't talk to me as if I was a sort of dumb uncle. It makes it so dam-hard when I have to tick him off."

"He's fond of you, Bill," I said. "Just what are you proposing to pay him, by the way?"

My eyebrows shot up when he told me.

"He's worth it," he told me calmly. "Some time I'll let you see some of the old books. Work things out per operative and you'll see why he's paid even more than Hallows. By the way, don't take him for any kind of a fool. He's got a dam-fine brain behind that show he puts on. I wouldn't like to be up against him sometimes when he's on a job."

"I gathered that," I said. "But how's he go down here? Popular, is he?"

"Everyone likes him," Bill said. "He's a good mixer. Never top-heavy. Always the same as you saw him just now."

In the saloon bar of the Prince of Wales in Crayford Street, Godfrey Prial and I had a pint apiece. I expected him to order a short drink for himself, but he didn't. Like me, he preferred beer, and I gathered he wasn't anything of a drinker unless it was essential in the way of business, and even then he hadn't a lot of use for it. In the next three years I was to come into close contact with Godfrey Prial and somehow he always seemed to open up with me. He spent quite a few evenings at my flat and Bernice liked him as much as I did. Quite a lot of things I learned about him that even Bill never knew. Incidentally, if he hadn't been so fond of Bill, I know he'd have set up in the same line for himself.

He was thirty-five that first time I saw him, and looked younger. His parents had died when he was still at a preparatory school—a motor accident, I believe—and he had no other relatives. Trustees had looked after him and the small estate, and after Felsted he had gone to Cambridge. At twenty-one he had come into his own money, some twelve thousand pounds, and after due deliberations he decided to spend the bulk of it on what he called experience. The way he went to work was unique, and typical. Through one of his innumerable friends he bought a maisonette in St. John's Wood and had it converted into two miniature flats. One he let to some quite nice people and the other was on a four-year lease, since four years was the time he gave himself. Then he left five hundred pounds on deposit at the bank and proceeded, gracefully, as he put it, to spend the rest. But not on wine, women and song. What he did was travel all over the world. When just over three years had gone he was in Chicago, and down to his last hundred dollars.

"The schedule had gone all cock-eyed," he told me, "and I was damned if I was going to cable the bank to help me out. I might have had to in the long run if I hadn't had the devil's own luck. Happened to do a good turn for a chap who was a key operative for a Canadian Detective Agency. He wangled me a job. Boy, did we bluff! But it worked."

"You liked the job?"

"When I got the hang of it and I didn't need to bluff. A dam-fine life, one thing with another."

He held that job for some months, thanks probably to his useful French and his likeable personality, and he quit with excellent references. Then he came home. He took over that flat, and he still occupied it. But that Canadian job had found him his *métier*. The detection bug had bitten him, as he put it, and not long after getting home, some chance brought him Bill Ellice's way.

"All the same it was queer your choosing that particular line," I told him.

"I don't know," he said. "I came home with no influence. I might have been on my uppers before I found what people think a high-toned job. Besides, I'd got to like the game. I still like it, and Bill's a good sort. Few better. It's a man's job of work, and to hell with snobbery."

In all my experience I never ran across any man with such a natural flair. What he found boring was the sometimes necessary fill-in, routine stuff and being one of a crowd, but when Bill gave him an assignment that meant single handling and brains and maybe a bit of a risk, he was in his element. Ours is the only Agency that advertises consistently in the best papers, and all sorts of gasping fish come to the Agency net. Prial's speciality was the handling of nervous clients taken in by con. men or gypped at shady night-clubs or false-fronted manicure saloons, or lined up for blackmail with a female frame-up, maybe, in the background. There was a big black-market racket he uncovered, and he handled one arson job so as to bring a bonus from the company concerned, and altogether, as I'd seen from the books, he far more than earned his keep. In fact he was a money spinner. The ultra-cautious Bill would have turned down more than one job if he hadn't had Prial at his elbow.

His secret? Chiefly, I think, that flair I mentioned, though women always fell for him every time, what with his looks and that natural charm of manner, and the pleasant, cultured voice that reeked of baronial halls and a mightily expensive education. And, of course, he didn't look like a hack detective or flat-foot or copper's nark. Then there was that happy-go-lucky side of him, and the fact that he was a generous spender. Bill would shudder with horror before even casting an eye over one of his expense accounts, and yet I'm positive that Prial never made a penny out of one of them. In fact he lost money. Take that car which he bought out of his five hundred when he got back to England, and which he had had laid up during the war. He ran it for the firm and the mileage account couldn't have covered expenses, and yet he never took the matter up with Bill. Money as such, even other people's, didn't seem to matter. What did matter was doing a neat and successful job.

In the office he was not only popular but respected as a top-notcher at the game. When he wanted a man to work with him there was always competition. Everyone called him by his Christian name. Bertha Munney, a trouper with only the vestiges of glamour, was always in a girlish dither if he so much as looked into her office. If he dropped into the staff room when two or three men happened to be standing by, there was never a dull moment. He had a wonderful gift of mimicry and impersonation, acquired the hard way as necessary, or so he conscientiously believed, to the stock-in-trade of a man who took a pride in his kind of job. I once overheard him doing an imitation of myself that was devastating in its accuracy.

Just one other thing I should mention, and there I don't want him to be misunderstood. There was nothing pornographic about Godfrey Prial but some people might have thought so in the matter of that snuff-box. In his little flat he had one or two nice period pieces and he had an eye for what I might call the domestically beautiful. He bought that snuff box—a lacquered one with a contemporary miniature of Napoleon on the lid—from an antique dealer in Cambridge who was quite unaware of its peculiarity. Godfrey had discovered that quite by chance, and thereafter he always carried that box on him as a kind of mascot. It was one of his diversions, and expected of him, to offer it to any newcomer to the staff.

"A pinch of snuff?" he would say, and offer the opened box.

The victim would take a pinch gingerly, unless he was that rarity of a modern snuff taker. Godfrey would close it.

"Nice box, isn't it?"

The victim would take it and maybe admire Napoleon.

"Funny sort of feeling if you squeeze the ends rather hard."

Then of course the ends would be squeezed and from some deft concealment along the bottom there would slide forth another miniature: this time a very salacious one of a couple embracing. It always brought down the house.

I was consistently treated by him with a curious sort of respect, though I don't know that I'd rather not have had the friendly familiarities and flippancies that ruled between him and Bill. But so much then for Godfrey Prial: likeable, generous, always good company and with never a touch of snobbery, and with a façade of cheerful indifference behind which lay a shrewd and agile brain.

I bought the business at the end of August though I carried on from the moment that Bill died. Almost as soon as I had control I was thinking of offering Godfrey Prial some sort of partnership. But before I could see my way clear, things had moved too fast for me, though I'm pretty sure now of at least two things—that he liked me, and that he'd have accepted. *If he'd lived.*

Chapter 2
THE CHIEF CONSTABLE

Towards the middle of September, Godfrey Prial finished a rather tricky assignment which brought little satisfaction to ourselves or the client concerned. It was just one of those things, but Prial was more than a bit depressed about it, feeling, I think, that he might have handled things better in a different way. His leave, with some arrears, was overdue, and on the twentieth he left for three weeks' holiday. I gathered that he had made no particular plans.

It was a week or two later that I got a letter from him. You will notice the ceremonial address. No Ludovic or Ludo for me, though I had long since got in the way of calling him Godfrey. There was no address on the plain sheet of paper but the postmark was London W.1.

> Dear Mr. Travers,
>
> I'm having a busman's holiday in a way. How's that for a facer! No competition with the firm, but just doing a favour, with expectations of a strictly confidential reward, for a newly acquired and charming friend. I don't know if you have any prejudices in the matter, but I personally don't mind who have the blondes provided they leave me the slinky brunettes.
>
> I was careless enough to spread myself, by the way, but most discreetly, which may be good advertising for the firm. Don't worry about any breaking of the golden rule.
>
> Love to Bertha, best wishes to yourself and Norris, and salaams to your charming lady,
>
> Yours as ever,
>
> G.P.

The letter both amused and mystified. I guessed long since that he must have innumerable women acquaintances, though what he called the firm's golden rule had been meticulously adhered to, and I'd never even met one of them, I did wonder if this was something more serious, though I could hardly imagine him as a married man.

But the following day something happened: a trifle at the moment but of immense importance later on.

I was talking to Jack Norris in the office when Bertha Munney came in. She should have buzzed through, but she didn't. She just tapped at the door and came in.

"Someone's been asking for Godfrey," she said in a blank sort of way. "A woman."

"What's wrong with that?" Norris said.

"Oh, nothing." The tone was a bit too off-handed. "Only it never happened before. People aren't supposed—"

"What'd she say, Bertha?" I cut in.

"Nothing, Mr. Travers, only might she speak to Mr. Prial. I said he was on holiday and before I could ask the name or if there was any message she just rang off—like that."

"What sort of voice was it?"

If there's one thing that years of experience have taught Bertha it's to classify voices.

"Husky, like a croonerette. Sounded as if she was about twenty-five to thirty."

I shrugged my shoulders. Norris was tapping the table impatiently with his pencil. Bertha caught my gesture, shrugged her own shoulders in a kind of reflex accord, and went mooning out.

"Poor Bertha!" I said. "A dam-nice girl but why doesn't she be her age? And what does she think Godfrey is? A ruddy trappist?"

That letter of his had been addressed to the flat in St. Martin's Chambers, and that evening I had another look at it. I hate unsolved puzzles and I wondered why a woman should ring the office. That business and pleasure rule is a mighty strict one with us. It has to be. It may not always be fool-proof but there's the stringent agreement that a man's private affairs must never enter the office except in a case of dire emergency and that what goes on in the office is deadly confidential all the time. I knew Bill sack at least two men who placed their own interpretation on that rule, and it's one reason why he always preferred single men.

But I did think I had an idea. If I read that letter aright, Godfrey had got himself entangled, pleasantly or otherwise, with some attractive brunette. She had told some tale of woe and he had offered to help. He'd spread himself, as he put it, by telling her his job. He must even have mentioned the office, though doubtless on a pledge of strict secrecy, but she had rung up to discover if what he had told her about us and his job was true. That called for a reprimand on his return, even if he had been somewhat frank and frivolous about it. It also seemed a good theory, and once more I slipped the letter into a drawer and proceeded to forget all about it. Then, on the Saturday before he was due to return, I had another letter. Again it was on plain paper but the post-mark showed Shireton, and the date of posting as the Friday morning.

> DEAR MR. TRAVERS,
>
> That little friendly job I mentioned has turned out to be dynamite. I don't know whether I'm due for the M.C. or a crack on the skull with a cast-iron mallet. I'd like to steer things in the direction of the firm, but it may be too hot even for you, though there may be a good bit in it.
>
> I'm dropping it unobtrusively till I can think things over. Shall be back in a couple of days or so, and I may tell you about it. In the meanwhile you have a vague hint. Sorry to be so cryptic.
>
> Till Monday.
>
> Yours as ever,
>
> G.P.
>
> *P.S.*—On second thoughts not the M.C. Something very different.

Cryptic wasn't the word for it. Beyond the obvious news that he'd bitten off something that had made some mighty uncomfortable chewing, that letter committed the unpardonable crime of telling either too much or too little. That bit about getting a Military Cross or a crack with a mallet made no sense, unless it was some kind of Intelligence slang which was meant to convey that he was due either for praise or blame. But from whom? Me, or the lady? I didn't know. As for the hints of trying to get the Agency to handle officially something that had burnt his own fingers, that didn't make sense. If we took over the Case—whatever it was—it had the look of something which he alone would have to handle. How could that make the Case no longer the dynamite which he'd described it? We could give no official backing like, say, the Yard.

That letter, in fact, was an annoyance, and the less sense and sequence I read into it, the more of an annoyance it became. And yet something would keep telling me that he would never have written it if he hadn't had good reason. Or written it in just that way.

When I got out of bed on that Monday morning that letter was the first thing in my mind, for in an hour or two I hoped I should know all the answers. While I was shaving I heard the telephone. In a minute Bernice was fetching me.

"Godfrey?" I asked with a lifting of eyebrows, but all she did was frown.

"Hallo?" I said. "This is Travers speaking."

"Mr. Ludovic Travers of the Broad Street Detective Agency?"

"Yes."

"This is Inspector Poorly, sir, speaking from Police Headquarters at Shireton. You have a man named Prial in your employ?"

"Yes, we have."

"Well, we'd be very glad, sir, if you could see us here straightaway. You have a car?"

"Yes," I said, and went on quickly for fear he should ring off. "But wait a minute, though. What's wrong? You haven't got Prial in custody or anything?"

"Nothing of the sort, sir," he told me gravely. "As a matter of fact there's been some sort of accident. In fact, he's dead."

It was half-past eight when I drew up outside police headquarters in Shireton, which shows how I'd travelled. I had a minute or two to wait and then the upstair room into which I was shown had CHIEF CONSTABLE on the door. Inspector Poorly was there too but he didn't do the talking. Loame did that. And he was the kind of Chief Constable with whom I like to deal: one who had pounded a beat and come up the hard way.

"We called it an accident," he said, "because we didn't want to show too much certainty. By the way, haven't I seen you somewhere before?"

I said it was likely. I even remembered some enquiries Wharton and I had made at Shireton a good fifteen years back.

"I was the one you saw," Loame said. "I was a Detective-Sergeant then. And I should have recognised your name."

He actually got up for another ceremonious handshake, and he asked after George Wharton. That made everything nice and cosy. I was able to show the Agency in the best light, and Godfrey Prial too, and to keep quite a lot to myself.

"On holiday, was he?" he said. "His movements were nothing to do with you then."

"Nothing at all."

"Wonder why he came here. No relatives, you say?"

"None. But he was at school at Felsted. That's not too far away, and I can't vouch for his friends."

You can't hurry another man's enquiry and I had to be patient and gather the facts in driblets. Prial had been staying for almost a fortnight at the Royal Hotel and had been due to leave on the Sunday. But on the Friday he left the Royal—said he'd been called away—and the curious thing was that he'd gone no further than the George. In a room at that hotel he was found shot; a room, as Loame emphasised, which was only at the other end of the town and a mile from the Royal. Medical evidence said he had died at about midday on the Saturday but his body wasn't discovered till the chambermaid came in at about eight o'clock that night to turn down the bed.

"Let's get right down to brass tacks," I said. "You can trust my discretion. You ought to know that. So tell me frankly. Was it suicide or wasn't it?"

"Well," he said, and drawled the word far too slowly. "There're rather peculiar circumstances. We don't know if he fired the shot, and there aren't any prints, except the faintest blur or two which isn't any good. No point in making the paraffin test either, because he had gloves on."

My mouth popped open at that.

"And there should have been the usual wallet or case or papers in his pockets. There weren't any."

While I thought that over, he was explaining how he'd got in touch with me.

"At the Royal he signed the book as from St. John's Wood, but at the George he simply signed as from London. There may be something about that which you might help us with. We got his address through the postal people and cross-checked through the number of his car. The people in the other flat put us on to the Agency and mentioned your name. I believe you know them."

"A Major Jones and his wife," I said. "Nice old people. I actually met them at Prial's place one evening. My wife and I were there."

"Well, all that took time," he said. "We didn't want to disturb you last night. This morning seemed as good. But tell me something. He was due back to work this very morning. Supposing it was suicide, was there anything to do with his work that he wouldn't be liking, say, to face? Money irregularities or anything?"

"Nothing whatever. His affairs were in perfect order. We expected him back. We were looking forward to having him back. He was first class at his job. I've told you that. We all liked him and I know he liked us."

"Any ideas at all?"

"I haven't a one," I told him. "But I'd like to see that hotel room."

The three of us piled into a police car which threaded its way through the stifled traffic of the narrow streets. After half a mile of that we turned suddenly and were in the yard of the George. It had a staid Georgian look, too much of a barracks, I'd have thought, for these times, but Loame told me it was well patronised. On the Saturday it had been particularly full because of some Farmer's Rally or Convention; I forgot what he called it.

He got the key from the desk and with the peering look of the clerk behind us, we went up the stairs to the second floor. Forty-one was the number of the room and its one large window overlooked the busy crossroads where the main town is entered from the east. It was a room I'd never have picked. Even at night the through traffic must have been disturbing.

"You'd better have these photographs," Loame said. "Nothing's been changed except the body's gone. And we drew the blinds for a couple of flashlights."

I stood just inside the door. To my far right was the window and, on the other side of the angle, the washbasin. Along its wall was a wardrobe and, near enough for me to touch, a small table on which was a folded copy of *The Times* and on it Prial's smart grey felt hat with the black band.

By the wall on my left was a chest of drawers. In the next wall was a fireplace adapted for an electric stove. Along the other wall, head in the corner and foot towards the window, was a single bed, made up but rumpled towards the foot as if someone had sat there. In the fairly ample open space of the room was an easy chair, wide and well sprung, its back slightly towards the window. A photograph showed Prial's body slumped in the corner of that chair, and by the gloved hand was the gun. An enlargement showed the fingers relaxed round the stock.

"The gloves," I said. "Of the chamois kind, were they?"

"Light coloured kid gloves," he said. "Yellowish. You've seen him wearing them?"

"Not necessarily," I said. "But he was a good dresser. I think he'd wear gloves with that hat. It was a greyish suit, wasn't it, with a faintly bluish stripe?"

"That was it. A West End tailor's tab on it too."

"What about the shot. Through the temple?"

"Clean through. Slightly backwards, though."

There had been a questioning look. I took it up.

"Too much trouble for the Inspector to sit there and for you to show me the direction?"

He didn't mind at all. He actually produced the gun: a little ivory-handled affair which he said was Belgian. "Ever seen it before?"

I shook my head.

"Know if he had a gun?"

"Officially he hadn't one," I told him. "Privately—well, I've never heard him mention one."

The gun was clapped to Poorly's temple. The angle was all wrong. Usually it's about sixty to seventy-five degrees with the line of the skull. This angle was the other way about.

"Well?" he said.

I shrugged my shoulders. I said Prial had gone out of his way to make an awkward job of it. Why twist one's wrist all that way round with eternity on the doorstep?

"Well, there it is," he said, and Poorly got up again. "On the face of it he'd been out somewhere—"

"Anyone see him?"

"Oh yes. He had an early breakfast and went out just before eight o'clock. No one saw him come in but it must have been after ten o'clock for the room wasn't tidied till then. But don't forget the place would be chock-a-block during the morning considering all the circumstances. But as I was saying. He did come in. On the face of it he came in, laid his paper and hat down there, sat on the bed for a minute, shifted to the chair, thought things over and then shot himself."

"On the face of it."

"That's right. On the face of it. Likely, do you think?"

I shrugged my shoulders again.

"Who knows a man's private troubles? A lot of things might have happened in the three weeks since I saw him. All I can say again is that he was a bit depressed. I told you about that. He certainly wasn't suicidally depressed. Just annoyed with himself, that's all."

"I see. And did anyone in your office get a letter from him? Or a postcard?"

I was glad he put it that way, though I'd have lied if he hadn't.

"I can enquire and let you know."

"Good," he said. "Anything you'd like to ask yourself?"

"Yes," I said. "Anyone hear a shot?"

"Unfortunately, no. A nurse on the floor beneath with a couple of children says she heard something she took tor a backfire. The right time, according to the evidence."

"Just the place for backfires," Poorly said. "Traffic lights right under the window. I was here yesterday—a Sunday mind you, sir—and I heard two inside an hour."

I said I quite believed it. But talking wildly; assuming that Prial had *not* killed himself, then his murderer didn't choose his bedroom.

"Anyone see anything suspicious? Anyone entering this room, for instance?"

"Not a thing," Loame said. "We've gone through the guests with a small toothed comb. Midday would be the very time when most of the guests were out. Lunch wasn't till one and it was a lovely morning."

"What about his belongings?"

"The car's in the garage. Everything intact apparently. What we took off him is back at headquarters."

Back to headquarters we went. All that was there was that snuff box—my eyes went first to that—the cigarette case, the lighter, a small ring of keys, a fountain pen, a pen-knife, a handkerchief, and the loose change that came from the trouser pocket. The valuable wrist-watch was unbroken.

"Wallet gone, if he had one," Loame said. "Never a scrap of anything. Here're the gloves. Here's his bag with his spare clothes. Never a thing in the pockets. That suggest anything?"

"Only that it wasn't robbery and murder."

"Why not?"

"A stranger couldn't have entered the room without his knowing it. There'd have been a struggle. And the wrist-watch wasn't taken."

"Any known enemies, had he?"

"Never a one. The most likeable chap in the world."

He grunted. He got up from his chair and took a turn or two about the room. I halted him with a question.

"Where did he go when he was at the Royal? Surely he must have said something to someone?"

"He didn't." That was emphatic. "He told one guest that he was interested in church architecture and was having a look at churches in the district. This person rather gathered he was writing a book. That's all we've been able to find out."

"I'd be prepared to swear he knew as much about church architecture as I do," I said. "And that, frankly, is dam-all. Maybe he was acting on the principle that used to operate with my old nurse. Ask no questions and you'll hear no lies."

He grunted again. I said I was sorry to be so unhelpful.

"Not a bit of it," he said. "I hoped when you got here that we shouldn't be up against the same brick wall. But there's time yet. We've hardly begun."

"Mind if I have a look at him?"

We went downstairs and along some corridors to the tiny mortuary. I was glad in some macabre way that one of those photographs had been a bit distorted and his skull was not the mess it had looked. As he lay there he was nothing but peace and serene indifference.

"When can I take him over?" I said. "I'd like to have him cremated here. He hadn't a relative and I'd like to be responsible."

"Tomorrow? Or the next day? I'll let you know. You can give me authority, if you like, and I'll fix it up. But what about a will? You don't happen to know if there was one?"

"I doubt if he was the sort to make one," I told him as we went back up the stairs. "Still, if you let me have his keys I'll go through the things in his flat. With one of your people if you wish."

"Mind if I go myself?"

"I'd like it very much," I said. "How soon?"

"In five minutes?"

"Fine," I said. "But one other thing. That snuff-box. It was a sort of private mascot. You'll think me a fool, perhaps, but it's curious seeing it lying there. It's like a part of him."

"You mean you'd like to have it?"

"I would," I said. "If there's a will, we'll see what has to happen to it. It's worth quite a bit, you know."

He and Poorly had another look at it. Loame had a tiny pinch of the snuff. I was on tenterhooks for fear he should actuate that second miniature, but it took too hard a squeeze for that. I'd have hated a dirty guffaw in the mood I was in at that moment.

"Here we are then, sir," Loame told me heartily. "Give Poorly a receipt and in five minutes I'll be ready."

What Loame had expected to find I do not know, but as far as that flat was concerned he might as well have stayed at Shireton. Our two cars drew up just after one o'clock and in less than an hour we were away again.

The little flat was tidy. Mrs. Jones, it seemed, had seen to it when Prial had left after the first week of his holiday. Everything seemed the same as when I'd last seen it.

In the bedroom Loame was rather inclined to sneer at the shelves stacked and packed with detective novels, mostly American and French, and it wasn't exactly intellectual arrogance.

"That kind of chap, was he?"

I didn't trouble to argue the point.

"Yes," I said. "Just that kind of chap. Interested in anything to do with his job. Even this sort of thing."

I was indicating the natty little bedside shelf with what I would call the text-books: volumes on medical jurisprudence, toxicology, ballistics, laws of evidence, famous criminal trials, unsolved murder cases, and so on. He merely nodded amusedly.

"Experience is what counts, believe me. Not cramming your brain with statistics and stuff."

Prial had been the meticulously tidy kind, and the few things his desk held were beautifully in order. There were no private papers except receipted bills. But there was no cheque-book. Since he'd paid at the Royal by cheque, there was no expectation of finding one. It was just an additional and unnecessary proof that a cheque-book had been taken from his pocket after death. And even that was no incontrovertible proof of murder.

We didn't even find a gun but we did find a will. Loame saw an immediate significance in the fact that it was dated the first week in September. Prial had expected trouble, that was his idea.

"I don't think so," I said. "I'd say an earlier will had Bill Ellice as a legatee. He made this one when Bill died, but not till he was sure he was going to like working under the new management, so to speak."

I seemed to be right, though I felt a bit queer as I read that will. I'd never have thought that his life had been so intimately bound up with the Agency. Except the bequest of their flat to the Jones people, everything was left in some way to the firm. Bernice was to have the little Queen Anne table she'd much admired and I, of all people, was left "my Napoleon snuff-box." Bertha Munney, none too happy with a married brother, was left Prial's own flat and contents. Jarvis, the man who often worked with him and whom we'd have to try out as his successor, was left the car. Hallows, whom I'd known to be a detective-novel fan, was to have all the books. Monies remaining after expenses were to form the nucleus of a staff welfare and benevolent fund. His bank and myself were named as executors.

"No motive there for anyone to murder him," I said to Loame when he'd read that will for himself. It was rather a petulant irony but he didn't notice it.

We looked for a book of telephone numbers, but there wasn't one. I'd rung the office before I'd left for Shireton that morning and now I rang again. Norris was to question any available staff, particularly Bertha and Jarvis, about receiving a letter or postcard from Prial on holiday. I also said that Loame and I would be along in about an hour. After that we called on Major Jones. His wife happened to be out.

Jones was a sapper who'd left the Service in the twenties: a charming old man with as charming a wife. Our news upset him pretty badly. Prial, as he said, had been more like a favourite nephew than a landlord. He was always in and out. That first week of his holiday he'd actually helped the Major do some jobs in the little back garden. On the Friday before he left he'd taken the couple to their old haunts near Chichester. They'd gone in his car and had a most enjoyable day.

"What about his nights?" I said.

"I believe he was nearly always out," the Major said. "These flats are side by side, as you know, and we're all very quiet people and hear little of each other. Just each other's wireless perhaps. But I don't remember hearing it much that first week."

"What about callers?" Loame asked.

Jones remembered very few: nobody unusual in any case. From his descriptions I identified both Hallows and Jarvis.

"No ladies?"

He got a sharp look at that—and a bleak reply.

"Just one important thing, Major," I said. "He spent the first week of his holiday at home. On the Sunday morning he left for Shireton. Did he mention why? Did he say anything at all?"

"He didn't. He came in late on the Saturday afternoon and told us he was having a few days away for a change. That was when my wife said she would see to things after he'd gone. He left his spare key."

"He didn't show any excitement, shall we say?"

"Not a bit. He was always, of course, full of fun and high spirits. But there was nothing unusual. He didn't mention where he was going. Now I come to think of it, I think he said something about just touring round in the car."

We went on to the bank which was not two hundred yards from the flat. We got a receipt for the will from the bank manager and learned that Prial's balance was just over four hundred pounds. Just short of half-past three we were parking our cars in Broad Street.

Norris had nothing for us. Neither Bertha nor Jarvis nor Hallows had heard a word from Prial. There seemed nothing else to do but tell Norris in front of Loame that if anything was wanted from us by Shireton, we were to help in every way. I said that I myself wasn't much in the office but Norris could be relied on all the time.

"Just one little thing, gentlemen," Loame said, and tried to make a joke of it. "This is a Detective Agency. Looks a very well run place too. But I take it you gentlemen aren't thinking of taking any hand yourselves in this business?"

"Business is the right word," I said. "We've too many overheads to indulge in that sort of thing, even if we were competent. We're rate-payers. We pay for people like you. Only a fool buys a dog and then does the barking himself."

"Thought I'd just mention it," he said. "Anything you get hold of, you'll turn over to us, and if we get anything we think might interest you, we'll let you know."

We said that'd be fine and he said he'd be getting back to Shireton. I suggested a cup of tea at the restaurant just across the street and he thought he'd just have time.

The place was pretty full so we couldn't do much private talking. It was when he was in his car ready to move off that I put my question.

"Reasonably sure now that it was murder?"

He shrugged his shoulders.

"Strictly between our two selves, that is?"

"Well, what do you think yourself?" he asked me, still hedging.

"The same as you," I told him, and he said that maybe I was right.

I watched his car till it took the sharp left-hand turn. I thought how ultra-cautious it was to be so cagey. Just a matter of professional snobbery, no doubt. He was the law and we weren't. Not that I gave a damn. I think I smiled to myself as I wondered just what he would think if he knew certain things. Just why I was going to be even less in the office. And what had been in those two letters that Prial had sent me on his holiday.

CHAPTER 3
JAMES MONAGHAN

"HALLOWS?" Norris said. "He's on that Birmingham job."

"I'd still like him," I said.

"You're the boss," he told me resignedly. "I might get him here by Thursday."

"Tomorrow evening, Jack," I said. "I'll leave something here for him to collect. Then I'd like him at my place at ten o'clock on the Wednesday morning. How long I'll want him I don't know. Charge his time to me personally."

Norris let out a sigh and said he'd do his best.

"I suppose it's no use asking any questions?"

"I'd rather you didn't," I said. "If you don't know then you can't tell. And didn't I just let Loame know that you'd handle everything?"

"But suppose he finds out what you're up to?"

"What *are* we up to?"

He looked at bit sheepish at that.

"Well, I can make a good guess."

"Then don't," I said. "But do something else for me." I'd been looking at our office photographs of Godfrey Prial. Each of our men carries our private equivalent of a Yard Warrant Card, and we like two photographs: one front-face and the other a profile. I wanted

Norris to rush through a dozen cabinet sized of Prial's pair. I said I'd collect them when I brought the stuff for Hallows.

"Might be a good idea to send a couple to Loame," I said, "just to show we're co-operating."

On the Tuesday morning I wrote a detailed account of everything that had happened at Shireton and drew a plan of the hotel room. I made a copy of each of Prial's letters and dated them, and interposed an account of that telephone call that had so perturbed poor Bertha. A covering letter for Hallows asked him to study the facts and be ready with his own ideas on the Wednesday morning. That Tuesday afternoon I had a meeting with Prial's bank people and arranged for them to carry on with his will. I left the Hallows stuff for Norris and collected the photographs. Loame had rung the office to thank us for the pair we were sending and to say there was no news.

"Just how's he handling this Case?" Norris asked me.

I said I thought he was playing for safety. He didn't want to call in the Yard unless forced. Meanwhile he could claim that things were balanced on the razor edge of suicide or murder.

"One thing I'm sure of," I said. "Whereas he'll expect to get from us anything that's likely to help, I'm open to bet that what we get in return will be dam-all—till he's dead sure."

I'd had a great affection for Godfrey Prial but Hallows was a man whom I'd always liked—if you can appreciate that difference. He was of Prial's age and had been with the Agency for almost twenty years, and was married and had a couple of boys. That makes for conservatism of outlook, but he was by no means stuffy. I'd call him the very opposite of Prial, which was perhaps why they were such good friends. In his dour way he always managed to arrive, taking few chances but always seeing the road ahead. His appearance was unobtrusive which is never a bad thing in his job: his height medium, his expression what I might call non-revealing, and the general look of him that of a business man, though what business, again, it would have been hard to say.

He was on time that Wednesday morning. Bernice was out and we had the flat to ourselves. I guessed that like myself he'd breakfasted early, and I had coffee ready. As soon as I clapped eyes on him I knew the Prial business had been a very nasty shock. We talked it over generally before we got down to the facts.

"It couldn't have been suicide," he said. "Even if everything pointed that way I still wouldn't believe it. It was murder, Mr. Travers. I'll lay everything I have in the world that it was murder."

I told him why I wanted him and what I'd arranged with Norris.

"You and I don't want to talk heroics," I said, "but my view is that if somewhere and somehow Godfrey can see you and me at this minute, he'll expect us to do just what we're going to do. He was a colleague. All he lived for was his job. Even his will showed that. If we had a kind of old-school tie, he'd have been proud to wear it. As I see it, Bob, he's still in the family. You and I as good as know he was killed. We're going to find out who killed him, and why. You're with me?"

"Just as long as I'm any use."

"That's fine. And now about those two letters. The time may come when we have to hand them over, and that's what I don't want. If the Press got hold of them, all sorts of things might be distorted and publicised. The yellower Press might make something very dirty out of the first one. We don't want that. We don't want his memory smeared. It wouldn't do the Agency any good either, though that's a small matter. You still agree?"

There was nothing sycophantic about Hallows. He meant it when he said I was right.

"Then we'll get to work," I said. "We've lost a valuable day but that can't be helped. You tell me first what you've made of things. Then I'll give you my own ideas and we'll argue the whole thing out."

There was little to argue. He read into those letters and what I'd seen and heard at Shireton almost exactly what I'd read myself. Prial had met an attractive brunette. She had asked his help when she'd gathered what his profession was. He thought that somehow or other—he dropping it by accident and she picking it up—she'd seen his Agency card, a neat little affair that looked like a visiting-card case. He'd been forced to tell her something though in strict secrecy. She'd nevertheless rung the office to check.

"I don't think I place too much reliance on the voice," he said. "It's the easiest thing in the world for a woman to do that husky stuff. I think if you try it, Mr. Travers, you'll see it's almost the only way a woman can disguise her voice without being sort of shrill and theatrical."

I thought he was right. In fact, it looked as if the natural voice of the woman was just the opposite of husky. Prial would know her voice and she wouldn't want him to think she'd broken the pledge of secrecy.

Hallows said that the job this woman wanted doing must be concerned with Shireton, or Prial would never have gone there.

"You know his way, Mr. Travers. Once he was on a job he simply ate, dreamt and slept nothing else. He'd work like a beaver. By the Friday or just before, he definitely got something, and it smelt. Either he knew he was being double-crossed, or else the whole thing smelt, as I said. Or both. It might have been something that would have got him in bad with the law, but he decided to get out quick. So he left the Royal. But he only went as far as the George. That shows there was either something he still wanted to know or someone he wanted to keep an eye on. But this woman traced him there and shot him there and fixed the room. The alternative theory is that she was actually staying at the George and wouldn't have minded being caught in his room. But it was she who shot him."

"You'd like to elaborate?"

"Yes, sir." He got to his feet at once. "I see you've got a chair here that looks like the one in the hotel room. Would you mind sitting in it?"

He told me on what his theory was based. Either the woman hadn't lost his confidence—she was still *persona grata*, so to speak—or else she'd thought of some good explanation for what had worried or antagonised him, and had come to the hotel to explain. He had been prepared to listen. He had sat in the chair and she, maybe, on the arm of it. She had got up and begun rumpling his hair, perhaps, or stroking his temples.

"Just like this, and sort of purring away to him all the time. Perhaps her head against his hair. All the time she's getting the gun out of her bag. She shoots, from just the angle I am now. That explains why it looked as if he'd twisted his wrist round."

I said he was right. That was the way I'd worked things out for myself. But if she was staying at the hotel, she must have come into his room dressed *and* gloved ready to go out. There'd been no prints.

"Just a minute," I said, "there's something I've got to find out."

I rang Shireton. Loame was out but I got Poorly.

"Morning, Inspector. So glad we could be of help about those photographs. I hope they'll be useful to you. . . . Yes, I happened to hear that from Mr. Norris. But there's plenty of time yet, as you say. . . . Yes, there was one thing I'd like to know. Did you test that gun for noise?"

He said they'd been waiting for extra ammunition and had got it on the previous morning. The gun, according to their tests, made no more noise than the crack of a whip. Two rooms away it had been inaudible unless one was listening carefully, and then it couldn't have been identified for what it was.

I thanked him and that was that. 1 went back to that chair and we demonstrated to our own satisfaction that the gun should never have been where it was found. Even if Prial was still very close to one side of the chair, how could his hand and the gun have fallen in such a way that his fingers were still loosely round the stock? The chances were enormously in favour of the gun falling to the floor and his arm dropping over the arm of the chair. As for his body, that should have slumped sideways and almost certainly to the floor.

Hallows asked me to sit still. He fired the imaginary shot, gun against the temple as the burn marks had shown, and with his other hand restrained the body from falling. No force was required to make my limp body settle to the corner where it had been found.

"The room was locked from the inside," he said. "She listened, then went through his pockets like lightning and put everything into her bag. She hadn't time to look things through. Then she slipped his gloves on and placed the gun. She unlocked the door and listened. Then she looked out and went down the stairs."

"Right," I said. "Let's take all that as a tentative basis. Why did she take his wallet and any possible papers? It couldn't have been to conceal his identity. His car and the hotel registration gave that away."

"There may have been some documents he'd unearthed. He may have made notes. There might have been one or two of her letters."

"That's it!" I said. "It was *her* identity she was going to conceal. Which brings us up against the real thing. Who was she?"

As I told him, he was nearer Prial than I ever was. The fact remained that whatever he was to me privately, he was an employee. To Hallows he was a colleague as well as a friend.

"What did he do with his nights?" I said. "Where would he be likely to meet this brunette? Did he ever talk about such things with you? Did you ever have a bachelor night and go anywhere with him?"

Hallows had been with him to a music hall show or two, and once to Leicester Square Hall to see some snooker, and Prial had spent an occasional evening at his house and just as occasionally he'd gone to Prial's flat. As for the rest, he only knew that Prial loved poking about, as he put it, in all sorts of places. He was an excellent dancer and didn't mind patronising a palais or dance hall. He'd occasionally spoken of night-clubs without mentioning any names. Hallows thought he did it for what one might call experience: seeing all sorts of life and meeting all sorts of people. That kind of thing was useful in his job. Though Prial had never given anything away, he must have had all sorts of connections to have carried through some of the seamier assignments. People don't lay themselves open to blackmail at prayer meetings.

"It's a tall order," I said. "If we put half-a-dozen men on and send them round with photographs it might take a month before we picked up a line. Time's too short. We've got to start somewhere else. What do you suggest yourself?"

"Shireton," he told me promptly. "He went there for something. Whatever he was unearthing, that's where it was. We'll have to start our own enquiries, whatever the police have done. He must have been seen somewhere in the town. He had to buy cigarettes and he always smoked the one kind. He must have asked someone the way to somewhere."

"That's your job," I said. "Fix things up at home and get away at once. Put up at the Royal. Register under your own name because of your ration book. When you ring me, let it be here. Use your own car and spend anything whatever that's necessary. Don't worry if you don't get immediate results. This is going to be tough and I know it."

He'd memorised those letters so he gave me the copies back. I remembered something. That Military Crossmallet business: could he throw any light on it? But he couldn't. He was of my opinion that it was some sort of slang for praise or blame.

"There *is* something that puzzled me," he said. "He says you've had a hint. A hint of what?"

"The letter's all hints," I said. "I think he was just talking generally. Maybe he meant that if he did put the matter up to me officially when he got back, I should have had some idea what it was."

He wasn't satisfied but we left it like that. At tea time that afternoon he gave me a ring to say he was settled in at the Royal. He'd digested a guide-book and ostensibly he was an exile returning to his native town and now revisiting the scenes of his early manhood. I'd have liked to be there with him, and but for that face and elongated form of mine, I certainly would. When the Friday came and there was still no news I was almost tempted to thumb my nose at Loame and at least have a meal at the Royal. Then that same afternoon Hallows rang up.

"That you, Mr. Travers? You-know-who speaking. I think I'm on to something. It's a long shot but we've got to try it out. Can you meet me tomorrow morning near a little place called Stadmore? Ten miles due west of Shireton? I'll wait while you get a map."

I fetched a largish road map and said I was ready. It was easy to pick up the main Cambridge road that passed within a mile north and south of Stadmore village.

"A mile south there's a lane coming into Stadmore to the east and then north," he said. "Just where it bends there's another road forking off to join the main road from Stadmore to Shireton. The fork of those two roads is known as Copley's Corner. I'd like you to meet me about a quarter of a mile south of that fork just past a farm where there's a copse on the left-hand side of the road and a pond on the other. You got all that?"

I said I had and I'd be there at ten o'clock if that wasn't too early. And could he give me a hint what it was all about? He said he'd rather not. All he'd say was that our friend had twice been seen in Stadmore. Another queer thing was that he had been absent one night from the Royal.

"There's just a chance of a link-up," he told me. "Everything's vague but I think it's worth talking over. And if I were you, sir, I'd bring a small bag in case you decide to stay the night."

I looked up Stadmore and found it was a village of six hundred people. The church was described as Perpendicular and there was a pub called the Ram. A house used as the vicarage was said to be a fine specimen of 16th century timber-framing. That was all and it seemed a curiously pastoral spot to have harboured the kind of thing that had ended in Prial's death. But Hallows would never have suggested that talk if he hadn't had good reasons, and theorising was useless till I'd heard what he had to say.

I was early in the morning; in fact I waited in my car in the place he'd suggested for a good ten minutes before he arrived, and it was still short of ten o'clock. He didn't seem to be troubling about secrecy. The first thing he said was that the place where we were was handy for seeing something. His small car had been drawn up behind mine. I got out and stretched my legs and we leaned over a gate as if we were discussing the sugar-beet of the field in front of us. The sun had come out and it was a perfect morning of early October.

First he told me how he'd picked up any trail at all of Prial's. The cigarette idea had seemed the best, for Prial had had expensive tastes, so Hallows had spent the first day and a half systematically working the shops. It hadn't cost a lot, he said, because quite a few of the shops hadn't stocked Prial's special brand, but wherever he'd found a likely shop he made a joke about his brother's expensive tastes and contrived to show a photograph. In the early afternoon of the Thursday he was working the outer ring of shops. At the very last one on the Stadmore Road he found the trail. The woman in the shop recognised Prial.

Her description of his car seemed to tally, and the really interesting thing was that on leaving the shop he had waved a hand and said, "This *is* right for Stadmore, isn't it?"

So Hallows went on to Stadmore. It was early closing day in the village. Shops were shut, including the post-office store, and he had to wait till the Ram was open. The pub had certain accommodation for guests, so Hallows asked if his brother was in. The landlord showed surprise, and so did Hallows. The brother had mentioned staying at the Ram and Hallows had expected to find him there. The landlord recognised the photograph. The gentleman had been in twice. Best part of a fortnight ago it must have been. On the first occasion he'd spent a whole evening in the saloon bar and had played darts. On the second occasion the landlord hadn't seen him personally, but one of the pub habitués had said something like this:

"You know that toff who was in here the other night? I just see him. Looked as though he'd been to the vicarage."

The landlord had expected him to come in, but he hadn't. Hallows gave plausible explanations and decided to put in an evening at the pub himself. As the usuals came in, the landlord naturally introduced him as the brother of the gent who'd been such good company a few nights back. Hallows let it be known that he was expecting his brother to turn up again that night, which gave the excuse to stay on. He was even able to show the company that couple of photographs. It was lucky that on recognising Prial earlier that evening, the landlord had called him Trevor.

"When I heard that, I thought I might be on to something," Hallows told me. "He wouldn't give a false name at a casual visit to a village pub. He wouldn't need to give a name at all. And it seemed to me quite likely that he'd put in the whole evening there because he wanted to do something after the place was shut. Then there was that second night visit when he hadn't come to the pub at all. Mind you, sir, there wasn't any certainty about that. I spoke to the chap who said he'd seen him, and said I knew he must be wrong, and he owned he might have made a mistake.

"What I did do that night was to sit with this one and that and try to find out what Godfrey had been after: what he'd talked about and got other people to talk about. I didn't have any luck at all till I tried another tack. I was with an old chap who looked like a farmer and I'd treated him to a pint and we were watching the darts. I said

I supposed nothing ever happened in Stadmore, and he reckoned nothing ever did.

"'Mind you,' he said, 'there was that business about old Monaghan.'" He pronounced it Monagan, not the Irish way. I asked what about Monaghan and this is what he told me. First of all I should say that I later on owned up to being a kind of Insurance Inspector. That seemed the right line as his story developed, and it gave me an excuse to make an enquiry or two the next day, at the other end of the village, well out of the way of the pub."

This is what Hallows learned about James Monaghan. He had come to Stadmore early in 1939 and had taken the cottage known as Copley's Corner. A medium sized van had brought his belongings from no one knew where. The cottage was just outside the village and Monaghan might have chosen it for that reason, for in Stadmore itself he was rarely seen. He looked about seventy, though the grey beard might have made him look older than he was. He spoke with an Irish accent, and he was reserved to the point of taciturnity. If anyone spoke, he would merely give a nod and a brief acknowledgement. In the spring and summer he pottered about, most ineffectively according to the village, in his garden, though apparently growing enough vegetables for himself. His method of growing flowers was to scatter a packet or two of seeds and thereafter forget all about them.

The village was definitely of the opinion that, though harmless, he was touched in the head. A mild religious mania was what it thought, for though he was never known to go to Shireford where was the nearest Roman Catholic church or to be visited by a priest, he was never seen even from his very first day in the village, without a rosary which he would tell automatically between his lean fingers while his lips inaudibly moved. It was a black rosary, by the way, and probably made of jet beads or of bog-oak. It was not known if he ever posted letters—he might have dropped them in the pillar-box after dark—and only very occasionally did he receive one. If he drew an old age pension it as not at Stadmore.

During the war he took no part in any kind of local activity, and, indeed, he was not asked. He was not rude to those who called for charitable reasons: he was known to have given small sums—never more than sixpence—to various callers, including the Salvation Army. The cottage was just far enough from the village to escape close observation, and only once was it known that he had a day-time visitor; who or of what sex was not known but a car described as big and smart was seen drawn up by the gate one August day in 1943. In the February of 1948 a car was seen drawn up there one dark night, and it was very shortly after that that the events took place which for a village so placid as Stadmore had been a nine-day wonder.

To go back to the 5th of February, the night when the car was seen. That car was drawn right in on the grass verge well clear of the road and its lights were off. It had been seen by a courting couple, and the swain, employed at the village garage, had thought it was a Buick. In any case he swore it was a big American car, but it was a pitch-dark night and, since the lights, quite lawfully, were off, he hadn't seen it any too clearly and he certainly hadn't seen its number. There was, by the way, no sign of a light in the cottage.

It was on the 14th, easily remembered as Valentine's Day, that the events occurred. The village policeman, Alfred Start, had been cycling towards Stadmore at about eight o'clock when he was suddenly halted by the vicar, the Rev. Charles Comfort. The vicar had been out for a constitutional—he had had a headache during the day—and he told Start that he had seen something which might or might not be suspicious—a man prowling about in Monaghan's garden. Start dismounted—he was then a hundred yards past Monaghan's cottage—and, the vicar volunteering to accompany him, went back on foot.

No one seemed about and the cottage was dark, but Monaghan, it was always thought, went to bed remarkably early. A light had more than once been seen in his bedroom at as early as eight o'clock. Start hammered on the door. There was a noise inside the cottage. A minute and there was a sound at the back door. Start ran as quickly as he could in the early moonlight and saw nothing. Then he heard a noise on the other and narrower lane—the one that cut round from the fork and by-passed Stadmore for the Shireton

Road. A car started up and shot off. All Start saw was the headlights switched on when it was quite a distance away.

He went round to the front again and once more hammered and called. Then he and the vicar went round to the back door which was found open. A light was showing from the oil-lamp in the living-room and when they went in they found Monaghan trussed up in a chair and a gag in his mouth. From the fact that one of his feet was unshod they deduced that he had just been taking off his boots and going up to bed when he had heard a knock. The caller had struck him down—a bruise on the skull showed that—and had trussed him up with a length of quite unidentifiable rope, and had then searched the place for whatever valuables Monaghan was supposed to be hoarding.

There were plenty of signs of a search. Even the bedding had been ripped. Everything was in what Start subsequently described as a proper old mess. But that wasn't all. Start cut Monaghan's bonds while the vicar was prising the gag from his mouth, and then the old man collapsed. In two days he had recovered, but he had spoken never a word. Early in March he was taken to the county Mental Home at Puckford, three miles north of Shireton. There he was just a harmless case of mental instability brought about by shock. His powers of speech had apparently gone and he mooned his time away.

Advertising had produced no relatives or a living soul who knew him. The vicar occasionally visited him, though it was a waste of time. His furniture was stored in a shed attic at the Ram since the enquiry for relatives was still apparently going on. The owner of the cottage had decided to sell it, prices being high, and it had been bought by some London man who used it as a sort of weekend place. That was all that Hallows knew—except one vital thing. That was something he had learned after he had rung me the previous afternoon.

"I called at the next cottage, sir; I'll show it to you as we go past, and said I was an Insurance Inspector and making enquiries about Monaghan. Godfrey had been there before me, asking all sorts of questions."

"'You're the second one who's been asking recently,' the woman said."

"I showed her the photographs and she spotted Godfrey at once. I worked out that date and it was that very night when he was supposed to have been in Stadmore and coming from the vicarage. Not only that. Her husband was as usual at the Ram and he was there when Godfrey called. Godfrey may have seen him go in the Ram and then taken advantage to slip along and have a word with the wife."

Well, there it was. It couldn't be denied that Godfrey had been interested. We'd picked up some sort of trail and that should have been exciting. But it wasn't. It was somehow like being told that there was the haystack so why not find the needle. I began polishing my glasses—a nervous trick of mine when at a mental loss or on the edge of an unusual discovery. But now it was the mental loss. Hallows was saying nothing either.

"Let's leave Godfrey out of it," I said at last, "and concentrate on the Monaghan affair. The Shireton police took over from the local man?"

Hallows thought so but he hadn't got that far yet.

"I don't know what you think," I went on, "but it looks to me as if the two cars, so to speak, within such a short time of each other, must be the same. That looks like a preliminary call of inspection. Monaghan had something someone wanted, and he wouldn't sell. The second visit was different. If the caller hadn't been disturbed he might have got what he came for. For all we know, he got it as it was. What it actually was, heaven alone knows. Monaghan can't tell. So where are we? We can't trace the car. The thing is, can we trace Monaghan?"

"You mean, find out his history?"

For Hallows that was a bit obvious.

"The only possible thing to do. We've got to do what the authorities either haven't been able to do or haven't thought of doing. We've got to find out if Monaghan was Monaghan: where he came from, why he came here, everything about him. All we've got to ask ourselves is how we begin."

"A tall order, sir." He shook a dubious head.

"This is what you must do," I told him. "Spin whatever yarn you like but find out two things: who had charge of the Case at Shireton and if they examined whatever Monaghan was allowed to take with him to the asylum. Even if they did, we may be able to have a look for ourselves."

"A telephone call might be the best for that."

"You're dead right," I said. "Give a fictitious name and it doesn't matter what you ask. And you can't be traced."

Then suddenly my fingers were at my glasses again.

"Wait a minute, though! Didn't you say most of his things were at the Ram?"

"Practically all his things. Besides, he wouldn't pick out anything to take to the asylum. That'd be done for him."

"Right," I said. "You show me the lie of the land and then I'll look in at the Ram."

CHAPTER 4
SLEMISH

HALLOWS LOCKED his car, took the ignition key and got back in my car again. We went round the bend, did about three hundred yards straight and he was touching my arm.

"Just round the next bend."

I slowed and there ahead of me was Copley's Corner. Our road turned only slightly to the left and the other road, more of a narrow country lane, swerved away right from the fork. In that fork was a cottage: and one common enough in East Anglia, with pinkish plaster walls and a tiled roof. The ceilings of its rooms must have been pretty low judging by the height of the eaves. Its garden, which began not far beyond it on the Stadmore side, was roughly triangular in shape and filled up the angle made by the twin roads. That garden looked in reasonably good order considering the time of year.

A small green-painted gate led from the road to the front door. The narrow path was invisible because of the bed of asters that bordered it. A water-butt stood under the eaves where the back roof came down to make a lean-to shed. Another small shed stood somewhat away from the back door. By it was the usual well-top with a brick surround and windlass. No smoke was coming from the one chimney, but in the morning sun it looked just what it was and no more—a little cottage which a few ideas and energy might make into an attractive place. An ideal weekend cottage, in fact, or where a man like Monaghan might spend his last days.

"Who do you say has it now?"

Hallows repeated what he'd told me before. Some London man or other had bought it; the name he didn't know.

"Well, we're looking at it," I said, "but it doesn't tell us much. It doesn't give me any ideas; I don't know if it does you. How far is the next cottage?"

Two hundred yards on, he said, just round the next bend and hidden now by that clump of elms. It was a thatched one and after it the houses began in a straggly way and merged into the main village.

"A natural place for Godfrey to ask questions if he wanted information about Copley's Corner," I said. "Seems to confirm what we've never been really sure of, that he *was* interested in Monaghan. What did Godfrey actually ask that woman at the thatched cottage?"

"I didn't like to be too anxious," Hallows said. "She was rather sticky with me. Said she wasn't in the habit of poking her nose into other people's business. The idea I did get was that he'd been more interested in the people who now have the house than in Monaghan himself. That didn't seem to make sense. I thought she was putting me off. She was standing with the door ajar, to give you some idea of what kind of an interview it was."

"Well, it's after opening time," I said. "You go back and get your car and turn up casually at the Ram. I'll be in the saloon bar. I shall try and get lunch there but I won't mention it till you come. Then you ask to have lunch too. After that we'll see."

Round the bend was the thatched cottage, a regular picture-postcard sort of place. There were more cottages as Hallows had said. Away to the left on a rise of ground a church tower was just visible among more elms. The road widened and gave a choice of ways to circle the village green. Across it I saw the Ram.

A middle-aged, pleasant-faced woman was behind the bar. She gave me a cheerful good-morning. I said it *was* a good morning.

"You can recommend the bitter?" I asked her.

"Nobody grumbles," she said.

"A pint then. In a tankard."

The bitter wasn't too good but I praised it. I said I was a stranger to Stadmore. The church looked a fine old place. And what was the vicar like?

"Nothing of a preacher," she said. "You can't expect much really, not here. It's a very poor living."

It was rather an amusing idea that a good living should mean good sermons, but 1 didn't pursue it.

"You want money of your own in a place like this," she went on. "Not that I've anything against Mr. Comfort—not really. They say he's a good living man."

Not really was the key phrase. Obviously she didn't like him at all. A temperance fanatic, maybe.

"Hard-up, is he?"

"I don't know how they manage," she said. "There's three children: Martin's about eleven, and then there's Paul and then the girl, Noel. She's about six. Then Mrs. Comfort. Quite a nice woman but always appears to be ailing."

"And no domestic help?"

"Never in these days," she said. "A woman comes in twice a week. Nobody in the garden hardly, though."

"Been here long, has he?"

"Just before the war, I think. That's it. Just before the war."

There was the sound of a car drawing up outside. A minute and Hallows came in. The woman's face lighted. "Morning, Mr. Trevor."

"Morning, Mrs. Price. How are you this fine morning?"

"None too bad, sir. How's yourself?"

"Just on my last legs."

She laughed.

"You'd better have something before you collapse."

"Perhaps I had. A pint o' shandy, I think. Where's the good man?"

"Gone to Shireton. He'll be home this evening, though. Heard any more about your brother?"

"He's doing fine. Might be this way in a few days' time."

He gave me a look as she handed him his shandy.

"What about you, sir?"

"I still have some. Thanks very much all the same. Oh, Mrs. Price. It is Mrs. Price, isn't it?"

"That's it, sir."

"Could I possibly have some lunch here? Anything will do."

"Well," she frowned, "I think I could manage it. One o'clock do?"

"It'll suit me fine," I said.

"What about a bite for me too?" Hallows asked her. "Trevor is my name," he told me.

"That'll be all right," she said. "One o'clock and no expecting it earlier. I'm single-handed, but for Ellen, now Ted's away."

I said I'd put my car in the yard. It was a fairly large yard with a range of buildings along one side. A lock-up garage had its doors full back and I guessed that the landlord had left them so when he had taken out his own car. I drew mine in and saw the flight of steps leading to an upper storey. A padlock was on the door and it seemed a likely place for Monaghan's furniture. From the far wall by the steps no window of the pub was visible.

I had to fill in my time so I made my way across the green to the church. It had a beautiful roof and very little else that interested me: no special monuments or carving, and a rood-screen that looked fairly modern and far too florid. I moved back down the nave wondering if there were steps in the belfry leading up to the tower. Then the door opened and the vicar himself came in. He gave me a rather peering look.

He was quite a big man, with smooth, pink cheeks, and I put his age at forty. But in spite of his pinkness there was something astringent about him. I think he would have passed me with merely a nod if I hadn't slowed and almost blocked his way.

"Good morning," I said quietly. "My name's Travers and I was going to call on you."

"Indeed?" he said, and his look again was curiously sharp.

"I'm a stranger here," I said, "but I happened to hear that your name was Comfort. I wondered if you were any relation of an old friend of mine, Canon George Comfort of Menlow Parva in Dorset."

I hope it sounded plausible but I was glad to see him shake his head.

"I'm afraid not," he said. "We haven't any relatives in Dorset. You're a Dorset man?"

"No," I said, and added the truth—that though a Londoner now of necessity, I was an East Anglian. My people had come from near Stowmarket.

"I can't say I know it," he said. "One gets about so rarely these days."

A moment of awkward silence and he was giving a quick little bow and mumbling an almost inaudible something which I just gathered was a request to be excused. I gave a feeble nod and smile and he moved off, gathering speed as he went. By the time I was at the outer door there was neither sight nor sound of him.

As I went along the churchyard path I was just a bit depressed, for I had counted on making Comfort's acquaintance. He was the one man in Stadmore who had known Monaghan at all well: the one who had been concerned in the events at Copley's Corner, and who still occasionally visited him in the asylum. Had Comfort been what I had anticipated—scholarly, friendly, and not too vicarial—we could have had a pleasant hour or so together, but the man I had seen rather repelled me. Mentally, or rather socially, I mean, though even about the prawnish pink of the plumpish cheeks there was something curiously unhealthy. There had been a frowstiness about him too: a cassock here and there frayed, and linen none too clean.

And then it struck me that those far too quickly formed views were bred of my disappointment. It had seemed necessary, in view of possible eventualities, to get on gossiping terms with Comfort, and because I now knew that the prospect was hopeless, I had vented a kind of childish spite on the man. With a sick wife on his hands, three children, a lean purse and no great competence for his profession, he should have had sympathy instead of my somewhat Pharisaical assessment. But even when I was aware of all that I still found it hard to feel a sympathy. Comfort, I couldn't help thinking, was the sort of man who'd resent sympathy. Or was I wrong? Hadn't he himself sufficient sympathy to visit the unfortunate Monaghan who hadn't even been a member of his Church?

I gave up thinking because I had come to that half-timbered building mentioned in that book I'd consulted. A side gate led out to a lane at the front of it and as I went through I heard the voices of children beyond the wall that separated churchyard and vicarage. I couldn't catch the words but a girl seemed to be reprimanding someone, and, by the sound of the other voice, probably a brother. The voices were lost as I came out to the lane.

It was a lovely house with quaint gables and beautifully carved timbers and barge-boards. The tiny strip of ground between the lane and its front was neglected, with here and there a spindly dwarf dahlia in the unhealthy bareness of dry soil. As I neared the gate a boy came out. He looked up and down the road.

"Have you seen a dog?"

He spoke nicely. I saw nothing of his father in him, unless it was that he was well grown. He was hatless and his clothes looked neat, and he was carrying a basket.

"What sort of a dog?"

He smiled in a boyish attractive sort of way.

"Well, a kind of terrier."

"I haven't," I said. "I haven't seen a dog of any sort."

"Oh," he said, and gave a little shrug of the shoulders. "I expect he's at the Smiths' again."

He gave a goodbye nod and off he went towards the green. I looked at my watch and saw it was almost one o'clock.

Hallows and I lunched on spam with mashed potatoes, followed by plum tart. It was quite a good meal and after it we went back to the bar. The dart-players had gone. Hallows treated himself to a glass of port. I said I ought to be on my way.

In a minute or two I was back.

"Something's gone wrong with my clutch," I said to Hallows. "I wonder if you'd mind lending me a hand?"

"Certainly," he said. "But there's a garage just down the road. Wouldn't they fix it better?"

"I know what's wrong," I said. "In five minutes you and I can fix it."

He finished his port and went out with me. As soon as we were in the garage he nipped up the stairs and picked the padlock while I kept watch. He came down and I went up.

What were certainly Monaghan's things were stored against the far wall of that attic room. There was some dust but the place was fairly clean and it was certainly dry. Some of the things looked reasonably good: a small sideboard, for instance, and a quite nice wheel-back grandfather chair. There too was a hair mattress, rolled and tied, but showing along the side where it had been ripped. A feather bed was similarly tied, and quite a lot of its feathers were on the floor. I noticed that the bed was a double one. If that indicated anything it was that Monaghan had been a married man.

I had a look at a wooden box filled with household crockery. A smaller box had more crockery and a couple of highly coloured vases, one of which was mended. There were one or two other oddments, including a pair of crude Staffordshire figures, each broken and clumsily mended. There was something else—a little mug with a curious sort of spout. I took it out. It was one of those whistling mugs where one blows down the spout, and I hadn't seen one for years. On it was a view of Skegness. I frowned at it, put it in my pocket, changed my mind and put it back in the box.

A small stack of pictures stood between a wash-stand and a painted deal chest of drawers. I had to reach through to get them out. All were cheap prints or lithographs, spotted and stained with age. A smaller one in a birds-eye maple frame looked like a photograph, though it too was discoloured with age. It showed a summer landscape with country rising to a dominating hill. In the near of the middle distance was a little farm, and the shape of its white-washed buildings told me that farm was Irish. I slipped it beneath my coat, looked cautiously out, and then came down the steps. Hallows nipped up and replaced the padlock.

I went off in my car to the spot where we had met that morning and ten minutes later Hallows joined me there.

I had prised the backing and tacks from that photograph with my pen-knife and the first thing I showed him was something printed and hidden by the closeness of the mount.

W. McCAFFERTY PHOTOGRAPHER
BALLYMENA

He was licking his lips at the sight of it. He said it gave us a lead. I told him about that little Skegness mug which might lead us to something too.

"Just what was Monaghan like in appearance?"

I wanted to know.

Monaghan, he said, was about six foot; gaunt and hollow-cheeked and with thinnish grey hair and a beard bushy round the cheeks but thinning off where it reached his waistcoat. I wondered if that would be enough to reconstruct a man of the date when that photograph was taken.

I got out of the car and leaned on that gate again and did a bit of thinking, but that was no use without jotting down my thoughts. When I came back I'd made up my mind. Too many things to do, that was the trouble, and it was a pity one man couldn't do them all.

"Look, Bob," I said. "I think this is our best course. You go back to Shireton and later on ring up Mrs. Price and get put up at the Ram for the weekend. Take a chance but find out every single thing you can about Monaghan. Find out why the cottage was sold and anything you can about the man who bought it. And we must know who handled the Monaghan affair. You can get that from the local man, Start. If Loame himself, or Poorly handled it, then we've got to move carefully. If not, you'll have more scope."

I asked if he had any other ideas and he mentioned the Puckford Mental Home. I said what about the Mental Home.

"Well, I might rig up some excuse to see Monaghan himself."

"He's there," I said. "He won't run away. Besides, it's a tricky business getting in places like those. The application to visit has to satisfy the Medical Superintendent. We don't want to slip up and start any suspicions."

"No," I said. "I honestly think what I've outlined is best. Tomorrow's Sunday, which makes it awkward, but I'll fly to Ireland on the Monday and take the photograph. I should be back by Tuesday midday at the latest. Be near the hotel phone and I'll try and ring you at two o'clock."

Some Ulster people named Anderson lived in one of the flats and after tea I showed them that photograph and asked if by any chance they could identify the place. Mrs. Anderson had smiled as soon as she saw it.

"Why, it's Slemish!" she said.

"And what's Slemish?"

"The hill," she said. "It's quite near Ballymena."

She should have known. Her husband was from County Down but she was an Antrim woman, from Glenarm.

"I suppose it's too much to ask if you recognise the farm?" I asked her.

That was beyond her. But anyone at Ballymena should know where the photograph was taken from, she said, and I had to be content with that. I wondered if her Ulster patriotism wasn't making her too optimistic, but she was right.

The train from Belfast got me to Ballymena early on the Monday afternoon. I walked the four hundred yards to what looked like the main shopping centre of the town. I found the post-office and asked if the W. McCafferty, photographer, was still in town. Nobody had ever heard of him.

I walked slowly back. An oldish man stood at a shop door and I asked him about McCafferty. He remembered the man and his shop, and told me he'd been gone from Ballymena for at least thirty years. His little shop at the lower end of Church Street was now a sweet shop. I showed him the photograph. Did he know where it was taken from? He squinted at it and frowned and gave it as his opinion that it had been taken from Broughshane. That turned out to be a village some four miles to the east of the town. I asked him where I could hire a taxi.

Let me make one thing perfectly clear. There are few things more musical to my ear than the speech of the Irish. I love it far too well to murder it with inane reproduction. But if I manage to give the talk a flavour of the Irish I shall be guilty of nothing worse than manslaughter.

The man who drove me seemed to take a personal interest in finding that farm. It was as if his own reputation was at stake, and he pulled up twice in Broughshane to make his own enquiries while I looked round at the soft countryside that seemed to gather and rise till it culminated in Slemish. After his second enquiry he came back with a beaming face.

"I have it for you, sorr. It's just a wee piece along."

The wee piece was about half a mile and then we turned into a narrow track. The car bumped and heaved and when it drew up, there was the farm. Brady's Farm was the name of it from some Brady or other who'd once owned it. The driver and I consulted the photograph and there wasn't a shadow of doubt. That farm had scarcely altered since the day the photograph was taken.

We saw the farmer and the driver called to him. His name was McCanlis and he looked about forty. He'd had the farm some ten years and before him a man named Johnson had farmed it. Johnson was dead, but he'd been at Brady's for certainly twenty or thirty years.

I asked if he'd ever heard of anybody of the name of Monaghan owning the place, and he hadn't. Then he had an idea. It was the driver he talked to, not me, as if it were still a personal matter between the two of them. The upshot was that I was to see a man of the name of Henry Cladden who lived back on the Ballymena side of Broughshane.

Cladden's place was the usual one-storied, white-washed cottage. It was back in a meadow and we left the car and walked along a grass track. Smoke was coming from the chimney and, as we neared, a stooped, elderly man came out to the turf heap. The driver hailed him and introduced me as a gentleman from London who'd come all that way to know if there'd ever been Monaghans at Brady's Farm.

Gladden was a man of over seventy, decently dressed even if he wore no collar. His hands were gnarled and twisted and but for his rheumatism, so he said, he would still be at work. He told us that and a lot more before he began on the Monaghans. He had a good look at the photograph and just when I was sure he would have some news, he baldly announced that there'd never been any

Monaghans, at least as far back as he could remember Brady's, and that was sixty years and more.

"Who had it sixty years ago?" I asked him.

"John Corkery," he said. "He had a son named after him and him and me was at school here in Broughshane."

"He was your own age—the son?"

"He'd be two years younger," he said.

He'd known the Corkerys till 1904, when the father had died and the place was taken by Sam Johnson. Old Corkery, I gathered, had been over-fond of the whiskey. His widow went to live at Coleraine and died there soon afterwards.

"What about the son?"

Young John Corkery had been what he called a hellion. The old man had been something of the sort too, and finally young John had been almost the spit of Synge's Playboy, for he had turned at last on the old man's bullying, knocked him down and bolted. I didn't gather if he had thought like that playboy of the western world that his father was dead, but the father definitely wasn't. Young John—he was eighteen then—went for a soldier and whatever news his mother had of him, Broughshane had none till he appeared soon after his father's death. He was in Broughshane only the day but Gladden had some speech with him, and now recalled that he had been through the South African War with the Fusiliers and was making some grand talk about himself and his prospects. He was married and had a son. I asked where the wife was living, and jogged his memory with a mention of various stations, and married quarters, but Gladden remembered no more.

And so to the real test. What had Corkery looked like in 1904.

"He was a brave bit of a boy," he said. "Not as tall as yourself but not far off it."

"About six foot?"

"Aye. He'd be all that."

"A longish sort of face and deep-set eyes?"

That was a bit too much for him but we talked round it in various ways and he didn't disagree. And that was all I could get out of him. He'd heard no further word of John Corkery and had hardly minded him till that day.

"You've seen him yourself, sorr—the same lad?" he asked me, and I had to shake my head. Then he was asking, with the driver listening intently, if it was a matter of a legacy. I said it wasn't. It was just some official business to do with a man named Monaghan. And nobody knew Monaghan.

I gave Cladden a note and told him to drink to young Corkery's memory, and I thanked him for what he'd done. Then we drove back to the town where I bargained to be driven straight to Belfast. Then I found a firm of Enquiry Agents and paid my driver off.

It seemed quite a good firm and I gave them the job of finding out what had happened to a John Corkery who had joined the Dublin Fusiliers in 1895 or 1896 and had served through the Boer War. Anything discovered was to be telephoned to me at Broad Street.

"You don't chance to know," they asked me, "what's happened to the original records?"

I had no idea. I knew the Regimental Depot had been near Dublin—the regiment had been disbanded at about 1920—but it shouldn't be hard to find out where the records had been sent. And I'd also like to know any details of Corkery's wife. He was said to be married in 1904 and to have had a son.

1 stayed the night in Belfast and was back in town before noon the next day. I was interested but not optimistic. Monaghan's build tallied with Corkery's and the only other point of agreement was that I had guessed Monaghan to be a married man. And considering the unassuming way that Monaghan had arrived in Stadmore, his retired way of life and what had happened in February, it didn't seem unlikely that at some time or other Monaghan had had another name. I didn't place much reliance on the fact that the Corkerys, so Cladden had told me, had been Roman Catholics. Catholics, even in Protestant Ulster, are numerous enough.

I almost rang Hallows from the airport, then kept to my agreed two o'clock.

"All sorts of things here, sir," was what he said. "Neither of our friends handled that business. A detective-sergeant did it, so that makes things easier."

He said he'd rather see me than talk over the telephone. I agreed to meet him at five o'clock at that pond near Copley's Corner. I didn't even have to unpack my bag.

CHAPTER 5
MORE COMFORT

LOAME HAD been to Stadmore at least once; just keeping an eye, Hallows imagined, on the Monaghan business, which was being handled by one of his sergeants. Apparently Loame had seen nothing more in the affair than the usual attempted robbery with violence in lonely country houses. Monaghan, to the knowledge at least of Stadmore, drew no pension, but he paid cash for what he bought, and that cash would be in the house. If the blow that had stunned the old man had actually killed him, that would have been a different matter, and Loame would have had a murder case on his hands. As for the fact that Monaghan had become mentally incapable after that attack, that was taken far less seriously than if he had not been considered mentally weak ever since his arrival. A man who talked to nobody but merely muttered to himself and twiddled that eternal rosary could never have been quite sane in the eyes of Stadmore.

I told Hallows what had happened in Ireland and he was inclined to be even less optimistic than myself. Monaghan, it now seemed to him, must be a far more important person than the possible private of the Dublin Fusiliers who had been born at the Brady's Farm of the photograph. When he told me what he'd discovered, I was inclined to agree.

First the sale of the cottage, which was due to the owner's leaving the district. He had bought it in 1927 for a hundred and eighty pounds. When he offered it, he put a reserve of five hundred on it, and it made five hundred guineas. But for its lack of any main services it must have fetched more. The agents had advertised it well and Hallows gathered they had been a bit disappointed. His information, by the way, had come from one of the agents' clerks.

"Now this is the first funny thing, sir," Hallows said. "Two people took up the bidding after it passed the four hundred mark and I'll bet you'll never guess who one of them was?"

I didn't try.

"The local vicar. Comfort, his name is."

I stared.

"But I thought he was as poor as his church mice!"

"That's what I heard. Still, there we are, sir. I'll guarantee the information's right. But he didn't want to appear in the transaction so he left a commission with the agents to go as far as the reserve. He said he was sure Monaghan would recover and then he'd like him to have his cottage back. And something else in that context. It was Comfort who had Monaghan's things stored at the Ram. He's paying Price for it."

"Then local gossip's all wrong about Comfort's means."

"Stadmore knows about him storing the furniture for Monaghan but it doesn't know about the cottage," Hallows said. "He *is* pretty hard up; there isn't a doubt about it. Mind you, sir; Comfort wouldn't have to be five hundred out of pocket all at one go. A Building Society would give a good advance on any sort of property nowadays. He might have had to find as much as a hundred and fifty, and then the interest. If he let on a short tenancy he'd get that back from the rent."

I didn't know what to make of it. Maybe I had been even less charitable in my assessment of Comfort than I had thought, though why he should so put himself out for Monaghan was beyond me.

"Did Comfort call on Monaghan regularly before all this business happened?" I asked Hallows.

"Never went near the man so far as the village knows."

"Curious," I said. "Still, it's the sinners that are supposed to be called to repentance. Maybe Comfort didn't take any interest in Monaghan till he needed help. But about the sale. Who did buy the cottage?"

"A man named Laver. Harry Laver of 14, Otway Mansions, N.W. After the agents held the bidding at five hundred on behalf of Comfort, Laver made it guineas."

"What was he like?"

"The showy type. Just too well dressed. Very smooth. Almost certainly a business man of some sort."

"He's been in Stadmore?"

Hallows said he was coming to that. Laver bought the property in May and he came down at once. His car—not a Buick but a new Austin twelve—was seen outside the cottage one weekend. Then he came down with another man, a rough sort of chap, and he and this man dug up the garden; at least the rough chap did the hard work and Laver seemed merely to be making heavy going of it. They worked all through the Sunday and left on the Sunday night. The next Saturday afternoon they were at it again, and the job was finished by the next evening. But on the Saturday night Laver came into the Ram. He didn't throw his weight about a lot but he did say he was going to make a smart place of Copley's Corner. Talked about a sunk garden and perhaps a little swimming-pool. That made Stadmore laugh. Where was he going to get the water from? And perhaps Laver tumbled to that too late. At any rate he got a Shireton firm to level the place off again and make something of the garden before it was too late.

I'd been pricking my ears at all that. I pricked them still more at what was to come.

"He was smartening up the place inside too," Hallows said. "Had a Shireton firm put it in order after he stripped all the old wall-paper and ripped out the old floor boards everywhere. It was a regular shambles when this Shireton firm got on the job, according to one of their men."

"How did Laver get the repair permit?"

"Ways and means," Hallows said dryly.

"And you say Laver still comes down?"

"Runs down very occasionally on a Sunday. That man he had digging there didn't come down again. Stadmore reckoned it was some navvy he brought down to do the job."

"Laver bring any woman down with him?"

"Only once. She was seen getting out of the car one Sunday morning in July. *A tallish brunette.*"

I sat up with a start. Then I was shaking my head. "Too good to be true. It couldn't be the brunette of Godfrey's letter."

"I don't know," he said. "The one who saw her was Pearce, the man who lives in that thatched cottage. He keeps a dog and I rather think he'd been out after a rabbit down the side lane somewhere, and he was coming back when he saw a car draw up at Copley's Corner. He got in behind the hedge and had a good view. What interested him was that Laver got out, had a good look towards Stadmore and then sort of beckoned this woman out. She nipped along the path and let herself in at the front door. Pearce had a good view of her. He says she was lanky—that's how he put it—and dark. In the twenties, he thought, and a very smart piece."

"And she's never been seen since?"

He reminded me that Copley's Corner was well out of the way. She might have been down but no one had seen her. Pearce had made her visit common talk at the Ram and if anyone had seen her again, all Stadmore would have known.

"We can't rule out that it might have all been normal," I said. "She came down to see what had been done to the cottage. To know what furniture would be wanted. Any furniture there, by the way?"

"A London firm brought some down. I don't know what or how much." He gave me a sort of exploratory look. "But that wouldn't explain why she scooted down that path. Why she didn't want to be seen."

"No," I said. "But let's pool what we know. Just what do you make of all this?"

He hesitated a moment.

"Well, if it didn't sound so melodramatic, I'd say Laver bought the place for what was in it. What he hadn't been able to get from Monaghan. He ripped out the interior to find where Monaghan had hidden it and he dug up the whole garden for the same reason. He was on the spot while the man he brought down did most of the digging."

"Then Laver's the man who made that attack on Monaghan."

"That's where it gets us."

I said it was just what I'd been thinking myself.

"That attack on Monaghan," I said. "The police seem to me to have taken something very much for granted—that he was going to bed when he admitted the caller."

Hallows had missed it too. He reminded me that Monaghan had had one boot off.

"I don't see it that way," I said. "Let's look at the whole thing again. Monaghan knew whoever it was that came or he'd never have let him in. The police found no forcible entry, or so I understand. The same known caller was able to strike the old man down from behind and truss him up when he was unconscious. Then he hunted the house and didn't find what he was looking for. So he came down to tackle Monaghan. What he was going to do was wait till he came round again and then burn the sole of his foot. Torture him, in fact, to get the information. He'd got one boot off when Start and Comfort arrived."

"Yes," said Hallows slowly. "I don't know, sir, that you aren't right."

"I'm pretty sure I'm right," I said. "Even if I'm not, we still want our own private look at Laver. But something else first. Do you think you can make an entry into the cottage?"

Hallows didn't see why he couldn't. Curtains were up and they should hide the light of a torch.

"I'd like to have a look inside the place," I said, and motioned him to be quiet while I thought things out.

"This is what we'll do," I told him. "You meet me at the back of the cottage at half-past eight. I'll go to Shireton and have a word with Loame and I'll ring up Start and make a fake call to get him well away from Copley's Corner. I'll also ring the office and get them to tell your wife you'll be home some time tonight. Unless anything unforeseen happens, you'll have to switch to Laver. We'll talk that over later when we've had a look inside that cottage."

I took the by-pass lane that brought me out half-way between Stadmore and Shireton. Just as I neared Police Headquarters I saw Loame coming down the steps and I stopped him as he was getting into his car. He put on a broad grin when he saw me and held out his hand.

"I thought it was you," I said, and he was asking me if I was in the town by accident or design.

"Just going on to Ipswich," I said. "Been seeing a man at Cambridge and this was my best road. Any news for me at all about poor Prial?"

He hesitated in a curious sort of way.

"Come up to my room for a minute," he said. "You've got time?"

I said I'd like to get to Ipswich before dark, which gave me a good bit of time, so up we went to his room. He offered me a cigarette and held the desk lighter.

"Funny you should ask about Prial," he said. "I'd been thinking of asking you to drop in. You people weren't holding out on us in any way, were you?"

"I don't follow you," I said. "Can't you be more explicit?"

"Well, you led us to think that he wasn't down here on a job of work."

"He wasn't," I said bluntly. "He was on holiday. I told you so. I as good as gave you my word to that effect."

His smile was quite benign.

"Well, there was something of his I forgot to show you when you were here the other day. If he wasn't on a job, how do you explain this?"

He had taken a small box from a drawer and was handing it to me. It was a little make-up box, complete with pencils, stain, spirit gum and two or three false moustaches. It was a remarkably neat little affair that would slip into a breast pocket.

"I neither can nor intend to explain it," I said. "I've never seen it before. I wasn't aware that he had it."

"You don't supply it to your men?"

"Good God, no!" I said. "Our men get assignments. How they carry them out is their headache, provided it's all strictly in order."

He waved a somewhat contemptuous hand at the box which I'd put back on his desk.

"Theatrical sort of cove, wasn't he?"

"Not to my knowledge," I said. "I can quite conceive of circumstances where a man might regard it as imperative to adopt some sort of disguise. I've had to do it myself. I admit it always made me feel as if I was playing at Indians."

"But why should he want to disguise himself on a holiday?"

I shrugged my shoulders. I said I could give quite a few reasons. To make a hit with some girl and not give himself away, for example. To frequent pubs or the local Palais de Danse without loss of face. To amuse himself by playing a part. After all, he was an excellent impersonator.

Loame took that for what it was worth. He wanted to know if I'd swear that Prial had been on holiday and hadn't been engaged on a job for the firm. I said if the time came for me to give evidence I'd certainly do what he said. I got in a question of my own about how things now stood.

"Where they were before," he said. "He was seen at one or two churches, so what he told that guest at the Royal seems to have some truth in it. But this"—his fingers rapped that box—"doesn't make things easier. If he was going about like an irresponsible lunatic in all sorts of comic disguises, what good are his photographs?" He shook his head. "I can't help thinking he must have given you people a pretty wrong impression of himself. This sort of thing doesn't exactly tally with what you told me."

"Sorry," I said. "I knew him well and what I told you was the truth. My only interest was to get the one who killed him."

"Who says he was killed?"

"Don't let's go round in circles," I said. "You can think what you like. This is a free country and I think he was killed. And I base it on what I knew of him and on what I learned from you when I was here last."

"Not a scrap of real evidence," he said. "Those papers could have been taken from his pockets by the one who was there when he shot himself."

"Good," I said, and got to my feet. "You find out who that someone was. And why he, or she, didn't come forward."

"Not very co-operative, are you?"

My eyebrows lifted.

"You as good as warned us against taking a hand! We've done everything you've asked of us."

"Leave it," he said, and got to his feet too. Maybe he was realising that he'd been a bit too short. "Sorry if I've been a mite touchy, but this Case has got me rattled."

We parted quite amicably. He went one way and I went another, but I took some side streets to the Royal and got dinner there. Loame didn't like me, I was sure of that. He was suspicious of my connection with the Yard and he had no use whatever for Detective Agencies. If it came to that, I had little use for him either. He'd deliberately kept that box up his sleeve and had tried to catch me out. But what I'd told him about it was perfectly true. Disguises may savour of Red Indians, but there are times when a man just has to do something of the sort. Science and detection may have moved on in line, but even science can't wave a magic wand and make a man look other than he is. For that sort of thing I'd still rather have a make-up box than a whole laboratory. And Godfrey Prial must have thought the same way too. He took a pride in his job, even if it was occasionally tinged with a kind of boyish, ironic delight.

It was a quarter to eight when I left the Royal. I stopped at a telephone kiosk on the edge of the town and rang the police-station at Stadmore. A woman answered.

"That Mrs. Start?" I asked gruffly.

She said it was. I asked if her husband was in and she said she'd fetch him, and what name was it please. I said she wasn't to bother. Tell him he was wanted at Shireton at once. The station-sergeant speaking.

I rang off before she could answer. I moved the car on pretty fast till I came to the lane again, then drove on more slowly with head-lights dipped. As I neared Copley's Corner I shut off the lights altogether, and I drew the car right in on the grass verge. There was a young moon and one could see clearly for a good thirty yards.

Hallows stepped from a gap in the garden hedge and startled me. He said he'd put a trip string on the front path, just in case. He nipped through the gap again and across a newly turfed lawn and we were at the Stadmore side of the house. We moved along the shadow to the back door. Hallows had it open and we bolted it behind us. The downstair windows had their blinds already drawn.

In the kitchen was a three-burner oil-stove and above the new sink a rack with oddments of crockery. The drawer of the small enamel-topped table held cutlery and some linen and under it was a new pail with water from the well. Furthest in the front from the

Stadmore side was the living-room. All it had was a folding camp-bed with a mattress, and blankets rolled up by its ticking pillow. There were two modern tubular steel chairs and a little round table that had on it the stains of glasses. On the mantelpiece was an empty ash-tray with merely the traces of ash. A painted deal cupboard had some tinned foods and three perfectly ordinary tumblers. A worn Axminster rug was on the floor, and there were ashes in the grate.

The other front room was a tiny one and completely bare, but its floor boards, like those of the living-room, were new. Its ceiling too had never a stain or crack. Laver had evidently intended it as a dining-room for a neat hatch had been made through to the kitchen.

That seemed all downstairs and Hallows went up to draw the bedroom blinds. He reported that only one room was used. The other had no curtains, nor had a kind of little box-room above the kitchen. That one bedroom had quite a nice divan bed, and a walnut chest of drawers in which was its linen. The commode stand by the bedside held a dirty chamber pot. On the commode top was a half-burnt candle in a pool of dry wax. The fireplace was clean but for some burnt matches.

We searched the floor to try to find a hairpin, but there wasn't one. A hairpin would have told us if a woman had definitely been up there and it should have given us an idea of the colour of her hair. So we came down again and began a search of the living-room floor. I wished we dared light that Aladdin lamp that was on the window-sill.

"What about trying to get a print or two somewhere," Hallows was whispering. "A tumbler ought to have one."

I shook my head. We couldn't take a tumbler away even if we did get a print. One out of three would be missed. On the other hand there were plenty of tins of food. We'd try one of them, I was thinking. But we didn't. *That was when we heard the noise.*

It was a queer noise but at the very first tremor of it Hallows' thumb was off the catch of the torch. We stood there in the pitch darkness, with never a breath. From the path beyond the window there had been something like a groan or a dull muttering, and then at last there was the sound of feet. I moved forward to the curtain. A man was just visible as he turned from the gate towards the village.

"Someone's been snooping," I whispered to Hallows. "He took the toss over that booby-trap of yours."

"Start?"

"He'd have stayed," I said. "You get everything shut up again and go to your car."

I unbolted the back door, had a quick look from the corner of the house and then nipped across that lawn again and through the hedge gap. My car was still warm and it started with little more than a purr. I drew gently round the sharp bend and the lights were off. I let the car idle in top gear until I saw something ahead, half-way perhaps between the thatched cottage and the village. I was within twenty yards of it. Then it was aware of the car and at that moment I switched on the head-lights. The man, whoever he was, darted across the road to the gate of the cottage, and his back was towards me as I went past. But it looked remarkably like Comfort.

I changed gear and shot on towards the village. At the green I turned right and drew the car up in the shadow of what looked like a barn. I nipped out and moved towards the church. A woman was coming my way.

"Is this the way to the vicarage?"

I had slipped my glasses into my pocket and had stooped a bit to disguise my height.

"Straight on," she said. "It's just on the left."

"Is that the front way or the back?"

"The front way," she said. "The back way's by the churchyard."

I walked slowly till she'd gone and then slipped into the church-yard. I found what looked like a back path leading to a door in the garden wall, and then drew back in the shadow of the church. I hadn't long to wait. I heard steps coming from round the tower. It was Comfort, and he passed within ten yards of me. There was no doubt of it in spite of the cap he was wearing and the muffler round his neck and ears.

Just short of the door he stopped. He drew back his waterproof and began dusting the knees of his trousers with his hand and there was a faint sound as of muttering. Then he lifted the latch and, slightly limping, went through to his garden, and after that there wasn't even the sound of his steps, and the wall itself hid the lower windows of the vicarage.

Hallows' car was just round the first bend beyond Copley's Corner. I drew up behind it and got out. Five minutes later we still had no clue to the mystery of Comfort. Hallows' guess seemed as good as any. Ever since that night of the attack on Monaghan, Comfort had had a sort of interest in the place. He had just been passing and on the spur of the moment had decided to have a look round.

I said he must have known what tripped him. And why hadn't he gone to warn Start? Hallows said it was because his trousers had been cut about. Perhaps he had thought that string a schoolboy trick.

"If he does decide to report to Start, Copley's Corner's going to be too hot for us," I said. "Start's bound to connect it with that fool's errand to Shireton."

"I don't know," Hallows said. "Comfort wouldn't like owning to Start that he'd been made a fool of over that string of mine."

That was when I thought of something. It was a theory and no more and for the moment I was keeping it to myself.

"All the same," I said, "we oughtn't to hang about here. You push off home now and first thing in the morning go along to Otway Mansions and get what you can on Laver. When you've got anything worth while, give me a ring at the flat."

He moved his car off and in a minute or two I followed. I didn't do much thinking till I was clear of that winding road and out at the turnpike, and then I began wondering about Comfort. In a very few minutes I'd explored my theory, and it seemed to fit.

I went back to the night of the attack on Monaghan. Comfort, it now seemed to me, had not been at Copley's Corner by chance. *He had been going to see Monaghan.* And why? Well, because he had for some reason or other seen him before, and some time after that first exploratory visit by the man who had attacked him that second vital night. Monaghan must have confided in Comfort. He had told him he was in possession of something dangerous.

That night then, Comfort had gone to see Monaghan by stealth, as it were. Something alarmed and scared him. Perhaps he saw the car parked in the other road, but whatever it was, he didn't knock or make a sound, for if he had he would have disturbed the man inside:

the man who at that moment was searching the cottage. Then Start overtook him and he told Start a garbled story of seeing something suspicious. But apparently he didn't tell Start what he had learned from Monaghan: what, in fact, the attacker had been trying to get. Comfort probably didn't know just what it was, except that it was both valuable, and dangerous to Monaghan, but he might have given Start an account of whatever it was that he *had* known.

And take Comfort's subsequent actions. Unless Comfort believed that that something was still in the cottage, why had he—a man notoriously hard up for money—tried to buy the place? Why had he visited Monaghan in the Mental Home, if not to extort somehow the whereabouts of that something? Why had he come to the cottage only an hour ago, and when the owner was away, if it were not to make some search of his own?

As for what that something was, two and two could surely be put together. Comfort was pressed for money, and therefore that something was worth money. It was worth an investment of five hundred pounds for an unwanted cottage. It was worth the risk of village talk about the Mental Home visits, and the risk of being seen by night at the cottage itself.

What exactly was it? I hadn't the beginnings of an idea. At the moment I hadn't an idea how to find out. To tackle Comfort himself would be folly. It would show my hand and merely make him the more careful. But there was the man Laver. He might be a kind of back door to Comfort. And there might be something in a day or so from Belfast about Monaghan.

Too many *somethings*, I was thinking. Everything far too nebulous, and like a waking moment when one almost recaptures the wonder of some escaping dream. But Laver, surely, would not be nebulous. He had not bought that cottage and hunted both it and its garden on some eccentric chance. That was what cheered me up as I drove on through the first suburbs—the thought of the morning, and Harry Laver.

CHAPTER 6
A BIT TOO CLEVER

IT WAS AT one o'clock the following afternoon that I got my telephone call from Hallows.

"Where're you ringing from?" I asked him.

"Hadenham Green," he said. "I'd like to see you if I could. It'll be at an A.B.C. almost opposite the Palais de Danse."

I had my car outside and I was away in five minutes, and heading north. It was an easy time for traffic and in just over half an hour I was in Hadenham Green, though traffic lights had been badly against me. Don't imagine anything idyllic, by the way, about Hadenham Green, even if that isn't its name. A hundred years ago it was a Green: now it's well inside the outer ring of suburbs and redolent of fried fish. How it grew God knows, but it's the kind of place one wants to hurry through, knowing that what's coming next can't conceivably be so dingy. Not that it hasn't its own crowded life and colour: the main road is lined with stalls, pavements usually chock-a-block, and buskers working the shop queues. Small factories are everywhere and here and there is a bombed space, and along the side roads one gets a glimpse of terraced houses, squat and monotonously depressing.

Hallows was waiting outside the restaurant and he told me where I could park my car. We ordered coffee and cakes and managed to get a seat at the window.

"Lucky I took my car to Otway Mansions," Hallows told me. "I've been over most of North London since I picked Laver up."

Otway Mansions was one of those blocks of flats built in the Holloway district between the wars. Their mere handiness to town made them expensive, but they were smart flats, Hallows said. He'd made enquiries at the office and all the flats were occupied, and the rents ranged from two-fifty to four hundred. Laver's flat he hadn't been able to investigate, for at ten o'clock he had picked him up. A man had brought the car to the front and Laver had taken the wheel and driven off. The man, not in chauffeur's uniform, had taken the seat beside him, and he had looked a bit of a tough.

Hallows had kept in touch with the car which had headed north and then turned off to the dog-racing track. It had driven inside and what had happened Hallows didn't know. But he had accosted an attendant and had learned that Laver was some sort of a big noise. His dogs ran there for one thing.

After about an hour Laver's car had driven out and had circled round towards the south of Hadenham Green. It had come out at that other main road which goes south to Tottenham, and there had pulled up outside an Amusement Arcade. It was the usual kind of thing: pin-tables, various slot machines, and a gramophone going full blast. It was a rather bigger place than most of its kind, and Hallows had wandered in and killed time by playing the tables, but he had seen nothing of Laver, though his man was there and talking to a rather frayed blonde who seemed to be employed at the place. When Laver did appear, and from a room that must have been the office, he was with a youngish man who looked like a spiv, and who was probably the manager. Laver was now carrying a small bag in which were probably the takings. The manager spoke to Laver through the door of the car before it moved off, and he didn't look too pleased with himself when it had gone.

The last stop was the Palais de Danse opposite where we were. Laver's car had been driven round to the back where there was an enclosed yard. Hallows had taken a look round but both Laver and his man must have gone inside, and there presumably they still were.

"What'd you make of Laver himself?" I said. "Just how he was described at Stadmore?"

"He looked a bit of a wise boy to me," he said. "Smart looking chap, though. Driving that Austin, by the way."

"We'd better find out at the flats if he ever had a big American car," I said. "He seems a pretty big shot himself. Owns that Arcade and probably the Palais de Danse. In a racket or two as well, I shouldn't be surprised."

Our problem was the next immediate move. Hallows pointed out that the Palais had its restaurant. He'd thought of going there for tea and questioning a waitress. That depended on whether Laver appeared before that and had to be followed again. I thought it didn't matter about following him any more.

Then I changed my mind. The logical thing to do was for me to go to that restaurant and for Hallows to keep an eye out for Laver. So I left him there and went across to the Palais de Danse. The main doors were open and a notice in the foyer directed me up the stairs to the restaurant. A pay-desk was at the top of the landing and through the swing door ahead of me I saw the cloth covered tables. The room was empty except for a single customer. It didn't matter where I sat for the windows didn't overlook the High Street, so I chose a table opposite a mirror which gave me a view of the room.

A waitress who'd been talking to the one customer came for my order. She looked well on for thirty in spite of the green dress that barely covered her knees and the frilly, yellow apron and fluffy cap to match.

"Too late for a meal, am I?" I said.

"You're only just in time," she said. "Plaice and chips is still on. Won't take above five minutes."

I hadn't lunched but I didn't feel hungry, but the plaice and chips seemed reasonably safe. The room itself was clean enough but its atmosphere was frowsty. The smell was a mixture of stale tobacco and vinegary sauce.

The garish mirrors made a false brightness but to me the whole place was nothing but a depression.

The last customer left and in another minute the waitress was bringing my order. She said it was a nice day.

"I suppose you were pretty busy a bit earlier?" I said.

Always busy between twelve and two, she said. But that was nothing to the evening rush. They were open till nine for the dance patrons.

"Pretty packed is it—the dance floor?"

"Packed?" she said, and tossed her head. "Like sardines gala nights and Saturdays. They don't seem to mind though. Can't say I like it myself."

"Mr. Collins the manager here now?"

"Collins?" she said. "I've never heard of a Collins. Mr. Ranger is here now. He was here before I came and I've been here over two years."

"Of course," I said. "I was thinking of another place."

The talk languished. She asked if the fish was all right. I said it was and then she sidled off. The last customer had left a picture paper and she took a seat at his table and began reading it.

The chips were greasy and the plaice watery, but I made a show of clearing my plate. I was thinking of slipping the balance into my own newspaper when the waitress came over again.

"Sorry, I thought you'd finished."

"Shan't be long," I said, and wondered how I could get the talk round to Laver. I thought I'd better ask her bluntly who was the boss.

"Mr. Laver," she said, and her voice had a kind of awe.

"Yes, of course," I said. "You ever on duty downstairs at all?"

She said she took a turn of duty at the soft drinks bar. It came only about twice a week. A rotten place for tips.

"Still, I suppose you've got to take the rough with the smooth," she said. "Interesting, though; watching the dancers when you're not too busy. A lovely band they have here too. Tony Athens and his Grecians. Excuse me!"

A man was coming through the door that led to the kitchen, and I had a good view of him in my mirror. He looked like the man Hallows had seen with Laver in the car. He must have had a good reflected view of me too—if it interested him. But he wasn't in the room more than a minute, then the waitress came back to me.

"That was Mr. Ranger?"

"Oh, no," she said, and sniffed. "That was Alf. I don't know what his real name is. We always call him Alf. He's Mr. Laver's sort of— well, sort of valet or secretary or something. You always see them about together. Any sweet would you like?"

"No sweet," I said. "I'm in a bit of a hurry."

I pulled out a handful of change as though deciding on the tip.

"By the way, just between ourselves, does Mr. Laver still have that lady friend of his? You remember: the brunette. Tallish. Sort of slinky, as they call it."

"I wouldn't know," she said. "I've never seen any brunette."

There was a queer reserve in her tone and I thought I'd better leave things like that. I put a shilling on the table and took my bill.

"Pay at the desk," she said. The tone was crisp and there was never a thanks for the proportionately generous tip. I went through the swing doors and then turned back as if there was something I'd forgotten. She was still standing by my table and her eyes were on those doors.

I crossed the road and looked in the window where I'd left Hallows, but he had gone. I went to my car and decided to go home and wait for a telephone call. Then I thought I might as well break the ride by having my own look at Otway Mansions.

They were a handsome block of buildings with a circular drive-way at the front and a largish car-park at the side. Only two cars were in it, and neither belonged to Laver or Hallows. As I neared the imposing entrance an attendant, looking like a cinema commis-sionaire in his plum-coloured get-up, was removing the autumn leaves from one of the handsome tubs with its trimmed evergreen that stood each side of the wide steps. I slipped into the huge foyer behind his back.

Wide carpeted stairs were at each side. I thought it best not to hesitate and took the ones towards which I had been veering. Flat Number 14 was at the end of the corridor and occupied a wide stretch of the angle. I went on and up to the next floor. The flats there were obviously not so large, and on the next floor they were smaller still. A lift was decanting an elderly couple and I took it back to the ground floor. Laver, I was pretty sure, had a four hundred a year flat, and one with a view.

The attendant at the door had finished his tidying of the tubs. I went past him and then turned back.

"Mr. Laver out, do you know?"

"I think so, sir. He went off in his car this morning. I haven't seen him come back."

"Did he take that big American car of his?"

"He parted with that some time ago, sir. He's driving one of the new Austins."

"So he sold that car, did he?" I said as if to myself. "A Buick, wasn't it?"

"Oh no, sir. It was a Hudson."

"Of course," I said. "I remember now. Hope he did well out of it."

I moved on but he was calling to me.

"Like to leave any message for him, sir?"

"It doesn't matter," I told him. "I can see him later."

That wasn't too adroit of me, but it couldn't be helped. And what I'd gathered was useful enough; in fact I was feeling on good terms with myself as I moved my car out again. Laver, I thought, had been pretty smart about Copley's Corner: smart, that is, according to his probable assessment of town smartness and rustic bovinity. What he hadn't allowed for was the countryman's assessment of city slickness, and an unpublished assessment at that. And the prevalence and potency of village gossip.

I had tea at the flat and just as I was finishing it, a ring came from Hallows. Laver had been at the dog-track again and then had left for his flat. Hallows was wanting to know if he should begin enquiries at the Mansions. I told him to come to my place straightaway.

Bernice, and I ought to say so at once, is gifted with an admirable discretion. When I'm working at the Yard she asks no questions and takes for granted my absences and erratic comings and goings. But this matter of Godfrey Prial was just a bit different. I'd told her what I was doing and she was as much for it as I. Most women, or so we're told, have a touch of the venomous, and because she'd had such a liking for Godfrey she seemed even more bitter about his death than I was, and maybe too because of that unknown brunette with whom he had become involved. It is true she didn't quite see why I shouldn't make use of the resources of the Yard. I suppose I should have taken that as a tribute to myself, who was actually less than an occasional cog in a huge machine, but I did try to make her see that the onus of things was on Loame. It was for him to call in the Yard. And even if he did, it was most unlikely that George Wharton would handle things.

All the same, if the Yard were called in, I might change my mind: at least to the extent of telling all that I so far knew. But in the meanwhile Hallows and I would carry on.

"Why shouldn't I go to that Palais de Danse?" she said. "You tell me what I have to do and I'll do it."

"Good lord, no!" I said. "You'd stand out a mile. That Palais at Hadenham Green isn't like a night-club."

"But I could go with Hallows?"

I'd thought of asking Hallows to take his wife there. This was a better idea. At any rate I said I'd see. Then she was wanting to know why I couldn't take her myself. I reminded her that I wasn't an asset to a dance floor but merely a menace. Besides, everything about me was just a little too conspicuous, and I wasn't too happy about the way that waitress had reacted to my last couple of questions.

Hallows came in and he and I talked things over. We planned a line of action into, which Bernice was to fit. He was to pick her up outside Finsbury Park Tube Station at half-past eight.

I walked the few yards with Bernice to Leicester Square. Her rig-out was of the neat but not too gaudy kind and I thought she'd rather overdone the make-up.

"Don't forget," I warned her. "Nothing to do but pal up with one or two likely customers. And go easy when you ask about that slinky brunette. And don't forget Hallows is the boss."

Her look was so pitying that I feared the worst.

It was just after midnight when the two came back.

"What was it like?" I asked Bernice.

"Not too bad," she said. "A very mixed crowd, but one or two quite decent. A bit smelly towards the end. I think I'd like a couple of aspirins."

Hallows had some beer and Bernice took her aspirins in weak whisky and soda. Hallows was saying he had drawn a blank.

"I got pally with the M.C. and got round to Laver and his brunette and he closed up like a clam. Mrs. Travers couldn't get any information either. She was awfully good, by the way."

"Did you actually see Laver?"

He said he'd seen him twice during the evening, but he hadn't come down to the actual floor. He had stood on the balcony for a minute or two, having a good look at everything below, and that man of his, Alf, had been with him.

"They might have been making a rough check of the takings," I said. "Everything looked just normal?"

"I don't know," he said. "A couple of flashy looking gents went up the stairs with a beefy looking, prosperous cove. I gave them a start and wandered up too. A chap at the top sent me back. Said it was private up there. Quite polite about it but took good care I went straight back."

"Gambling games going on?"

"I wouldn't be surprised," he said. "I saw one or two others drift that way and they didn't come back."

I said he'd better push off home and I'd see him in the morning. Bernice went to her room and I walked down with Hallows. I don't know if it was the clear sharp air of the night that cleared my wits, but suddenly my depression went and what had seemed awkward, to say the least, was as suddenly all to the good.

"I ought to have a personal look at Laver," I told Hallows. "I think I know how."

When I told him, he wasn't excited.

"But look, Mr. Travers: suppose that waitress at the restaurant reported that you'd been asking questions and the same with that commissionaire at the flats. Wouldn't Laver identify you?"

"That's what I'm hoping," I said, and he stared.

"You're an unknown factor," he said. "I think you ought to stay so. He may be given your description but he couldn't possibly find out who you are—if you keep clear of his haunts."

"I want to make him even more uneasy," I said. "My scheme will scare the innards out of him if he's what we think he is. Once I've done that, I can drop out again. He'll have to make some new move. He may go down to Stadmore again. Whatever he does, you'll have to watch him. It'll be tough for you but it's just got to be done. So you do what I said. Ring him in the morning soon after nine. Say you're my secretary. Try it with a fake address and make my name Peterson."

When I woke in the morning I still thought that scheme of mine a good one. Then about half-past nine Hallows rang.

"It's all right, sir," he said. "You're to see him at half-past ten this morning. He didn't question the address."

"What'd he sound like?"

"A bit suspicious at first. Then he cupped the receiver and asked me to hang on. If he was looking up the Telephone Directory for Petersons he'd have found his hands full. I think he was talking things over with someone. Alf, perhaps. It was over three minutes before he spoke again and he was just a bit too hearty."

"Right," I said. "You get out there and pick him up when I've finished with him. Don't question a soul at the Mansions. You're to keep under cover."

When I got out of my car just short of half-past ten, I was looking quite a smart professional man in a neat grey suit and hat and a leather portfolio under my arm. The attendant spotted me as I walked in and gave me a flick of the forefinger. I went on up the stairs to Flat 14. I pushed the bell and while it was ringing I heard the voice telling me to come in.

I walked into a handsome lounge. The carpet was thick and the chairs huge and comfortable. A radiogram-television set, big as a Victorian chest of drawers, stood in the near corner. Sporting prints were on the walls, and an open cocktail cabinet was just by the handsome mahogany desk at which Laver had been sitting.

The tortoiseshell glasses had been something unexpected. He hooked them off and laid them on the desk and got to his feet as I entered. He too was well-dressed, though a bit too in at the waist and out at the shoulders for my tailor's liking. Hallows had been right: he was good-looking in a flashy sort of way, but I put his age as nearer fifty than forty. His nose had a hook and the lips weren't all that fleshy.

"Mr. Peterson?" he said.

"Yes," I said, and with my best smile. "You're Mr. Laver?"

"Yes, I'm Laver. You wanted me about something?"

"That's right," I said. "My secretary fixed this appointment. I hope I'm not giving you too much trouble."

His own smile had shown a beautiful set of teeth. I didn't like his eyes. They hadn't smiled as well. They were a cold sort of grey and already they'd contrived to take in every inch of me.

"No trouble at all," he said. "You'll have a drink?"

"Thank you, but it's just a bit early. And you must be a busy man."

"Take a load off your feet," he said, and waved me to a chair. "What's on your mind, Mr. Peterson?"

When I sank into that chair I knew what it was like to try to swim in the Dead Sea. I had to heave myself up again.

"Well," I said as diffidently as I could, "it's like this. I've had to go to Stadmore once or twice recently—my wife has some relations quite near—and I happened to see that cottage of yours. Copley's Corner, I believe the name is. I thought it might be nice for a week-end place as my wife's relatives are so close, so I made an enquiry or two and it appears you don't use it a lot. I got your name and address from the agents who sold it, by the way. So I wondered if you'd like to part with it."

"I see," he said, and the eyes that had narrowed had never left my own. He looked away and frowned.

"I might," he said. "Depends what you offer. You say you want it as a weekend place?"

"Yes," I said. "It's secluded but it's not too secluded. I like the country round that way, too."

He leaned back in his chair, finger-tips together and his thumb hard against his chin.

"It has no main water and no indoor sanitation or electric light."

"When in the country you expect to do as country people do," I told him cheerfully. "That's all part of the fun, as it were."

He didn't smile. The eyes narrowed just a bit more frowningly.

"I think electric light's coming at any moment," he said. "You could have an electric pump from the well and indoor sanitation, or make do with a hand rotary pump. But you'd have to have septic tank drainage. All that would cost you a packet. I don't know if you're a wealthy man."

"I manage," I said a bit fatuously. "But I do realise I'd probably be faced with pretty big charges if I wanted a bathroom and so on."

"You know the place well?"

I didn't fall into that little trap.

"But how could I? I've just formed my own impressions from the outside." I smiled as if I'd only then realised something. "But if I'm a buyer, aren't you going the wrong way to work? I mean, one doesn't cry stinking fish."

"Just wanted you to know," he said. "Nothing like having things open and above-board."

There was a tap on the door back to his left. A man came in and I saw he was Alf. He gave only a quick glance at me. I saw the cauliflower ear that faced me as he turned sideways towards Laver.

"Excuse me, sir, but what about Harris? Oughtn't I to let him know?"

"Tell him anything you like," Laver told him impatiently. "The man's a ruddy pest."

Alf went soft-footed out. Laver gave a grunt.

"About the cottage, Mr. Peterson. What do you offer?"

"You can't expect me to be buyer and seller too," I told him craftily. "What price do you want?"

"Twelve hundred," he said, and there was something a bit supercilious in the way he said it.

"Good lord!" I said. "That's a bit steep, isn't it? You only paid five hundred and twenty-five."

"I got it cheap," he said. "I'm not worrying, Mr. Peterson. House property is still right up there. Someone'll want it. If you want it badly enough, twelve hundred isn't all that much. You do want it badly, don't you?"

I wasn't falling for that either. I said I didn't want it badly at all. I'd just liked the look of the place and had hoped to buy it at a reasonable price.

"And what is your idea of a reasonable price?"

"What you gave for it—or a bit less," I said, and was scared as hell for fear he'd take me up.

"Nothing doing," he said, and his lip was drooping as he got to his feet. "Sorry, but there we are. Twelve hundred. Take it or leave it."

I looked as disappointed as I could. He shook hands and was saying he'd let me know if he changed his mind. Perhaps I'd better leave my address. He hadn't taken it down from my secretary. I'd been a fool. I didn't know what address Hallows had given him.

"I don't think it's necessary," I told him coldly. "In fact I've changed my mind. At anything like your price that cottage has ceased to interest me."

He gave a casual nod as he closed the door behind me. I went straight downstairs to my waiting car, and I'd been careful not to leave it in the car park. I didn't want Laver to trace me from its number, and I took a different way back by Islington and the City, for I wanted to see Norris and was wondering about some news from Belfast, and as I drove through the not too crowded side streets, I was thinking all the time about Laver.

He was tough, there wasn't a doubt about that, and almost certainly as ruthless. Clever too, but whether he'd have risked his neck over murder I didn't know, though often the clever ones make mistakes. I didn't even know whether or not he'd taken me at my face value, which shows how smart he'd been. Nothing on his face had told me a thing about that waitress or the commissionaire. As for the ridiculous price he'd put on Copley's Corner, that might have been a try-on. On the other hand he might have wanted to see if my interest in the place had been twelve hundred pounds worth. As for what he'd now do, I hadn't an idea, and as I was then in the traffic of the City, I hadn't a chance to do much theorising.

But I was soon to know. I drew up my car outside the Agency, got out, and gave my long legs a preliminary stretch. It was then that a taxi passed me. It was travelling slowly and it went straight on and turned left at the far end of the street. But I'd recognised the man who was in it. *It was Alf.* He'd had a newspaper but he'd covered his face just a bit too late.

And I couldn't do a thing about it. I'd taken too much for granted and underestimated Laver. Alf, it was obvious, had had his ear against that door. Some word of Laver's had been a signal for him to come in, and that blether about a certain Harris had told him to get on my tail.

And now Laver would know that I was connected with the Broad Street Detective Agency. It wouldn't be too hard to find out my name and where I lived. But it couldn't be helped. As far as I was concerned he'd no longer be up against someone unknown. I should have stayed under cover, and Hallows had been right. Or hadn't he?

Maybe everything had been for the best after all. Godfrey Prial had been an employee of the Agency, and that connected me with him. In poking my nose into Laver's affairs I could only have told Laver that I—and the Agency—was after the one who killed Prial. If he was the killer, or connected with the killer, then surely he'd be pretty badly alarmed. Looking at things from a melodramatic point of view, it almost seemed as if he'd have to do something drastic to me in order to protect himself. But he couldn't do that. He couldn't eliminate a whole Agency. But he'd have to do something, and it was that something for which we'd have to be on the look out. And there was at least another cheerful thought. Laver might know all about myself but he hadn't got the same line on Hallows—as yet.

CHAPTER 7
DEAD END

THERE WAS nothing for me from Belfast, but no sooner was I at the flat again than Norris was ringing me. Just after I'd left, the Belfast firm had telephoned their report. He hadn't an idea what it was all about but was sending me what had been taken down.

I was having lunch when it came and I read it on the way from door to table. John Corkery had joined the Fusiliers in 1895, had served throughout the South African War and had married in 1903, holding then the rank of corporal. His wife was a Clara Masters of Withbourne, Lincolnshire. His son was born in December, 1903, and in the Spring of 1904 he was reduced to the ranks for drunkenness. By 1906 he was back to full corporal again, and in 1907 was again reduced to the ranks. In 1908 he was sentenced to two years' detention and dismissed from the service for striking an officer. Nothing else was known about him as far as regimental records were concerned.

Once again I was back where I was before. Complete as the report was, it offered no connection between Corkery and Monaghan. If it added to my knowledge at all, it was to confirm in a mild sort of way what old Cladden had told me about Corkery at Broughshane: that in 1904 he had paid a visit home after his father's death and had talked rather big about his prospects. Those prospects were simply that he was telling himself that he'd turn over a new leaf and soon be made up to corporal again. Cladden too had seemed to be dead right when he'd described Corkery as very much of a hellion.

At the end of the report was the question as to whether we wished Belfast to carry on enquiries at Withbourne. I rang Jack Norris and asked him to say we'd tackle that end ourselves. Meanwhile would they send their bill, and if subsequently anything else turned up, we'd pay for it. After that I had to wait till Hallows should ring me, and that wasn't till after two o'clock. I told him to come to my flat, and while I was waiting for him I packed my bag.

Hallows wasn't happy about things. He'd picked up Laver after I'd left, but not till a good hour after. He'd seen Alf go off in the taxi that had passed me in Broad Street and he'd seen him come back in the same taxi, and it was a quarter of an hour after that when Laver and he had left in the Austin. But Hallows soon spotted that Alf was sitting at the back with his eyes on the following traffic. Laver was plainly suspicious, and Hallows didn't dare to take a chance. What he'd done was to drive straight to Hadenham Green, park his car in a different side street, and then watch for Laver's arrival at the Palais. Laver had duly arrived and had still been somewhere inside when Hallows had rung me.

I told him about my morning and put the best face on things that I could. I wanted his views on what Laver was now likely to do. He hadn't an idea.

"What *can* he do, sir? He can't bolt. That'd own he did kill Godfrey—if he did. All he could do would be to keep that brunette well under cover."

"That's it," I said. "What we've got to find is that brunette."

He gave a wry shake of the head.

"Surely we can make some contact," I said. "There must be somebody at the flats who's seen her? What about nobbling one of the staff? I take it they're service flats?"

He said they were service flats all right, but how was he to do the nobbling business? Godfrey, now, with his appeal, would have walked away with such a job. He could have told the tale to any woman.

"I'm not that sort," Hallows said, and he was dead right. "Besides, wouldn't Laver take precautions? Wouldn't he complain to the manager and get him to warn the staff about any snooping?"

"Money talks," I said. "It's a question of who pays most—we or Laver. Even that commissionaire might open his mouth if the bait looked good enough."

There was the same wry shake of the head.

"Look, Bob," I said. "I'm off to this Withbourne place to find out anything I can about Corkery. You go bull-headed for that commissionaire. Try him with a tenner to start with and see how it works."

He said he'd try, which was good enough. I told him I couldn't be back till at least the following evening, and we made a tentative arrangement that he should report to me personally at round about nine o'clock.

I rang a hotel at King's Lynn and then set off in my car. I had tea at a place just beyond Cambridge and turned up at my hotel well in time for dinner. In the morning I had an early breakfast and was away shortly after eight.

That fen country in the Wash corner was even duller than the Cambridgeshire flats of the previous afternoon. But the road was good and I was through Long Sutton half an hour later. I had another look at the map and found the side road for Withbourne. For two miles it ran alongside a canal, then turned sharply right. I went through one hamlet and then two miles on I came in sight of Withbourne church.

It was an ugly village lying below the road along which it was strung out. Another and sunken kind of road was below me and it joined my road where a bridge crossed a wide dyke. Beyond were a few more houses and a farm. I had to stop somewhere so I drew the car in by a little shop. The post-office-shop had already been passed. This was a small grocery and general store. I wondered if it would be open. It was, and a woman of about fifty came in from a side door at the tinkle of the shop bell.

"I wonder if you could possibly give me any information," I said. "I'm enquiring about a woman named Masters, Clara Masters, who left here a good many years ago. She was married in 1903."

"Masters," she said, and licked her lips. "Yes. There were Masterses here. I just remember them."

"What I was wondering was this," I said. "Could you tell me any very old person in the village who'd be likely to give me the information? Someone aged, say, about eighty? I'd be quite prepared to pay."

She had been smiling.

"What about my mother?" she said. "She's eighty-four. Wait a minute and I'll ask her."

She went back through the door and I could hear faint voices. That showed at least that the mother wasn't deaf. What she turned out to be was as alert and sprightly as a good many women of seventy. Even her cheeks hadn't the yellowish ivory of age, but were plump and vividly red. Her eyes were none too good, she said, and but for that she was as well as ever she'd been.

"You want to know about the Masterses," she said.

"A Clara Masters who married a soldier named John Corkery," I told her.

"I know," she said, and almost aggressively. "She was a servant up in London when she married him. Got her into trouble, he did, and married her."

I interrupted her only once. She said, "Look here, young man, you let me remember things my own way, else you'll get me all muddled." So I let her go on till she'd finished. The sequence of things was apparently this.

Clara's father had died. The Masterses, as old Mrs. Privet called them, were consumptive. The father had been a small farmer and when he had died the widow, Rebecca Masters, had retired to a small cottage which she had bought from the proceeds of the farm sale. It was the second cottage on the left, Mrs. Privet said, as one entered the village.

John Corkery she described as a bad 'un. The description she gave of him tallied with that I'd had from Gladden. The married couple hadn't come to Withbourne at all after the marriage, but in about 1908 Clara came home bringing the boy. I didn't mention the fact but it was plain that the wife had come home because her husband was serving that period of detention. About a year later, Mrs. Masters had died, also of consumption. About a year after that, Corkery had joined his wife at Withbourne. He was a soft-spoken, blarneying chap and had lived on what his wife had inherited from her mother, and then he took a job with a cousin of the family, a farmer named Smeeth. Two years after that he was sentenced to two years' imprisonment for breaking into a private house at Long Sutton. Smeeth took the boy, for while Corkery was in jail Clara died. Corkery gave instructions from the jail that everything was to be sold. When he came out he took both the money and the boy and that was the last the village ever heard of him.

"What was the boy himself like?" I said.

"Young John Corkery?" she said. "A nasty little varmin, that's what he was. Always up to something no good and real crafty with it. Took after his father. I'll lay you he came to no good."

I kept on at her but she could remember little else that seemed of importance. She said that Clara was a nice little body, and so was her mother. Corkery was said to be a Roman Catholic but acted more like a heathen. The boy had had an accident with a saw and severed his little finger, and it was discovered that the saw had been stolen. Those were all the kind of oddments she mentioned, and there seemed no point in staying on longer. I thanked her and her daughter and wanted her to buy herself some small present, but she wouldn't take any money.

I managed to reverse the car in the narrowish road and drove back the way I'd come. It had been a wasted journey and there was only one thing that cheered me in the least. Corkery had left Withbourne not too long before the outbreak of war. He would have had money on which to live for some time, and if the boy was as big and tall at eleven as one might expect from a father of the build and height of Corkery, then he might have passed for more. But that wasn't important. The thing was, just what would Corkery be likely to do when he had spent his money. Surely as an old soldier he would have joined up, *and under another name.*

But the records of the Army couldn't be searched for Monaghans, nor would it be possible to advertise. Nor could one hope to pick up the trail of the boy, unless he had turned out a criminal like his father and the Yard had his record. If Corkery served right through the war without mishap or trouble, his boy would have been seventeen or so when the couple were united again. But doubtless a boy so cunning and adaptable as Mrs. Privet had described him, would have gone his own way while his father was serving somewhere abroad. Both father and son had disappeared and, to face up to facts, it looked as if we were hunting not only a cold scent but a false one. Godfrey Prial's death might be somehow connected with

Monaghan, but to find a connection between Monaghan and Corkery seemed futile. And yet two things stood out. Why had Monaghan had that photograph of Brady's Farm? Why had he kept that small mug which had been a present from Skegness? Skegness was the natural seaside resort for Withbourne. It could have belonged to the boy and the boy might have taken it with him when he finally left Withbourne with his father.

But there it was. A glimpse, as it were, of something, and then that something gone. And it was a pity the Smeeths had gone too or they might have told me things that Mrs. Privet had forgotten. Everything was a pity.

Everything brought a depression: a monotony of depression like the monotony of that flat sameness of the country through which I drove.

I didn't stop for lunch but drove the car hard on. Soon after one o'clock I was at the flat. Bernice was out but I had a service meal and then went to the Yard. Wharton wasn't there but I saw someone who knew me well enough, and Norris too for that matter, and who could do the job.

"I think I might possibly do you people a bit of good," was how I put it. "We're handling a case and a certain John Corkery has cropped up, and I have a faint idea he might turn out to be on the run. You might look him up and see if you're interested."

"Corkery," he said. "John Corkery. What was his line?"

I said I didn't know. That was his baptismal name and he'd now be forty-five years old. He was probably about six foot, and might possibly speak with an Irish accent. Only known connection—Lincolnshire. I added what I knew of his father, with special reference to the conviction after the Long Sutton business, and I threw in for weight the guess that the father had rejoined the Army in 1914.

"You're not in a hurry?" I was asked.

I said I wasn't, though I'd like the information that afternoon. I was told to come back soon after four o'clock, so I went to my club and glanced through the periodicals and had tea and it was half-past four when I reported back at the Yard. There was nothing for me. Records had nothing on a man whose baptismal name could be traced to John Corkery.

That again was that. I went home and was wishing I'd arranged to see Hallows earlier. Then my wife came home from some tiring committee meeting or other. I had a second tea and suggested going to see a well-reviewed French picture. That passed the waiting time, though I didn't tell her that, and when we were home again and nicely through the evening meal, Hallows turned up. I told him what had happened in Lincolnshire and the Yard. His own story wasn't much more exciting, even if he had nobbled Cox, the commissionaire. As a matter of fact he had left Cox only a few minutes before coming to the flat,

Cox had been off duty and by arrangement had met Hallows at the Fox and Geese. Hallows had hinted he was working for the Commissioners of Inland Revenue and had brought in the brunette by hinting that Laver had probably used her as a kind of stooge for tax-dodging. He had promised Cox handsome payments for results and had given him a couple of pounds on account.

"But surely Cox must have known something about the brunette already," I said. "You're not asking him to do things in the future. You wanted to know what happened in the past. Was Laver seen about with this brunette. What was her name, and so on."

"I know," he said. "I was coming to that. Cox swears he knows nothing about a brunette—any particular brunette. According to him Laver has various women. You know: first one, then she isn't seen any more and another shows up. Naturally some were blondes and some brunettes. All he could think of was a widow who used to have Flat 15 in the early days of the war. She sounded far too old for me."

He added that he didn't trust Cox an inch. He looked a twister and acted like one. In fact Hallows was of the opinion that that night's interview would reach Laver's ears. Cox would try to string us along and take pay from both sides.

"A pity," I said. "I thought money might have talked. I mean one-sidedly."

"Not our kind of money," he said.

I didn't see it. Laver's income might be considerably more than my own, but it seemed to me that I had quite enough to tempt a man like Cox.

"It isn't exactly money," Hallows said. "It's more subtle than that. It's the sort of personal relationship. Laver calls him Fred. Laver's there all the time. Besides, Laver's a dog man. What we can give Cox is just pickings compared with what he picks up in the course of a year from Laver. Think of the straight tips. 'Watch Trap so-and-so for the second race, tonight Fred,' or, 'You might have a bit on my So-and-So tonight, Fred. Do it with a bookie, not on the Tote.' That's what I mean, Mr. Travers. Laver can put more pounds in Cox's pocket than we can shillings, and without parting with a cent. And Laver'll be there all the time long after we're gone—or Cox thinks so."

He was right and I had to admit it. I also saw the implications. If Cox was the double-crosser that Hallows suspected, then from our point of view he was a dangerous liability.

"No more Cox," I said. "We'll drop him like a hot poker. And the devil of it is that neither you nor I ought to show our faces anywhere near Otway Mansions again. We're neither of us under-cover. Cox will pass your description on to Laver."

Altogether I seemed to have made a mess of things. Most of what I'd done had been done against the advice of Hallows, and yet Hallows, for that matter, hadn't put forward any concrete ideas to take their place. And we couldn't afford to remain static. Time was on Laver's side. If there was anything that our appearance on the scene had shown he had overlooked, he'd now be only too busy putting it right.

But what could we do? I didn't know and neither did Hallows. All either of us could suggest was to go on making him uneasy: to rag and irritate till he made some new move. But how could we tell what the move would be?

"What about putting a new man on?" Hallows said.

"Just a question of time before he was rumbled," I said. "And where could we plant him? Laver wouldn't bring his private affairs to the dog track."

"Wait a minute," I said. "A dog track's a big place. You could move about there and no one would know you. There'll be regular bookies and their clerks. They'd know Laver. One of them might put us on to the brunette."

That seemed the best chance and Hallows said he'd give it a try. I wondered too if we might get hold of some other owner who was a cut above the Laver class and might be trusted to hold his tongue. Hallows thought that a far more likely line. He had never been to a track himself but he thought it would be like the lay-out of things at a race-course—a select stand or a special part of one where owners were very much in each other's company. And he could spend the next morning interviewing a sporting writer he knew on one of the popular papers, and go to the dog track duly primed.

The problem for me was what to do with my time. I reviewed every angle of the case and for the life of me could think of nothing. Then it suddenly struck me that I'd never clapped eyes on Monaghan himself. But even if I could scheme a visit to that Mental Home, I didn't see what a mere sight of Monaghan could tell me. And yet when I was in bed that night the idea kept gnawing at me, and in the morning I made up my mind.

I went by train to Shireton and took a taxi at the station. It was a matter of only ten minutes before I was there, and I told the taxi to wait. What my line of approach would be I still didn't quite know, and I was trusting largely to bluff and charm.

The Mental Home was a magnificent place with a range of handsome red brick buildings, and we had made our way to it along a superb drive. In the wide courtyard before the main entrance were beds of autumn flowers, and trees and shrubberies were everywhere. I might in fact have been calling on the owner of some modern country estate.

I walked in. A man in some sort of uniform had his back to me in the enquiry office and it looked as if I could have gone right through the corridor ahead of me without his knowing, but I halted, and coughed. I asked him if I might see the Medical Superintendent, and I had to own that I hadn't an appointment. He looked dubious, asked my name, and then got to work on the telephone.

What was said I don't know, but I was asked to wait in a room that was pointed out to me. It was a room bare of everything but chairs and just when I was getting restless, a woman whom I took for a secretary appeared. She wanted to know my exact business and then gave me a smile and said she'd report back. Five minutes later I was being shown into a nearby room.

Dr. Goodrow was a heavily built man of over fifty. To me he looked somewhat grim, and he merely nodded when I repeated my name and gave him one or two references. Then he wanted to know precisely why I wanted to see James Monaghan. I said that by a curious chance connected with the British Legion, I had come across a James Monaghan of whom traces had been lost, and enquiries at Stadmore had shown that the James Monaghan now in the Home was of the same build, and was also a Roman Catholic. I was working on behalf of the wife whom he had deserted some years before. She had thought he was dead and as she now had the chance of marrying the man to whom she was housekeeper, she wished to be sure. Those, I said, airily, were just the main outlines.

To my surprise he saw no reason why I should not see the man. It was not a visiting day but I should be needing only a look. That settled he became almost genial. He asked me about myself and the British Legion and I told him quite a lot that I hadn't known before.

He even accompanied me back to that waiting room. I wondered if he were going to do any telephoning.

Another five minutes went by and a male nurse arrived and escorted me along a couple of corridors to another room. It was a largish room and in it were only two chairs. In one of those sat the man whom I knew at once for Monaghan. The nurse, who had been there, moved back by the open door. I went forward.

Monaghan was raw-boned and gaunt but his ramrod back was that of an old soldier. His hair and beard were snowy white, and he had the look of some old Hebrew prophet. His deep sunken eyes seemed to see me and not to see me: there had been, as it were, a flicker of life in them, and then they were fixed on nothing, unless it was the blank wall of that room. In his fingers was a crude sort of rosary and his lips almost imperceptibly moved. I watched for a moment or two and tried to read the scarcely moving lips. Once I thought the rosary had slipped from his fingers and then I saw it was fastened to his waistcoat. It was the one he had always been seen with at Stadmore, and made, or so it looked to me, of various sized black beads.

I took the other chair and sat almost facing him. I smiled gently at him, and his eyes met mine and then moved away into that same vagueness of space. I leaned slowly forward and whispered.

"John Corkery."

The fingers checked their movement. But only for a second or two.

"John Corkery."

This time the fingers failed to check.

"Brady's Farm . . . Clara . . . Withbourne."

There was never a sign that he heard me. I shook my head and got to my feet. There was no point in outstaying my welcome.

"Is he always like that?" I asked the attendant.

"Always the same, sir."

He said the doctor wanted to see me before I left but I'd better wait where I was. I drew back while he gently took Monaghan by the arm and led him unresisting away.

In two or three minutes I was with the Medical Superintendent again. I said I was sorry I'd troubled him. Monaghan definitely wasn't my man. My Monaghan had had a wart by his left eye, for one thing and a scar on his right hand.

He didn't seem too interested. I thanked him and said that if he was in town he must have lunch with me at my club. That led to some quite cheerful chit-chat and it was another ten minutes before I left. At Shireton I had only ten minutes to wait for a train. It was a slow one but I was back at the flat in time for lunch.

What I learned was precisely nothing. As far as concerned what might be called the imponderables, I was worse off than before, for as my mind's eye kept seeing that poor devil of a Monaghan, I had an unease that cast a gloom upon everything, and made a hopelessness of all we had so far done! Lunch failed to cheer me up and in the afternoon I took a walk in the Park. Then the sun came out for the first time that day and I felt a bit better.

When I got home I learned that Hallows had rung. I waited and in another hour he rang again. A Sir Philip Stangate was a likely man to approach. He said he was a well-known sportsman who ran his dogs at the same track as Laver. I said I'd see what could be done.

I'm lucky in having a pretty wide social experience, if that's the name for it, so I hunted about in my mind for someone of the same possible tastes as Stangate. I tried one man and he put me on to another. He knew Stangate personally and said I might use his name, but where Stangate was at the moment he had no idea, though I might try a couple of clubs.

It was too late then to go chasing anything so elusive, but I found Stangate's town address in the Directory and rang it on chance. A woman's voice said he was out.

I gave my name and asked if I could see him in the morning. I gathered I could try it but not before eleven o'clock.

So at soon after eleven o'clock I went to Eaton Square. Stangate was in a kind of library room and he looked a man of my own age. I introduced myself and mentioned what I might call my backer, and I was hoping he would notice my tie. He did. We unearthed a mutual acquaintance or two and everything was fine.

"But about this business of mine," I said at last. "It's highly confidential and I'm quite prepared for you to look me in the eye and tell me to go to hell. I simply ask you if you know a man named Laver. Harry Laver."

"A friend of yours, is he?"

"God forbid," I said piously.

"I know him," he said. "A very unpleasant piece of work."

He gave me a shrewd look and asked if there'd been any kind of swindle.

"Oh, no," I said. "This is some dirty work to do with a woman. I'm being a kind of Galahad since she happens to be a friend of mine—and a good sort. All, in fact, that I want to know, and I promise you I shan't bother you again or divulge a single word, is if you've seen Laver with any particular woman lately."

He thought for a moment.

"Yes," he said slowly. "Up to a month or two ago he used to have a woman with him. About twenty-five or so as far as I remember. A rather showy piece."

"Blonde or brunette?"

"Not a blonde," he said, "if you mean one of those long-haired platinum wenches. To the best of my belief she was a dark haired girl."

"Tallish?"

He frowned, then shook his head.

"I'll have a word with my daughter if you don't mind waiting here. Women remember these things."

In under five minutes he was back.

"Pen says she was tallish. Very stream-lined, if that's any help to you. She hasn't been with him for some weeks now. The last one he had in tow, so I'm told, was a shattering blonde."

That was all. Hallows was waiting at my flat and we tried to assess the value of what we'd learned. Whatever we made of it didn't cheer us. Cox had evidently told us the truth about one thing—that Laver changed his women. Our slinky brunette had had her day and had been succeeded by a blonde. And that left us hopelessly stuck. We had no authority behind us like the police. We couldn't have interviews with the staff at Otway Mansions and try to trace that brunette. Otway Mansions was, in fact, the last place where we ought to be seen. What then could we do? The brunette had gone. Perhaps she had never set foot in the Mansions at all. Where could we start? Where could we find a lead?

And since that waitress at the Palais, and Cox, had almost certainly blown the gaff, and Laver knew we were very much interested in that brunette, his policy must be to keep her well under cover. He might have parted company, but he'd keep an eye on her and he'd warn her of the dangers of saying a word or committing any act that might connect her name with his.

But there did seem one possible line of approach. Hallows must at all costs keep an eye on Laver, even if he had to change his cars and adopt some sort of disguise. There must have been night-clubs or hot spots in town that Laver had frequented in company with that brunette. He might visit one again. That was the kind of place at which to carry on enquiries. It was even possible that though she and Laver had parted company, that brunette was still frequenting the old haunts. Why shouldn't she be, unless Laver had warned her off.

Hallows worked at that for over a week and I was getting more and more bored with idleness. Laver was followed to a place in Wardour Street but Hallows hadn't the high sign and wasn't let in. Then Hallows found a nightclub to which Laver had been and there he got vague news of a brunette, but that brunette hadn't been seen there for at least a couple of months. And that was how things were drifting on: Hallows working like a beaver and things refusing to happen.

But meanwhile one thing did happen, and it was surprising enough. Norris went to Shireton to give evidence at the re-opened inquest, and a virtual murder verdict was brought in. I didn't know the reasons for that *volte face* on the part of Loame and, according to what Norris heard, there was no new evidence, but within a very short time we heard something else: that the Yard had been called in and that a Chief-Inspector and Det.-Sergeant of our acquaintance had gone to Shireton.

The other thing that had happened I learned myself when, bored by that same idleness, I had paid another visit to Stadmore. It was that Copley's Corner was in the market again. It was being advertised by different agents from those who had handled it before, and when I drove slowly past it I saw that men were at work. I stopped my car and got out, and they told me they were making those very improvements that Laver had suggested to me when I had seen him in his flat. What I knew was that Laver had convinced himself that the thing for which he had searched was no longer there, and all he wanted now was to get his money back, and perhaps make a profit.

But, as I said, things just drifted with me and Hallows and it was plain that we were wasting our time. Finally we faced up to things, and were virtually resigned to placing our information at the disposal of the Yard. And then, just at the last moment, something suddenly happened. It was the opening of what I might call the Second Phase.

PHASE II
MYRA COWLE

CHAPTER 8
OUT OF THE BLUE

I suppose one could call it coincidence. As things were to turn out, I should have been wrong if I had even thought of it as luck. It happened to me personally because of that enforced idleness which I have mentioned, and because, to kill time, I had got back to my morning calls at the Agency. Then Norris had to go to Birmingham where we had undertaken to investigate a pretty extensive matter of pilfering, and I was the one who had to take over. Norris left in rather a hurry. He rang me in the late afternoon of the Sunday and put it to me that he ought to go to Birmingham, and would I run things in the office for a couple of days.

I went along rather early the next morning and had a quick conference with Bertha. I went over the various assignments and got in touch with everything again, and it was after ten o'clock when we'd finished. It was then that Bertha told me I had an appointment in twenty minutes' time. A Miss Cowle had asked for it and she hadn't been willing to give the least idea what her business was.

"What'd she sound like?"

"Sort of so-so," Bertha said. "A youngish woman. Not a bad voice but nothing off the top shelf."

I gave a non-committal grunt and got on with the correspondence. The minutes went so quickly that I was surprised when Bertha buzzed through and said that the Miss Cowle was there.

"What's she like, Bertha?"

"On the quiet side. Beautiful clothes. Looks about twenty-five."

"Right," I said. "Bring her in."

I'd hardly pushed my papers aside when the door was opening. The woman, or should I say girl, was a tallish blonde. I smiled and was shaking her gloved hand.

"Good-morning, Miss Cowle. Mr. Norris is away and I'm acting for him till he gets back. My name's Travers. Take this seat, will you?"

She gave me a little nod and a shy kind of smile. Her hair was almost a silvery blonde and her eyes brown. It was a coldish morning and she was wearing a New Look coat of brown velveteen, and she had just the height to carry it. Beneath it was a glimpse of a blouse of old gold, and the brown of the hat was lightened with a cluster of something that caught up or repeated the colour of the blouse. Her gloves, her bag—everything about her was what Bertha would call class.

"You found it cold outside?" I said.

"It is . . . a bit," she said. "But I rather like it."

There was a nervousness in the way she looked quickly up and then down again.

"People think that detective agencies must be rather terrifying places," I said, and gave what I imagined was my most avuncular smile. "They're not really—as you see. Not even so bad as going to a dentist."

"Everything is confidential?"

"Implicitly so," I said. "If you were to tell me that in that charming bag of yours were some jewels you'd just lifted from a shop— well, that'd be that. I shouldn't telephone the police."

"But I haven't done anything like that."

Damn the stupid woman, I thought, and told her that of course she hadn't. I'd just been saying in so many words that whatever she said in that office would never get outside. I was thinking as I told her that, what a pity it was that so good-looking a girl should not only be so slow in the uptake, but the owner of a voice which, unlike her clothes, had not come quite off the top shelf. Not again that it mattered to me. I never recall a peeress on our books.

"Just what is it you'd like us to do, Miss Cowle?"

"Well," she said, and gave me that part shy, part nervous look again. "It sounds so silly now I'm here. I don't think I ought to ask you to do it."

"Can't you leave me to be judge of that?" I told her gallantly.

"Well," she said, and hesitated. "If you won't think it *is* silly, I'll tell you about it." She ventured on her first real smile. "After all, you can always turn me down."

"We shan't do that," I said. "But first, your full name, Miss Cowle."

"Myra Cowle."

"Miss . . . Myra . . . Cowle," I was saying in my best bedside manner as I wrote it down. "And the address?"

I looked up to see her eyes curiously on me. She flushed slightly and probably at having been caught in so close an examination of my features.

"Perhaps you'd better hear about everything first before I give you the address. I mean, because you might not want it. . . . If you think I'm being silly after all."

"Good enough," I said, and leaned back in the swivel chair. "So suppose you tell me what it really *is* all about."

She had the story ready because she began in the right place by telling me just who she was. Her father had been a doctor and she was his only child. He and her mother had been killed in a plane crash in 1946. With the money she inherited she bought a half-interest in a Beauty Salon. Then in February 1948 her uncle—her father's elder brother—was murdered by his manservant.

"My uncle was Bertram Cowle," she said. "I expect you read all about it."

I had to shake my head. Unless a murder case was sensational the Press—at least my Press—had little room for it.

"Then you've never heard of my uncle?"

"I assure you, Miss Cowle, I've never heard the name of Bertram Cowle in my life."

She was looking at me as if she couldn't believe it. It was incredible, apparently, that what had been so important somehow to her had been quite unheard-of by me.

"Well," she said, and gave that shy smile as she looked away. "That doesn't make it any easier."

"Why not?" I said. "But where did this murder take place?"

"At Marland. My Uncle's house was called Danlow."

"Marland," I said. The name rang a distant bell. "I can't say I've ever heard of it. Where is it exactly?"

"Well," she said. "The nearest big town is Shireton. It's seven miles away."

Would it have been a shock to you? It was to me, though I'm positive I didn't show it.

"I know Shireton," I said. "I was there quite recently on a rather distressing business. Do you know it at all?"

"Not in the least," she said, "except for getting out at the station and taking a bus to Marland. And that was only twice in my life."

I'd seen Marland sign-posted somewhere in the neighbourhood of Stadmore but I didn't mention the fact. What I did say was that the murder must have been a bad business.

"I knew my uncle so little," she said. "When I was a girl he was always abroad. Then when my parents died he wanted me to go and see him, so I did. I only stayed the one night. He was very eccentric: I think that's what you'd call it."

I gathered that he had had a small but most expensive jewellery business at Nice and that he had managed to get back to England in 1940 with the loss of most of what he had, and after suffering privations which had turned him into the eccentric he was. But he must have salvaged something or have had money salted in England, for he bought the house known as Dowland and employed a married couple to look after him. He was sixty-seven when he died and he'd been living partly on capital, for all the invested cash he left was nine thousand pounds. Myra Cowle was his heiress and with what she inherited she bought out her partner in a Beauty Salon and took in the next shop as well.

"How's it doing?" I said.

"Quite well," she told me with that diffident smile.

"Fine," I said. "And it's something in connection with your uncle's murder that you'd like us to investigate?"

There we were, at the difficult part. I had to cajole and go round in circles before she would tell me. Perhaps I'd better give her story some sort of sequence.

When she had visited her uncle he had told her she was now his heir. He was nice, she said, but queer. He had, for instance, his own room which no-one was allowed to enter and when he was in it he kept it locked. When it was cleaned he kept an eye on whoever was cleaning it.

"Mrs. Baker told me about that," she said. "She was the housekeeper. She'd been with him all the time."

When she went down the second time, which was in the November before he was killed, he hinted that there would be a surprise for her when he died, if not before. What that surprise was may have come out at the trial, when it was proved that Bertram Cowle had been collecting diamonds. Since those stones had been specifically about three-eighths of an inch in diameter—that is, about four carats—they had cost big money, and, judging from the small amount he had left, it was clear that whatever collection he had wanted was practically complete. The Hatton Garden man who had sold him what were apparently the last two stones, had said that his only remaining commission was one further stone of the same size and quality.

The murderer was apprehended and hanged in Shireton Jail and those stones were missing from the safe, that was what I gathered. But I wanted to know more.

"Would it distress you too much to tell me more about the actual murder?"

She winced. She didn't say anything for a moment.

"But couldn't you read all about it?" was what she asked me. "It upsets me just to think of it. That was why I didn't really like coming."

"You had to be a witness at the trial?"

"Oh, no," she said. "I had nothing to do with it—not like that."

"I see," I said, and then my smile took on a certain roguishness. "And may I be permitted to guess that what you'd like us to do is try and find those diamonds?"

She was all blushes and confusion. She knew it was foolish, she was saying, and that was another reason why she had wished she had never come. If the police hadn't been able to trace them, then perhaps nobody could. And yet. . . .

The *yet* consisted of every kind of feminine reason. She would naturally like those diamonds which were hers by right. And she knew, or she'd been told, that the police weren't infallible. And though she wasn't in actual need of the money they represented, it was always nice to feel there was something like that behind one. Business mightn't always be as good as it was.

You see a something? So did I, though it was wishful thinking to connect it all up with what had happened at Copley's Corner. At the worst it was a strange coincidence: only at the best it might be very much more.

"I don't see what you had to be nervous about," I told her. "What you'd like us to do is the very kind of thing we're here for. I think we shall be pleased to do what we can for you. I don't promise results, mind you. These supposed diamonds disappeared months ago. If they were still unmounted, individual stones, heaven knows where they are. But we can at least try."

"Will it cost a lot?"

"It's a case where we should prefer to work on results," I said. "We can't afford a lot of time but I can assure you that our organisation is capable of fast work. No results, no fee. Doesn't that strike you as fair?"

She smiled. She actually admitted I was being generous.

"Well, that's the way I prefer to work on a case like this," I said. "We like satisfied clients. We mayn't succeed but we'll have a good try. And if we don't succeed, you won't be able to give us a bad name for wasting your money."

"But I'd never think of doing that."

"I'm sure you wouldn't," I said. "But may we leave things like this. Could you be here tomorrow morning at the same time?"

From her look I judged that to be a bit awkward. Maybe that Salon kept her busy. But when she'd frowned a bit and wriggled delightfully on her chair, she thought she might manage it. But naturally she wanted to know why the business couldn't be settled then and there.

"To protect your own interests," I said. "We wouldn't even undertake the job at all if we didn't see some hopes of a successful conclusion. We should require a small retaining fee, for instance, probably about ten pounds. I'd like to look up the facts of the case as brought out at the trial. Tomorrow morning I hope to tell you we've decided to act for you. You do understand, by the way, that confidence is expected on both sides. If we undertake the commission, it's to be a strictly confidential matter between the parties."

"I should never dream of saying a word," she told me.

"That's fine," I said, and handed her a sheet of paper. "Will you be so good as to write down the address with which we can communicate with you at any time."

She took a pair of tortoiseshell glasses out of her bag and they gave her the look of a young, charming and slightly flustered schoolmistress. Maybe it was a fellow feeling, but I suddenly liked her when I watched her writing that address. But she didn't give it to me—not at once.

"Will you be very careful," she said, "to put *Personal* in the corner, like this. My secretary opens the mail and I wouldn't like her to have even a suspicion."

"Most certainly, I'll see that it's done."

"Besides," she said, "nobody at the Salon has ever connected me with that dreadful business. Someone did notice the similarity of the name but I put them off. Don't you think I was right? I mean— well, it wouldn't be good for business."

I took the paper and said I agreed.

SALON MARGUERITE—29 Rochway Street, W.

That was the address. I said I thought it was just off New Bond Street and she said I was right. Then I thought of something else.

"What did your uncle's solicitors think about all this?"

She didn't understand.

"Did you go into the business of the missing diamonds with them?"

"I didn't," she said. "I met them here, in London. I just had to sign some papers, that was all. I only saw them twice. I didn't like them."

I raised my eyebrows at that.

"They were all stiff and starchy," she said. "I don't want to have anything else to do with them."

"You wouldn't like us to consult them in any way?"

"I'd hate it," she said. "I don't want to have anything to do with them."

"You didn't by chance tread on their toes?"

"I don't know what you mean by that," she told me just a bit tartly, and I hastened to tell her that I didn't know myself. But she could rely on her wishes being respected. If we took the case we'd make do without any information from the lawyers.

"They couldn't know anything about the diamonds," she said.

"Of course they couldn't," I said. "In any case the police must have questioned them."

She had gathered that the interview was at an end and was getting to her feet.

"Well, that's all for the moment," I said. "I'll see you tomorrow morning. I hope everything hasn't been frightening after all."

She was putting her glasses back in her bag. She smiled up at me.

"I *was* scared, you know," she said. "But you were so nice."

I probably blushed at that. I went to take her arm in an avuncular way but she was already at the door. I didn't push the bell for Bertha but saw her out myself. I'd rather expected to see a taxi waiting, and she told me she'd come by taxi but would catch a bus back. She gave me another smile and I watched her move off. Smart, sometimes charming, and even rather likeable, I thought, and who the hell cared about the very top shelf?

Bertha was peering out of her door as I turned back to the old-fashioned corridor.

"What was she like, Mr. Travers?"

"Almost as nice as you, Bertha," I told her flippantly. "Mr. Hallows rung up at all?"

She said he hadn't.

"Try him at his home address," I said, "and if he's there, tell him to get here at the double."

Bertha's mouth gaped slightly as I went on. It was lucky, I thought, that Bertha hadn't been listening in. Sometimes it was a sound precaution, but that morning I'd slipped back the catch.

Even before Bertha told me that Hallows was on his way, I had changed my mind. To wait even a half hour is foolish when a tooth nags beyond endurance and a dentist is on one's doorstep. And it struck me that it might be wise to let Hallows discover things for himself and for me to hear his reactions, rather than the other way about. So I wrote a note. He was to go to the office of a certain paper and make a digest of a murder trial—the murder of a Bertram Cowle by his manservant, at Marland, early in February, 1948. I asked him to get the main facts and meet me at Broad Street as near three o'clock as he could.

I left Bertha in charge and made my own way to the office of quite another paper, and asked to see the files for February onwards. I found the actual murder report almost at once. It had taken place on the night of February the third, and the issue of the paper was that of the following day. It merely said that Cowle had been found suffering from severe head wounds and had died almost at once. His housekeeper, a Mrs. Baker, had been found with him, also suffering from head wounds and was in Shireton General Hospital. A detective was at her bedside.

The issue for the 5th of February said that a man had been taken into custody for the murder of Cowle, and would appear at Shireton that day. I turned quickly to the issue for the 6th and found just one paragraph. I read that paragraph just the once and the words stood so starkly clear in my mind that there was no need to read them a second time.

> At Shireton yesterday William Mallett, gardener-hand-yman, was formally charged with the murder of Bertram Cowle at Marland, Essex, on the night of February the 3rd. Mallett was remanded in custody.

Mallett. That word hit me like the kick of a mule. What was it Godfrey had said? Something about being cracked on the skull by a cast-iron mallet. Cracked on the skull. *Cowle had been cracked on the skull by William Mallett!*

I looked at the paper again and found another paragraph. Mrs. Baker, the housekeeper, had died as a result of her injuries, and it was not known if she had been able to make a statement. I whipped over the pages but there was nothing till I came to the trial itself. That had taken place at the end of March.

The account was short enough for Mallett had had no defence. The housekeeper had been able to make a statement for her own head injuries had not been too severe, though she had subsequently died as a result of them and from a heart attack. She, it appeared, had been with Cowle ever since he had bought the house known as Dowland, and with her husband had constituted what is known as a Married Couple. Her husband died in the summer of 1947 and Cowle advertised for a man whose duties were to lend a hand in the house and fill in his spare time in the easily worked garden. Mallett had got the job. What his references had been was not known, though it subsequently appeared that they must have been forged.

Mrs. Baker was in bed when the tragedy occurred. She had heard a shouting at about eleven o'clock and had come hurriedly down, thinking her master had been taken ill. A light was on in the study and she had arrived just in time to see Cowle lying on the floor and Mallett, fully dressed, apparently about to leave. Mallett had struck her down with the same poker. It had all happened very quickly and the only other thing she remembered was that the safe door was open. Mallett was actually closing it when she came into the room.

Mallett was hanged in Shireton Jail, but there were snippets of news before that, and especially since he had made no appeal. His record was bad. His speciality in Canada, where he had had various aliases, was the same sort of thing that had led to his taking the job with Cowle: a position as valet or personal servant or even butler, and then robbery and disappearance. He had served one sentence of five years and then the Canadian police had lost track of him and it was thought he was in the States. He reappeared in Boston in 1940, where he had had a job as attendant to an elderly man. He had been apprehended after the usual robbery and on that, and another count, served a sentence of seven years. He claimed to be a citizen of Eire and was deported in 1947. He got the Marland job the same year.

1 found one other piece of news—a chatty account of how a post-mistress had helped to catch Mallett. The hue and cry was out, and on the morning of the 4th of February, a man had entered the post-office at the village of Bawford, which is not far from Cheshunt and just off the main Cambridge to London Road. He had bought a letter-card but hadn't written it, as was usual, in the post-office, though he had gone to the table provided, and when the post-mistress happened to look just after he had left the place, she found he

had taken a pencil which she had only just put there. She rang the police at once and within a couple of hours Mallett was arrested. He had gone back to the main road and there thumbed a lift in a lorry and was caught as that lorry was at some traffic lights on a by-pass.

It later emerged that on the night of the murder, or rather in the early hours of the morning after it, Mallett; had got a lift from another lorry driver on the Cambridge Road some two miles south of where it passes Stadmore to the west. That lorry had stopped near Cheshunt and Mallett had got off, saying he would get a bus for London. He had said he was from Grimsby and was going to friends at Brighton who thought they could find him a job. He was a Canadian who'd been a lorry driver during the war, and that was why he preferred to thumb lifts from Grimsby rather than take a train. And he wasn't too well off for money.

If I'd hunted the issues through I might perhaps have found more, but I had more than enough. As it was it was alter one o'clock, so I hopped on a bus that took me on to the City and found a place for lunch. The service was bad and the lunch worse, and when I got back to Broad Street, Hallows was waiting. And he looked full of questions.

I've laughed or wept enough in my time at the antics of George Wharton, but you can't work for years with a man you admire at heart and not pick up some of his tricks. George likes rabbits out of a hat, and effective curtains, and I couldn't help letting Hallows imagine that some amazing prescience had made me unearth an old and none too sensational murder case.

"How you got on to it, sir, beats me," he said. "But talk about a turn up for the pack! Just what the doctor ordered."

I wanted him to elaborate. In a couple of minutes it was clear that his brain had been working much better than mine. He hadn't known a thing about that morning's client.

There was the word *Mallett*, of course, and Cowle's crack on the skull. There was the nearness of Marland to Stadmore, and of Stadmore to the spot where Mallett had thumbed his first lift. There had been an open safe and a robbery and yet nothing had been said about what was found on Mallett at his arrest. Surely that meant that Mallett may have deposited the proceeds of the robbery with

Monaghan at Copley's Corner. The housekeeper's bicycle was missing—that was news to me—and had been found behind a hedge near where Mallett had thumbed that lift. But judging by the time that had elapsed between the murder and the lift, Mallett might have gone straight to Stadmore, deposited the loot, and then gone off again. It was that loot that Laver had been after.

"Must have been jewels of some sort," he said. "Cowle was a retired jeweller, according to my paper. That would make Monaghan some sort of a fence. And he couldn't have been. He hadn't got the brains for that—unless he was putting on an act." He clicked his tongue exasperatedly. "If we knew just what was taken, it might help."

"It was diamonds," I said. "Beautiful stones that matched each other. Diamonds four carats each."

He stared. I came off my high horse and told him how I knew. I took my time over it and left nothing out.

"Old Cowle's niece," he said, and then was staring again.

"Wait a minute, sir! Myra Cowle, you said."

"That's it. Myra Cowle of the Salon Marguerite, Rochway Street. The dead man's niece."

"Yes," he said, "but the name! Myra Cowle. M.C. . . . The M.C. of that letter of Godfrey's!"

I did the staring. Right under my nose so to speak, and I'd never had the gumption to spot it.

CHAPTER 9
ALL CLEAR AHEAD

HALLOWS' MEMORY is better than my own but we didn't trust to it. We went hot-foot to my flat where we had a look at Godfrey's original letter. That second letter.

It didn't take us too long to see, at least to our own satisfaction, what lay behind it.

I don't know if I'm due for the M.C. or a crack on the skull with a cast-iron mallet.

The first part seemed to mean that he was on the track of the diamonds and might expect to get a good reward from Myra Cowle. It would have been easy to find out that she was the murdered man's heiress. He had most definitely not approached her or she would have mentioned the matter to myself.

The second part, what might be called the alternative, meant that the job was being far from easy. It was dangerous, in fact, or he wouldn't have called it dynamite. The danger would come from someone connected with Mallett, or in the know. Since Godfrey, both from his own nature and that of his job, would be acquainted with every murder case mentioned in the Press, he had expected me to know that that holiday job of his was connected with the Mallett-Cowle murder, and the mention of a crack on the skull was merely a reinforcement.

Meanwhile you have a vague hint. Sorry to be so cryptic.

That also was an underlining. It deliberately said he was being cryptic and invited me to identify his various allusions.

On second thoughts, not the M.C. but something very different.

That meant, if it meant anything, that he'd been too sanguine. We had a good look at that letter under my glass and it seemed almost a certainty that that postscript had been written some time after the main body of the letter, and with a different pen. But the writing was his. There wasn't a doubt of that.

And according to it he wasn't going to get that reward from Cowle's heiress. He looked like getting something else. That something else might have meant anything: a crack on the skull himself, or a bullet. He'd made some slip or other, and he'd dropped out, as he'd called it. He was lying low at the George till he got things straightened out, or the danger had passed.

All that was reasonably obvious. It was cheering to know it. It was a tremendous step forward, and yet in some ways it wasn't. It planked us down, so to speak, in the middle of things, and gave us no hint whatever about the beginnings. While he was being cryptic, why didn't he give us some sort of a line on the brunette? Who *was* the brunette who had started him off on that job? Was she the somewhat nebulous woman who had been with Laver to the dog track, and of whom Hallows had heard faint echoes, as it were, at a night-club? How could we know? In fact we were back just where we were before.

"What we've got to do," I said, "is to work back from the other end. What we've been doing is working back from Godfrey to that brunette. Now we can start at the murder and work forward."

That was how Hallows saw it. Myra Cowle's call at the Agency had been a godsend. It made sense and furnished motive where events had had neither. It clarified the obscure and gave a simplicity to what had been bewildering. If anything, it seemed almost too simple. There had been a murder and diamonds had been stolen. The murderer had parked the diamonds at Copley's Corner with Monaghan, who had probably been an old associate in crime or else a fence. The Laver gang had got wind of it and had tried to get the diamonds from Monaghan, but he'd refused to part.

"Just a minute, sir," Hallows said. "That doesn't explain the brunette who approached Godfrey. What about this for an explanation?"

His theory was that two parties were looking for those diamonds. Laver had been one, and at first that brunette—his lady friend—had been associated with him. Then he had given her the go-by, as we knew, or thought we knew, and then she had begun looking for the diamonds on her own. Chance had thrown Godfrey in her way and he had been well on the track of the diamonds when the Laver party decided he knew too much.

I'd never known a theory that fitted more snugly. All I could add was that Myra Cowle's interest in the diamonds had been just too good a stroke of luck for us. Just when we'd been absolutely flummoxed, along had come the clue to everything. Not that Myra Cowle wasn't in every way open and above-board. She was a genuine person: honest-to-God flesh and blood, so to speak, and not something nebulous like that mysterious brunette.

"What she did was just what any woman would do," Hallows said. "Both the police and her lawyers would tell her the diamonds had gone for good, but you don't separate a woman from diamonds as easily as that. She was like someone who buys a ticket in a big sweepstake. Did it just for devilment and knew there wasn't a chance. Then you know how people like that are. They can't help wondering if the million to one chance mightn't come off. Then they begin planning how they'd spend the money if it did. That's how she was. Got round to thinking there might be a chance, after all. Then she saw the Agency advertisement and that did it. She screwed herself up to coming. I think she'd made up her mind to risk a certain amount on the off-chance. Probably she got herself to that pitch the previous night, but when she got to the Agency in the morning, things didn't look all that rosy. She knew she'd been a fool. That's why she was sorry she came. If you hadn't convinced her otherwise, she'd have gone again."

As I told him, I'd certainly done some wheedling. As soon as I'd begun to get the implications of what she was telling me, I knew I had to have her for a client. There was not only what she had told me: there was what else I might have the chance to learn.

"As you've said," I told Hallows, "she was all over the place this morning. She knew she'd been a fool, and she was just a bit scared of what she'd done. Heaps of people are like that when they step inside that room. But wait till I've seen her the next time. I think I can get her talking. She might tell me about Mallett, if she ever saw him. She might let something else fall about her uncle. You never know when something important is going to pop out."

Hallows agreed. But there was something he didn't understand. Naturally he didn't know the business arrangements usual in the office, but he too, like Myra Cowle, thought that working on a results basis was strangely generous.

"Of course the Agency wouldn't do anything of the kind," I told him. "We've two simple rules: no divorce cases and no pledge of results. A client has to take our word that we'll do everything in his interests, and he's expected to pay for what we do, results or no results. We have to keep our side of the bargain because if we didn't get results we'd never get clients. But this isn't going to be an Agency case; it's going to be a private one of my own."

"I get you, sir," Hallows said. "We'd have gone on working in any case, and now all you stand to lose is nothing at all. You even get a ten pound fee."

"That's it. And for that ten pound retaining fee we'll have a genuine crack at finding those diamonds. Not that I give a damn for the diamonds. The importance of those diamonds is that they've given us just the clue we needed for knowing why Godfrey was shot. We're not after diamonds. We're after the one who got Godfrey."

Neither of us had any doubts about that. Finding those diamonds months after they'd disappeared was a million to one chance, and but for the fact that we just had to get her as a client, Myra Cowle would have been told so.

"All the same, I think we should know a bit more about her," Hallows said. "The more you know about a client, the better. And if we're going to use her for information, don't you think it might be as well to know just the kind of person she is?"

"Why not?" I said. "You might discover something I could find useful when I see her in the morning. Just what were you thinking of yourself?"

He suggested having a look at the Salon Marguerite. Perhaps there was a flat above it, but if Myra Cowle didn't live there, then he might have a look at where she did live. And what reputation she had with her neighbours. I said he'd better go easy on that last bit. Myra was restless, and at the least alarm she might turn the Agency down.

We left for Rochway Street and I began jotting down the various things that I ought to ask Myra Cowle in the morning. Maybe I was a bit too cocksure about my bedside manner but I'd never a doubt that the morning's meeting would soon develop into a cheery chat between old friends. In the first place she ought to jump at the offer I'd made her. Except for a retaining fee, and that only put in to give things an air of the official, she had everything to gain and never a thing to lose. All I could hope was that she didn't broadcast my generosity. A few more clients like Myra Cowle and the Agency would find itself in Queer Street.

We'd left it that Hallows wasn't to drop in again unless he had anything to report. I was just a bit alarmed when he did turn up again, and soon after eight o'clock. But everything had been satisfactory, and he'd merely come to tell me so.

He'd gone straight to the Salon, and it was just after five o'clock when he'd got there, and that turned out to be closing time. He saw only one client leave, and some ten minutes later two employees left. Shortly afterwards three more left, but it was not till almost six o'clock that Myra Cowle appeared, and with her was a woman who was probably the secretary. The two chatted for a minute or two at the door and then Myra made for Bond Street Station. She evidently had a season ticket, so Hallows got a sixpenny one from the machine and hoped for the best. He managed to squeeze into the same carriage and he followed her at Oxford Street where she had to change. He stood quite near her in that train. At Bond Street she had bought an evening paper, and she put on her glasses to read it, and Hallows thought they spoilt her looks.

"I thought they gave her a nice, homely sort of look," I said.

She ought to have had rimless glasses, he said, not tortoise-shell. But at any rate, she had read that paper till the train was slowing for Swiss Cottage where she got out. He followed her for a brisk five minutes to a quiet road called Oak Avenue, where she let herself in at Number 10A, which was an upper flat of the kind of pair into which the semi-terraced houses of the Avenue had all been converted.

He saw the light go on in an upstair room and the curtain drawn and then he explored the Avenue. Then he knocked at the door of Number 10B, flashed a card and said he was an inspector from the railway claims' department, looking for a Miss Someone who'd put in a claim. Unfortunately he'd lost the number of her flat but he had an idea it was number ten. The Miss Someone was a short, stout person. The quite well-spoken and definitely married woman who'd come at his knock was able to tell him he was at the wrong flat, and he learned that Myra Cowle had had her flat for over two years. She was described as a very charming girl indeed and the ideal person to have on the flat above.

"What was the actual Salon like?" Bernice wanted to know.

Hallows said it was two premises made into one. The window display was very tasteful, and the whole place had an expensive look. The girls he'd seen coming out all looked chic, and altogether he thought that Salon must have a high-class clientele. Not surprising considering it was as near as nothing to Bond Street.

"Why shouldn't you try to fix an appointment there yourself?" I said to Bernice. "I know I'm being a philanthropist, but I'll foot the bill."

Hallows laughed. Bernice had to show a polite reluctance before she graciously agreed. And that seemed all for the moment. Neither Hallows nor I could get very far till Myra Cowle had signed on the dotted line.

Next morning I waited till Bernice had rung the Salon Marguerite. She gave her maiden name of Haire—it had an awkward sound but at least was something she couldn't forget—and said she was up from the country and was looking for a reliable place to have her hair done whenever she was in town. Her present place in the country was most unsatisfactory. What she wanted at the moment was a shampoo and set. And, if possible, that morning or afternoon.

She was told that it couldn't be done. Then she was asked to hold on, and it turned out that she could after all be squeezed in at three-thirty that afternoon.

"Who was doing the talking?" I said.

"The secretary. She'd be a kind of receptionist as well. She sounded quite nice."

I hurried off to Broad Street and looked through the correspondence with Bertha. Just before ten o'clock there was a telephone call. It was Myra Cowle. She made sure it was I who was listening.

"Oh, Mr. Travers, this is You-Know-Who. The one who was in yesterday."

"You needn't worry about being overheard," I told her. "No possible chance of that here. It's Miss Cowle, isn't it?"

"Yes," she said, "and I'm so sorry, Mr. Travers, but I've been thinking things over and I think I must change my mind. I don't think I want to go on with it, so will you let the whole thing drop?"

That was a shock. Somehow or other I had to make time.

"But why?" I said. "It can't be that ten pound retaining fee that's bothering you?"

"It isn't that. It's because I realise you couldn't possibly find what I was asking you about—not after all this time. You couldn't even know where to begin. I wouldn't even know myself."

"Plenty of things to begin at," I said, "if that's the only reason."

"Well, there's my business as well," she said. "I'm terrified of anyone connecting me with what happened. People get things so twisted round."

"Listen," I said. "Let me slip along and see you, just for a moment. Not that you need worry about the Salon. We'd neither see you there or telephone or communicate in any way except by post. We wouldn't even send in the usual reports unless you specially wished it."

"Reports?"

"Yes," I said. "It's the usual thing. Just to let the client know how we're getting on. To prove we're as good as our word and really working on his behalf."

"I didn't know that," she said, and just a bit apologetically. I didn't see what difference it made, but I did some striking while the iron was hot.

"Even if you are busy, surely you could slip out for a moment some time this morning? Cassoni's is almost on your door-step. Why not have coffee with me there at, say, eleven o'clock."

"I couldn't possibly," she told me. "But just wait a moment."

She must have cupped the receiver for I couldn't hear a sound. In about a minute she was telling me she might manage to spare me a very short time at a quarter-past eleven.

"That's grand," I said. "I'll be outside Cassoni's at a quarter-past."

"I'd rather you waited inside," she said. "I might be a minute or two late."

I hurriedly drafted out that contract and made it simplicity itself. In so many words it said that Ludovic Travers *of*—not *for*, mark you—the Agency, agreed to try to find certain articles which were the legal property of Myra Cowle, but at present lost. The client agreed to pay a retaining fee of ten pounds and would be under no further financial obligation unless the articles, all or in part, were recovered, in which case she would pay fifteen per cent of their value as agreed by an independent valuer. I agreed to devote a period of three weeks to the search and to furnish, if so desired, a report at the end of each week.

It was short and to the point, and I hurriedly made two drafts— one for her and one as it affected myself. Then I told Bertha I was called away for an hour or so, and went in search of a taxi. I found one and it got me to Cassoni's with a few minutes to spare.

She was five minutes late. There were plenty of tables and she spotted me at once even if I was at the far end of the main room. She was wearing the same get-up she had worn when I had seen her first. She gave me a nervous sort of smile and said she was looking frightful. The morning had been a dreadful rush and she hadn't had a moment except when she had telephoned me, and that had been with an exasperated client waiting. I said I saw no signs of it. If she would pardon one old enough to be her father, she was looking perfectly charming. But since she was so busy, perhaps she would like to read the contract. She put on her glasses and was just about through it when the coffee and biscuits arrived.

"It seems all right," she said, "but I'd rather read it through when I have more time. Might I take it with me, then I could post it to you tonight with the cheque."

"Don't forget my own Personal on the envelope," I reminded her. "I'm most anxious to meet your every wish about secrecy. Nobody in my office will know a thing about you except myself."

The coffee was hot. She made a face as she sipped it, and smiled as she caught my eye.

"That's better," I told her. "You've got to relax, young lady. Don't let things get you down. Once you've signed that contract, you can forget everything. Any headaches will be mine."

"I still don't understand why you're so generous."

"To be perfectly frank," I said, "we're rather slack at the moment and I've a certain amount of free time. A big job's coming on in three weeks' time and that's why I've got just the three weeks to spare. And also we always try to give special terms to a new client. You probably know how it is. Every satisfied client recommends us to another—or we hope so—and that's how a business grows. Which reminds me. How did you get hold of our name?"

She'd seen our advertisement in *The Times*, she said, and one of her girls had once been told something about us by a client.

"There you are," I said. "And about the reports. Would you like them?"

"They sound very exciting," she said. "Perhaps I would. But you do understand about the Salon, don't you? It may sound silly to you, but a lot of people mightn't think it very nice if I was connected with a horrible thing like a murder. I know a girl who had a business and her place was burgled and all sorts of rumours got about: you know, that she'd done it herself for the insurance, and so on. She must have given some horrible old cat a grudge or something, but you wouldn't believe the harm it did her."

I told her again that she needn't worry, and I was just wondering how I could get her to talk about her uncle and the murder, when she was looking at her wrist-watch and saying she must fly. She gulped the last of her coffee and though she smiled charmingly as she held out her hand, she wouldn't let me walk back with her to the Salon. By the time I'd paid the bill she was away along the opposite pavement and I was only just in time to see her turn into Rochway Street.

I turned back towards Piccadilly, and I was thinking how disappointing those few minutes had been, and in spite of the fact that she now looked like signing that contract. But what the hell good, I told myself annoyedly, was the contract? I didn't want a client. I wanted to be on friendly terms with Myra Cowle: to get her to talk: to have her on tap, as it were, if there was something needed in the way of information. She would have been supposed to think it was information that might lead us to the diamonds, whereas all I wanted was something to lead me to the killer of Godfrey Prial. And there she was, worried about that Salon, and shutting herself up in some goddam ivory tower. And why couldn't I have seen her at her flat? Or was she prudish about such things? Did I have the look of a wolf? I very much doubted it.

But by the time I was at the Tube Station I was a bit more reconciled to things. I told myself I ought to be grateful. But for Myra Cowle we shouldn't have been bothering about the Case at all. We might even have handed things over to the Yard. And instead of that we'd had handed to us something of incredible value: and something against which it seemed childish to set the fears and the even excusable precautions of one who knew her business as well as Myra Cowle professed to know hers.

At the office I had lunch brought in. At two o'clock I had an appointment with a client, and then this and that cropped up and it wasn't till half-past five that I got back to the flat. Bernice had had tea and she was most enthusiastic about the Salon Marguerite. The charges were high but everything had been perfectly charming, and she pivoted round for me to see the results for myself. I never like Bernice's hair when it has been newly manipulated, but I summoned an enthusiasm of my own. One never knew when I might like her to pay a further visit, and, since the bill was mine, it was poor policy to tell myself that I'd had less than my money's worth.

"What's it like as a business?" I said. "Flourishing?"

"Darling, it's a gold-mine," she said. "The place simply reeked of money and it was buzzing with activity. Everything was absolutely up-to-date. All the latest gadgets. And every kind of beauty and toilet preparation: things I haven't seen for years. And they have a service at clients' own houses. Manicure and massage and all that kind of thing. Strictly for women, of course."

I don't know why she added that, unless it was because I had raised my eyebrows.

"You saw the fair Myra?"

"Oh, yes," she said. "I think it was just routine as I was a new client. I thought her very charming. And the most lovely hair."

I hadn't thought it so good, but I didn't say so. No blonde looks real to me. Maybe it's the prevalence of the synthetics that has spoilt my taste and made me suspect that there's no blonde living for whom God did all. Not that these days did I profess a knowledge of things feminine. I know a pretty girl when I see one and I know what I like, and if it comes to a matter of preference, then I'm like poor Godfrey—give me the brunettes. I'm no authority, but you seem to know where you are with brunettes. To a certain extent, of course, and I make the reservation because I married one.

I rang Hallows that night and told him to go on taking a breather and to report at the flat after lunch the next day: say at about half-past one. We'd almost certainly be going to Shireton and he should put a bag in his car. Unless anything unforeseen cropped up, I'd be going with him.

The next morning I was up uncommonly early and I was round at the Agency at the inhuman hour of eight o'clock. The post had arrived and there was my letter, and it had the Swiss Cottage postmark. There was no covering letter but just the signed contract and a cheque for ten pounds. I signed my own contract and addressed it to the Salon. A receipt for the cheque was enclosed. Then I posted the Myra Cowle cheque to my bank and asked for it to be paid into my account.

Bertha came in at a quarter to nine and looked mightily surprised at the sight of me. I said I was getting things ready for Norris.

"Something I want you to do for me, Bertha," I said. "That client who was in yesterday morning. If you made a note of her, just erase it. I don't want a word to a soul."

There was something faintly gratifying about the look she gave me. If there was a cloven hoof, at least she wasn't being shocked.

"Not what you think, Bertha," I said. "That is if you're thinking what I blush to think you're thinking."

"Mr. Travers! As if I should!"

I had to laugh. I nearly chucked her under the chin.

"Well, keep everything under that bonny beret of ours," I said. "And if any letters should happen to come for me marked Personal, don't let them go into the office. Keep them till I collect."

I thought of something else.

"And if by chance a lady should ask for me personally, and I happen to be here, give me the tip. If I'm not here, just say I'm away."

Norris was coming in and I gave her a grin and nipped through to the office. Norris and I were busy for most of the morning, and by the time I'd finished lunch at the flat, Hallows was there. In five minutes I had my own bag in and we were off. I began telling him what had happened, and by the time we were clear of the inner suburbs, we were planning the next moves.

I said we had to avoid both the Royal and the George, so he recommended the Suffolk which was on the Stadmore road. As for what we'd do when we got there, that looked obvious. The *Shireton Herald* would have far fuller reports of the trial of Mallett, so we ought to go through their files. And maybe because we were actually moving towards Shireton, and away from the hamperings and obscurities we had met with in town, we were both a bit optimistic. We even felt that we might get the connection between Mallett and Monaghan, and the connection of Laver with both. The moment even came when I had to laugh, for if half our optimisms were realised, we'd wasted time in packing our bags.

But I needn't have worried.

CHAPTER 10
MUCH AND LITTLE

WE COULD HAVE consulted those files in the public library. I preferred to go to the fountain head—the *Shireton Herald* itself—and to the office library.

In my time I've had various dealings with provincial dailies like the *Herald* and, according to the one with whom I'd made friends at the time, I've consulted files in sub-editors' rooms, reporters' room and, more often, in the advertising department, but what I always preferred was the office library. Anything more than a year old is kept in bound volumes in that library. In pre-war days when paper was thicker, the bound volumes were three-monthly. Now they're usually six months to a bound volume, and kept in a long range of cupboards. They're always heavy and generally dusty, and if you consult a volume that's more than three years old, you find the paper has yellowed and it tears almost at a touch.

All that doesn't sound promising, even if the issues for the current year are there as well. But what I like is the office librarian, for generally he's what one calls a character: something between a mole and a ferret, with a provincial accent and an elephant's memory. Since he spends most of his time clipping and filing cuttings and is supposed to be able to check any reference at a moment's notice, he has what I might call a strong attachment to scissors and paste. He would have clipped and filed that murder case under heaven knows what cross-references, and he was the one who could save us considerable time.

Hallows found out that his name was Trank. I asked to see Mr. Trank, and an office-boy took me in tow with Hallows trailing behind, and downstairs we went to a room where electric light was never off. It was the same old office library with the same old smell, and the shelves of reference volumes, the filing cabinets, and the two large tables with their litter of press cuttings and envelopes. It was pretty warm down there, and Trank was in his shirt sleeves. He was a tallish, stooping man with a straggly overhanging moustache, and he peered at us over a long thin nose.

Hallows introduced himself and me. He was Hall and I was Trave, and I was supposed to be writing a book on famous murders, which was why I wanted all I could get about the Mallett case.

"Writin' a book, are you?" Trank said to me. "Reckon I could write a book myself if I sorta set myself to it."

Those last two words had been pronounced *toot*, and there had been the clipped *ing* and the peculiar sing-song that speaks the Suffolk man.

"You're not an Essex man, Mr. Trank?" I said.

"Me?" he said. "No, I'm from Suffolk. A little place called Eye. Don't reckon you know it."

"Eye," I said, and smiled. "I was born at a little place called Savenham. I don't reckon you know that."

"Savenham!" he said, and his face lighted. "Do I know Savenham! Reckon if I had a pound for every time I'd bin in Savenham Waggoners, I wouldn't hatta do no more work."

It wasn't till five minutes later that I could get to the job in hand, and there wasn't any need to consult the files. Under that bald cranium of his he had things that weren't in the files at all: snippets of information and gossip picked up in the reporters' room: oddments and stray deductions that the paper had never put into print. The Mallett Case had been pretty sensational for Shireton; for Trank it had been something happily removed from the humdrum.

He told us about the night of the murder. Mrs. Baker—obviously a light sleeper—had been awakened by faint steps outside her door and had guessed it was Bernard Cowle going down for something. That was why she was already awake when she heard the frantic shout from downstairs. Cowle had surprised Mallett at the safe and had let out the yell when Mallett had attacked him. Trank had said that Mallett's counsel had proved that Cowle's skull was abnormally thin and that the blows hadn't been intended to do more than stun the man.

"Reckon he might have got away with it," Trank said, "if he hadn't attacked that housekeeper as well. No use saying her skull was thin, 'cause it weren't."

"Cowle was what they call an eccentric, wasn't he?" I asked him.

"Don't know as he was," he said. "Queer, perhaps, and a bit of an invalid and didn't go out—not a lot. Unless you're referrin' to that room o' his he never let no one in." He gave a dry chuckle. "Wouldn't mind havin' a room like that myself. Somethin' my missus didn't have to go tidyin' up."

"You think that was why he wouldn't let anyone in the room?"

"I reckon so. They tell me he was one o' these writin' fellows, like yourself. Writin' a history of jewellery and so on. He'd been a jeweller. You knew that?"

I said I'd heard it.

"That's why the room was all papers and books and things," he said. "Didn't want no one messin' about with 'em. Then there was that safe where he kep' them diamonds and no one know what. Not much of a safe neither, so they tell me—not to Mallett."

"Mallett had a bad record?"

"Yes," he said. "Best me, though, how he faked them references what he got that job with."

I asked if he had the full record handy and he turned it up at once. It was just what I'd seen in the London paper, with one addition. Mallett had married in Canada, and his wife and daughter had left Canada shortly after he had received that sentence of five years.

"Anything ever discovered about the wife and daughter?" I said.

Trank said it hadn't been relevant to the trial. He had an idea that the wife had been connected with either the stage or burlesque. When I asked what Mallett's age was, he put it at about forty-five to fifty. I began comparing dates and it seemed to me that when the wife had left the country—probably for England—the daughter had been about four or five. That would make her now about thirty, if she were still alive. Trank gave me a shrewd look and was wondering if I knew her. I said that till I entered that room I hadn't the least idea that Mallett had been married.

"What did he look like?" I said.

"A dark, thin, tall sort o' chap," he said. "They were too clever to put him in the box, though. Never opened his mouth once, so they tell me. Only sorta sneered when the judge put the black cap on and told him what he was for."

I said I'd like to see the actual scene of the crime and he told me the way to get there. Then I asked if there wasn't a niece of Cowle's.

"Niece?" he said. "You mean the one what come in for his money. She weren't at the trial. Didn't know nothin' about her till afterwards."

"How was the crime first discovered?" Hallows asked him.

Trank said Mrs. Baker had come round and had managed to telephone. That's why the hue and cry was on almost at once, even if Mrs. Baker had collapsed again as soon as the police began questioning her.

I was hardly listening. Something had been dawning on me, and that something had brought a something else. Trank might be a god-send in the matter of information. And the way to get information was to share judicially what one knew one's self.

"Keep this under your hat, Mr. Trank," I said, "but I've just thought of something. Doesn't it strike you that Mallett knew the whereabouts of his wife or daughter or both? And they were in England?"

"You mean that letter-card what he wrote that mornin' when they caught him," he said. "The police took that up but never got no farther. Least, I've never heard nothin'."

Was I deflated! But worse was to come—or was it better?

"I suppose you've had several people consulting the Mallett files," I said, and with a vague hope of getting something on Godfrey.

"Don't know as we have," he said. "Except one, though, and that's somethin' I'll have to ask you gentlemen to keep under your hat."

He went to a filing cabinet and came back with a photograph.

"You don't know *him*, I suppose?"

How I kept from starting, I still don't know. What I was looking at was one of those photographs of Godfrey that we'd passed on to Loame! Not the original but a copy, and a moustache had been pencilled in on the upper lip, and horn-rimmed glasses round the eyes.

I shook my head. I passed the photograph to Hallows and contrived to tread on his foot.

"You don't know this chap, do you?"

Hallows shrugged his shoulders. He asked Trank if he were anything to do with the murder case.

"Keep it under your hat, as I said," Trank told us, "but that's the chap what was found shot at the George not so long ago."

"Not another murder case?"

"That's what the verdict was. This here photograph was one we was supposed to publish when the police were lookin' for information. I happened to be lookin' at it a day or two ago—last Friday it was—and somethin' told me I'd sin him afore. Just like a young chap, he was, what come down here one afternoon to see the files, just as you two gents are doin' now. So off I go to the police. A couple o' Scotland Yard men, they was, and as soon as they'd done that bit o' pencillin', I knew he was the one what had been down here. All they did was to thank me and told me to keep it to myself."

"Good lord!" I said. "And what files was he interested in down here?"

He said he couldn't rightly say what particular item he was looking up, but he'd asked for the January-June file of the current year.

"He couldn't have been looking up the Mallett trial," I said. "That'd be too much of a coincidence."

"Don't reckon he was," he said. "Quiet young chap, though. Didn't say much. A Scotchman by the way he spoke. Tapped his ear as if he was a bit deaf. I didn't pay much attention to him. Happened to be busy at the time."

There was a moment or two's silence. Hallows sensed that we'd got enough to chew on. He took a look at his watch.

"Yes, we must be going," I said. "Hope to see you again in a week or two's time, Mr. Trank."

"Always glad to see you," he said. "Like to have another talk about Savenham. Which reminds me. Did you ever know old Eli Barnes what used to live at Church Farm?"

I said I faintly remembered the name.

"Now there was a character for you," he said. "The yarns I could tell you about old Eli! You'd know him though if you'd ever sin him. Walked all bow-legged. A hoss kicked him and busted his knee."

Curious how a thing like that could send through my mind a flash of this and that—Savenham itself, Church Farm, a farm at Withbourne, old Mrs. Privet. . . .

"Yes," I said. "You and I must have a drink sometime and a good old yarn. But talking of peculiarities. Had Mallett any peculiarities of any kind? Anything he could have been spotted by?"

"Don't know as he had," he said, and frowned. "Unless it was that little finger o' his, if you could call that a peculiarity. Lost it, he had, except for the bottom joint."

The first thing I told Hallows, as we hurried instinctively back to the Suffolk, was that from then on we must avoid the *Herald* office as if its staff were all sickening for cholera. Give Trank the idea that we were too interested and he might drop a word to our friends of the Yard. At any time they might be down in that library and questioning him again. Even if Trank had told them what he had told us, that he hadn't had an idea what Godfrey Prial had been interested in, they'd simply have to worry him again as soon as they found themselves at a dead end. It was lucky, I said, that some instinct had told me to say I shouldn't be seeing him again before a fortnight. And that I'd taken a chance and changed my name.

"What did you say the name was, sir?" he had asked me when I'd shaken hands.

"Trave," I said, and he had shaken his head and said he didn't remember any Traves. But of course I'd been after his time.

What we'd gathered was bewildering for the suddenness with which it had come and the light it shed on things. It kept us talking through our meal and after the time when we should have been in bed. And somehow it never ceased to be bewildering. After what we'd done, and the dead ends we'd come to, and the hopelessness we'd felt, that night was like an Englishman's first week in an Eire hotel—an unaccustomed stomach bulged almost to nausea with more food than it had tackled in the previous six months.

But there it was. That trip to Ulster hadn't been wasted. James Monaghan was John Corkery, and Mallett was young Corkery. The young Corkery had almost certainly arrived in Canada under a different name. Maybe his father had gone there too. The two might even have operated together, and the Yard could find most of that out.

But as far as we were concerned, the time pressed too quickly for that. The wife and daughter of Mallett—it was easier to go on calling him that—had come to England, and almost certainly under another name. It seemed to us that the wife wouldn't have left Canada if she hadn't intended to cut herself adrift from her husband, and therefore she must have been of a different moral fibre. Mallett had been sentenced under the name of O'Brien—I gathered he'd had numerous aliases—but it wasn't even certain that that was the name under which he had married, and which his wife and daughter bore. Add the complexity of her changing her name to something quite different, and it looked hopeless to try to find traces.

But both Hallows and I had an idea that the mother must be dead, if only because no woman of approximately the age of fifty had anywhere been glimpsed on what might be called the Prial-Monaghan-Mallett scene. But there had been glimpses of a likely daughter. That elusive brunette had been about twenty-five. And there had had to be someone to whom Mallett had written that letter-card.

So we got down to a general reconstruction of the crime and what seemed beyond doubt to have followed. Mallett must somehow have made contact in England with both his father and his daughter. Most likely it was when visiting his father—that would probably have been by night—that he had seen Cowle's advertisement. The job had struck him as one with possibilities. He had presented himself and again almost certainly with references from Canada which Cowle hadn't been able to check. But his manner must have been convincing and his competence beyond question.

He didn't hurry things but preferred to feel his feet, for this was to be the first job he was to pull in England—as far as we knew. That safe, to an expert like himself, would have been little more than opening a child's money-box, but the room had been hard to reconnoitre. His chance was to come on that night when he had been surprised by Cowle.

If Cowle had been dead, could he have pretended that he had surprised a burglar, and that the burglar had killed Cowle? I doubt it, for the police would have unearthed his record, and he knew it. Then the appearance of the housekeeper had been a further disaster, and after he had struck her down, he had grabbed the diamonds— if he hadn't had them in his pocket already—and panicked, and bolted. He had intended going in any case, and almost certainly on the housekeeper's bicycle, but not in the way he went that night. His plan must have been to rob the safe and to be well clear by the morning when his absence would be discovered. Now those plans had to be violently changed.

So he went to Copley's Corner and left the diamonds with his father. That was a safe place, for no one knew of the relationship. Then he went on to where he could thumb a lift to London, and he would be making for London because of his daughter. But he guessed the hue and cry would be out, so he wrote that letter-card to warn her to be prepared to see him, and he told her that he had left something valuable with her grandfather, and she was to collect it if anything happened to himself. That that something was the diamonds she would learn when the information was given in the Press.

So far, so good. And so, too, to Copley's Corner. Monaghan— it seemed as well to call him that too—had had at least one visitor and that visitor had come by car a few years before the Cowle murder, and when Mallett was still in jail in the States. The visitor would have to be the daughter, and, judging by Monaghan's taciturnity and queerness of mental outlook at even that time, she couldn't have enjoyed the call. But at least she knew her grandfather's whereabouts when she received that letter-card.

What happened? A car was seen at Copley's Corner on the night of the 5th—the night of the day when the card was received. It was probably Laver's car, and therefore the daughter was as probably Laver's mistress. Whether Laver went alone, or she with him, we had no means of knowing, but whoever went, Monaghan was either stupid or dumb. He either professed ignorance of anything having been left with him, or else he refused to give that something up. So much for the 5th.

But by the 14th, news had got out about the diamonds. Laver went to Copley's Corner again, and this time meaning business. If Comfort hadn't been suspicious, he'd have tortured Monaghan and got the whereabouts of the diamonds from him. Copley's Corner had been dangerous from then on, but Laver had managed to buy it. Then he had ripped the innards out of it and dug up its garden, and even then he hadn't been able to find those diamonds.

"They must be on the place somewhere," Hallows kept insisting. "We've got to think of somewhere that Laver might have missed."

Funny how those diamonds could fascinate Hallows. I had to remind him that as far as we were concerned, they were incidentals. The answer to that was that they hadn't been incidentals to Godfrey Prial.

But that was something that was largely surmise, and when we tried to work it out in the light of the new knowledge just how he'd been concerned, the best theory at which we could arrive, and based on the maximum of available evidence, was this. And remember too, that he had come on the scene four months after Mallett was hanged, and seven months after the diamonds had disappeared. Adopting Hallows' own theory that Laver and the brunette had parted company, but that each was still hoping to find the diamonds, then the undoubted fact that Godfrey was working for, and possibly with, that brunette should be proof that the Laver party had killed him. And there again one thing couldn't be ignored. He might have been killed because he *had* found the diamonds.

But to go back to the beginning. He had met that brunette—the one who was almost certainly both Laver's mistress and Mallett's daughter—and she had discovered his profession. She had set out to attract him and he had been far from unwilling. Probably he had spread himself, as the letter had said, by telling her that the diamonds were as good as found.

But what did *she* tell *him*? We couldn't begin to guess. But surely nothing about the Mallett murder or she'd have been hard put to it to explain her own connection. One could think of dozens of things—that she had told him Monaghan was an old family retainer who had stolen the diamonds, for instance—but none had the faintest proof to give it backing. We knew, in fact, the things she daren't have done, but we had no idea of the things she did. But whatever she did, she made a mistake. Godfrey had remembered diamonds in connection with the Mallett Case, and he had gone through the *Herald* files. Did what he discovered there make him realise that the brunette had only been stringing him along and that everything she had told him was nothing but lies? Would that have made him drop out, and nevertheless still keep a surreptitious eye on her? We didn't know.

Everything was surmise and it led us nowhere, so we got back to safe ground. That evening we had made some important discoveries. They were a new basis, and we had to know the best use to be made of them. One thing did seem a certainty, though it would need proof. Monaghan simply must have been suggested to Godfrey as one who had had the diamonds in his possession: if not, why had he gone to Stadmore? Wouldn't it have been imperative, then, for him to have visited the Mental Home and seen Monaghan for himself, and tried, even though others had failed, to elicit information?

"I'll try to pay another visit to Monaghan myself," I told Hallows. "Not that I particularly want to see Monaghan."

I outlined the scheme and he thought it a good one: risky, perhaps, but the likeliest one on hand. I said I thought the afternoon would be the best time, but the morning needn't be wasted. Maybe he could make contact again with that acquaintance of his and find out if Copley's Corner had been sold and if so, who was the buyer. I'd go to Marland soon after breakfast and have a look at the scene of the murder. Not that I expected to learn anything. All I could hope was to get a kind of background: to see, in fact, whether my preconceived notions of the place made a true fit with the little I'd been told.

I was away soon after nine o'clock and getting to Marland was no trouble at all. The lie of the land is simplicity itself. Take an almost perfect equilateral triangle, with Shireton at the apex. The triangle is wedge-shaped, with Stadmore at one corner and Marland at the other, and the distance from one to the other is about six miles.

I met a milk-float as I entered the village and asked the whereabouts of Danlow, and found it was clean through the village past the church, on the right-hand side. It was a timbered house standing by itself, and I couldn't miss it. The people who now had it, I was told, were called Gill, and the man was a retired gentleman who'd been somewhere out East. I moved the car on as directed and drew up with the house in full view.

It was a charming Tudor house that had probably been a farmhouse, for there was a large building at the back that had the look of a converted barn. The gardens were quite small but pleasant, and the house itself looked ideal for a man like Bertram Cowle—fairly secluded but not too remote. Cowle almost certainly hadn't had a car for near that converted barn some workmen were building what was obviously a garage.

I drew up in front of the house and went to the front door. A woman of about sixty, almost certainly the owner's wife, answered my ring. I asked if I might see Mr. Cowle. She looked surprised. She said he'd been dead for some months. I was surprised too. I'd been out of England for a year or so and, happening to be that way, I'd thought I'd look him up. He hadn't been exactly a friend, I said, but a fairly close acquaintance.

She asked me in and we went into a lounge where her husband was reading his paper in front of a cheerful fire. She explained my visit, and I gave my name as Trave. I remarked on the brass top of the low coffee table and that got us to Egypt where he'd spent most of his life and I'd soldiered, and all that was why he made no bones whatever about telling me just what had happened to Cowle. I was horrified.

"And it didn't put you off buying the place?" I said.

"The house suited us," he said, "so we didn't mind the associations, so to speak. In fact I think we got it more cheaply for that very reason. But that sort of thing is only a nine days' wonder. We had a few sightseers when we first came here, but you never see them now."

"It's a charming place," I said. "I don't think a murder would have put me off either."

"You'd like to have a look round?"

I wouldn't give him that trouble but he insisted. I'd said I'd never been in the house before and that may have made him so eager: that, and a wish to display his knowledge of the crime. He told me frankly that he'd been interested.

So I saw the room where Cowle had been killed, and just where the wall safe had been, and the french window through which Mallett had bolted. The Gills did have at the moment an aversion to using that room. They preferred to use the lounge, though that room, with its delightful view, would have been preferable.

They insisted that I should have coffee, so I thanked them and stayed on. While we were having it, I asked if by any chance they had met the owner—Miss Cowle. I thought one of them might have met her at the lawyer's office in town.

"Oh, yes," Mrs. Gill said. "She actually called here to see how we were settling down. Most thoughtful of her. We thought her very charming, didn't we, Jim?"

"Very charming indeed," Gill said. "A very good-looking girl too. But of course you know her, Mr. Trave."

I said I'd met her once, to the best of my recollection. I didn't remember her very well except that she was blonde and very charming, as he'd said.

I finished my coffee, refused another biscuit, and said that I'd really have to be on my way. I had business in Shireton which might keep me there for a day or two, but I couldn't be sure. I thanked them again and Gill went with me to my car. They were nice people and I'd have liked to see them again.

But what was worrying me as I drove back to Shireton was how to reconcile the fact that Myra Cowle had called on the Gills with her explicit statement to me that she'd been in Marland only twice in her life. All I could think was that she had meant me to realise that she'd been referring to visits to her uncle, and that the subsequent call on the Gills had been nothing to do with that matter of the diamonds which at the moment, we'd been discussing. But, as

I've said, I hate loose ends and a lack of clarity, and that's why it worried me.

I took a wrong turn but didn't panic, since all roads would lead back to Shireton. I actually came in from the north, and knew I was on the Puckford Road, and I had an idea I should have to turn somewhere to the right. I was looking about me for someone to ask, and was just letting the car move and no more, when I saw something that made me put the brake on hard. On my left was a church, and coming from it was Comfort. With him was a woman, and they were both talking to another man in clerical dress. They were near the gate when I first saw them, and in a minute they were through it and making their way south towards the town.

I guessed that the woman was Comfort's wife, and I don't know why unless it was that she had been on Comfort's left and the strange parson on Comfort's right. Her face had looked pale, like that of a convalescing invalid, but it had been a pleasant face and she had looked a nice, superior sort of woman, if you gather what I mean. And I don't know either why I got out of the car and made my way through the gate and into the church. The usual notice-board had said it was the parish church of St. James the Less.

In the comparative gloom I polished my glasses and then looked about me. By the far steps to the choir a woman was doing some cleaning, and I made a slow way towards her, and then let my steps be heard. She looked up.

"Pardon me," I said, "but was that the vicar I just saw going out?"

"The vicar's ill," she said. "That would be Mr. Comfort."

"Of course," I said. "And the lady with him was Mrs. Comfort."

She didn't contradict so I took it as read.

"But who was the other clergyman?" I said.

"That was Mr. Voles," she told me. "He's Chaplain at the Prison. A very nice man."

I said he looked it. And that was that. Except perhaps that when I got into my car again I was wondering just why we'd been neglecting the Rev. Charles Comfort.

Chapter 11
PINCHES OF SNUFF

HALLOWS WAS in the smoking room of the Suffolk when I got back. He hadn't needed to make contact with that acquaintance of his for he simply walked in and asked about Copley's Corner and whether it was sold. The young clerk at the desk said it wasn't, and wanted to know if Hallows was interested. Hallows said it depended on the price. The price turned out to be fifteen hundred pounds! Hallows said he *wasn't* interested, even though the clerk had given that figure with a look in his eye that hinted that one might take less. The clerk had also added that electricity was coming that way at once, and a lot of improvements had been made. Hallows said he didn't care if the place had been rebuilt. At that price he still wasn't interested. I went to the telephone and rang the Mental Home and asked for an interview that afternoon with the Medical Superintendent. I gave the same name as before and mentioned the interview I'd previously had.

"The Medical Superintendent's away," I was told. "You'd have to see the Assistant Superintendent, Dr. Upstone."

1 said it was all the same to me, and was told to hang on. When the voice came again I was asked my business, and I said it was what it had been before—to do with an inmate of the name of James Monaghan. Then I waited again and at last was told I could see Dr. Upstone at two-thirty.

It was a lovely afternoon with a late lingering of summer. Hallows drove the car and he must have taken a different turn at the fork, for we came to a notice which I'd never seen, and it directed one to a private road to the Home. It was only when we'd taken it that I saw another notice saying that one came that way at his own risk. That would be, we guessed, because it was open to certain of the inmates, though those we met looked harmless enough.

The huge spread of buildings had always been in sight and we came to a T-head with a choice of ways. Before us was a wired enclosure where scores of women were strolling aimlessly about. There were children too. It was a depressing sight and we hastily took the track to the left. We circled round and went past a second enclosure reserved for men. Hundreds of them there seemed, walking briskly but aimlessly and never a one talking to another. We hurried on again and I recognised the chimney of a power station, so we turned that way and found ourselves almost at the main entrance.

I left Hallows in the car and went in. There was the same procedure as before and then at last I was in the Superintendent's room again. Upstone was a vastly different man from his superior: younger, for one thing, short, plump, and almost hearty, and the old-school tie cut no ice with him. I didn't know if my previous visit was on record but I told him about it, and added that the woman in whose case I was interested was still unconvinced. I said it was all very annoying, but I felt I ought to do what I could.

He did remind me that I should have known it wasn't a visiting day but he too didn't seem to mind whether I saw Monaghan or not. So out I went and waited as before and after a bit an attendant came along and I was taken to the same room. The same male nurse or attendant was waiting there with Monaghan. It might have been because of the tip I'd given him—I definitely hoped so—but he recognised me.

"Here again then, sir?"

"Shan't be more than a minute or two this time," I said, and slipped something into his hand. That something was a pencil, five pound-notes, and a piece of paper on which was written:

Where and when can I see you when you're off duty?

I merely put it into his hand and, as if nothing had happened, went at once to Monaghan. He looked for all the world as he had looked before: the same sunken-eyed expression, the same gaze at nothing, the same fingers at the same rosary and the same almost imperceptible movement of the lips. I moved my chair so that I almost faced him, and my back was towards the attendant.

I wondered if I could read his lips. I knew most of what there was to know about rosaries. There was the crucifix at which one said the Creed, then—on his rosary at least—a larger bead for the Lord's Prayer—and three beads for the Hail Marys; then a larger bead again to indicate the beginning of the Sacred Mysteries. Fifty-five beads, that would be, in a series of five elevens: an introductory bead for the Lord's Prayer and always ten Hail Mary beads to follow it, and the words would be almost mechanical, for as one told them one was supposed to be thinking of the Mysteries: the Five Joyful, the Five Sorrowful and the Five Glorious.

You see what I was thinking? Maybe Monaghan wasn't saying the Lord's Prayer or the Hail Marys. Maybe he was talking to himself: about himself and his distorted remembrances, and seeing through the peep-holes of sanity beyond the heavy cloudiness with a numbed but groping brain. So I watched the lips carefully but they scarcely parted. Then I saw his fingers, that they were not telling the beads at all. The beads were dark, and looked to me now as if fashioned of bog-oak. Some relic of his days in Broughshane, maybe, and that was why he clung to them still. But the fingers weren't moving, except aimlessly from this bead to that, and then as aimlessly to no bead in particular. But the fingers kept moving and the lips kept moving, and I shrugged my shoulders and got to my feet.

Then I stooped and my face was not an arm's length from his. His eyes met mine and went beyond again.

"John Corkery?"

Nothing seemed to happen at that whisper, unless it was that the fingers closed unmovingly about that rosary.

I shrugged my shoulders again and moved back to the chair.

"That's all I want," I told the attendant.

He said nothing. He merely gave me a nod, but as I passed him his hand went to mine and mine closed about that pencil and the paper. I put both into my pocket and hurried on.

Upstone had a file on his desk and seemed to have been looking into the case of Monaghan. I told him that I shouldn't have to bother anyone again. Monaghan was definitely not my man, and I was sure I could convince my supposed widow of the fact. But what I wanted was to get him to talk about Monaghan and let something fall, maybe, that would help. So I said that Mental Homes were depressing places for a layman like myself. He didn't rise to that, so I said that Monaghan wasn't so pathetic as some. Still speaking as a layman, I'd call his a case of a one-track mind, and not too much of that. It wasn't religious mania exactly, as the last vestiges of sense making, as it were, a final stand in religion.

"From what I was told at Stadmore," I said, "he wasn't very mentally bright when he first came there. I suppose he's been deteriorating ever since, and then that burglary business finished him off."

That amused him.

"You fellows always insist that you're laymen," he told me, "and accuse us of talking medical jargon, and yet you always manage to produce some extraordinary jargon of your own. The whole thing's quite simple. In what you call layman's language, his brain was injured a good many years ago, probably as a result of an accident. There's an old lesion to prove it. Strictly between ourselves, I shouldn't be surprised if he'd been in an institution immediately after it, and made a sufficient recovery and was discharged."

That certainly was something. It showed where Monaghan might have been lying dormant, so to speak, for quite a few years. But I didn't want to show an undue interest in the man, so I thanked Upstone, repeated that I shouldn't trouble him again, and then left. When the car moved on, I didn't say anything for a minute or two, for I was trying to think something out. If Monaghan had been discharged from some Mental Home, and just before he came to Stadmore, then someone must have helped him to a very considerable extent. He might have been found that cottage and, except for a few personal things such as that photograph and the Skegness mug, he would have had to be set up with furniture and household things. And would he have had money to live on? And who could have done all that if it wasn't Mallett, working through his daughter. That supposed that Mallett's wife, who, as we had argued, had dissociated herself from Mallett entirely, was dead, or else living entirely apart from her daughter. All surmise, perhaps, but you see where my thoughts had brought me. Wherever one turned in that Case one came up against that brunette.

I let out a breath and then remembered that attendant, and I felt as if I was going to read a telegram that might bring bad news.

Saturday afternoon, 2.30 at Kozy Kaff just before Odeon.

That was what was written. I passed it to Hallows, who drove with one hand while he read it.

It was a Thursday and, as he said, there were two more days to wait. He also said we passed the Odeon on the normal way back to the town. In fact we were almost there, and as we neared it, he slowed. Just beyond it we spotted the cafe. I couldn't bring myself to think of it by that emetic of a name.

Hallows went to inspect and I moved the car on. From the shrug of his shoulders when he came back, I gathered it wasn't palatial. He called it a good pull-up for carmen.

After we'd had tea and talked things over, I thought we might take another look at Copley's Corner, so we drove out towards Stadmore and took the side lane that avoided the village. As we neared the cottage I saw that the men were still at work.

We reversed the car and got out. It was almost five o'clock and near knocking-off time. A couple of men were already getting their things together, but another man, with a boy to help him, was finishing off a cement top a foot or so below the ground above the well where the windlass had been.

"Crowned the well in, have you?" I said.

"That's right, sir. Electricity's coming next week."

"And that small hole you've left is for the pipe?"

"That's it," he told me. "A pipe with a suction valve right down in the well. Little electric pump in the kitchen to take water up to the tank in the roof."

"Plenty of water, is there?"

"Not so bad," he said. "Ought to hold five or six foot if there ain't a bad drought. We had to deepen the old well pretty considerable, though."

"Find anything at the bottom?"

I'd known all sorts of things found at the bottom of old wells when they'd been cleaned out or deepened.

"Nothing worth talking about," he said. "An old pair o' pattens, all rusted up, and an old brass candlestick what the parson reckoned he could clean."

"The parson?" I said. "You mean Mr. Comfort?"

"That's it," he said, and waved a casual hand in the direction of the church. "He weren't much comfort to me though. Soon as he got wind of this well being deepened, blowed if he weren't here the whole darn time. Don't know what he expected us to find, but soon as the bucket came up he'd be looking in it and turning it over with his fingers."

"Well, he did get a candlestick," I said. "And between you and me, I don't know that I wouldn't have been here myself. I've known some remarkably funny things drawn up from the bottoms of wells."

"You're in that line?"

"No," I said. "But I'm a countryman."

"Thinking of buying this place, are you?"

"Don't know," I said. "Depends what I think of it when you fellows have finished."

The job was done and he was getting the kinks out of his legs. Hallows and I moved on round the cottage and made a show of inspecting the place. Five minutes later the truck that had been parked in the lane moved off with the men. Hallows and I went back to our car.

"Funny how that parson keeps cropping up," Hallows said as he moved the car on.

"Yes," I said. "Anyone might have thought he was expecting to find those diamonds at the bottom of that well."

"Just what I thought myself," Hallows said. "He knows something, sir. I wouldn't mind betting a fiver he got something out of Monaghan."

"When?"

"Probably the night when Monaghan was attacked. There'd be he and Start, and why shouldn't Monaghan have told Comfort something privately before he collapsed? When Start wasn't there. You know, sir. 'The diamonds! He didn't get the diamonds!' Something like that."

I said it was likely. I also said that Comfort was a gentleman whom we'd singularly neglected, and the time had come to do something about it. Just what I couldn't at the moment say, but it was something worth talking over.

When we got back to the Hotel there was a message from Bernice asking me to ring her. So I rang and she told me there'd been a telephoned enquiry from the man who was handling Godfrey's affairs for the Bank, asking if I could see him the next day. She had his private number, so I said I'd see him at ten o'clock in the morning as he'd suggested. I'd take the seven o'clock train from Shireton and drop in at the flat on my way.

That fitted in well as a killer of time till Saturday afternoon and the Kosy Kaff. And Hallows would have plenty to do. I thought of coming back early on the Saturday morning, and he could concentrate on Comfort. I told him what I'd seen and heard at St. James the Less, and I thought he might pay another visit to Stadmore. He might even make some excuse to call at the vicarage.

It was short of nine o'clock when I arrived at the flat. I hadn't breakfasted but I didn't have time for more than coffee and toast, and as soon as I'd smartened myself up, I had to be off. But I did remember to put that Napoleon snuff-box in my pocket.

Everything was concluded satisfactorily about Godfrey's small estate and in a day or two everyone would be in formal possession of what was coming to him. Even the Shireton police were relinquishing the car and the personal things they had held, and I gathered that the Yard men had been over them and found nothing worth their while.

"This is that snuff-box, by the way," I said. "Perhaps I'd better write myself a receipt."

While I was doing that, my fellow executor had a look at it. He called it a very nice example and worth at least fifty pounds. I think he'd have increased his valuation if he'd have known about that sort of secret panel underneath, but I didn't say a word. I did stand him a lunch on the strength of it, and because my duties as executor were as good as over.

It was at my club that we'd lunched and after he'd gone I stayed on for a time, and I was wondering what to do with that snuff-box. In my unregenerate days I might have carried it about with me as Godfrey had done and had considerable fun from the reactions of those who'd be unexpectedly aware of that secret panel, but my taste for that sort of thing had gone. Not that that miniature was grossly sexual except to a pornographic mind. It was a work of art, but of the kind I didn't feel like risking in the flat. A museum was the place for it, and yet I didn't like parting, even to a museum, with what had been a personal and affectionate gift.

I suppose my fingers must have stiffened instinctively as I held that snuff-box, for I was suddenly aware that that secret miniature had slid out, and it was as I moved it back that I saw something I had never noticed. It looked like a sliver of paper, so I drew it gently out, and it came with all the ease in the world. But it wasn't exactly a paper. It was a piece of perfectly plain paper on which something was fastened with a sliver of what looked like stamp paper. There were two somethings and I saw they were a couple of finger-prints!

A piece of plain paper just smaller than that miniature, say two and a quarter inches by one and a quarter, and attached to it two smaller and different pieces of paper on each of which was a finger-print, dusted and sharply clear. But not the firmly pressed down, official kind of prints, but what I'd call casual prints, and clear in detail as I've said. One was on a thin piece of what looked like cheap manuscript paper and the other on plain paper slightly thicker. Each piece of paper was of a size to contain the print, and little more.

I got out my pen-knife and gently prised the prints from the main paper which held them, and placed them carefully between the folded pages of a letter in my wallet. I had another good look at the snuff-box and even shook it, but nothing else had been hidden there, so I put it in my pocket and had a look at the paper on which the prints had been stuck. It had been neatly cut to size from what I thought a sheet of cheap, thin, plain paper, and it was when I held it to the light to see the watermark that I saw something else. That sheet must have been part of a block or pad, and someone—Godfrey almost certainly—had written on the sheet above it with such a pressure of pen or pencil that my paper still retained a faint trace of what had been written. But what I saw, of course, was a part of that original sheet: a fragment only of what had been written.

There was at that moment no one but myself in that room, so I took it to the window and held it against the light. That was useless. The light was too strong and coming through the indentations, so I held the paper so that the light came sideways, and at once those marks were more clear. I doubted if I'd ever see them clearer.

First was what looked like a telephone number, but woefully indistinct. It was this—

UN 1003

except that it needn't have been a 3 but an 8. I looked at it under the big reading glass but I couldn't be sure. All I could tell myself was that I'd bet, if I had to bet, that it was a 3 rather than an 8. As for the UN, it took me some time to find that, and it was thinking of Godfrey that brought me to it. *C(UN)ningham*, that was what it must be. His was a CUNningham number.

I had a look at what I could see beneath. This is what I made it:

vols plus additi
ry fortnight unl
e expert not tel

The first line beat me. *Vols* might be *volumes*, or it might be the end of a word, and at that moment all I could think of was *frivols*. The last word would be *addition*, or *additional*.

The next line looked like *every fortnight unless*. The last line beat me again. The initial *e* could be the end of innumerable words, though *the* looked the likeliest, and the same with that final *tel*, though *tell* looked as reasonable as any. But what the whole thing originally was I had no earthly idea, and I doubted if I should ever have.

But at least I could try that telephone number, so I nipped up at once and went to the telephone and asked for enquiries. I tried to be exceptionally charming and spun a yarn that I'd lost a certain number and name, but thought the number I wanted was Cunningham 1003. If I could be told the name of the subscriber, I'd know at once if that was really the number I wanted.

The whole thing sounded pretty fishy to me, and when there was a silence, I thought enquiries had hung up on me. But I could still hear a faint something that said perhaps the line wasn't dead, so I held on. It was three minutes before the voice came on again. The subscriber was MASTERS Miss E., of 8, Chester Hall, St. John's Wood.

I went back to the reading room to think things over. *If*, and it was a mighty big *if*, that number was correct, then the lady might be one of Godfrey's innumerable friends. Chester Hall, I knew. If one went to Godfrey's flat by Lord's cricket ground, then it was north of Godfrey's place, and about five minutes' walk away. Its high-sounding name was a kind of show title for yet another of those blocks of flats with which the suburbs are sprinkled, and, as far as I remembered, they were expensive looking too, and there again it was a question of nearness to town. And then I asked myself why I was still sitting there. Inside five minutes I had hailed a taxi and was being driven towards St. John's Wood.

I told the driver to wait. We had stopped just beyond the flats and on the way there I had been puzzling my wits. One never knew, I had told myself, and with a face and form like mine, I had to keep under cover, so to speak, and get my information at the same time. And I couldn't help remember how I'd been far too clever at Laver's place.

But I needn't have worried. An elderly postman was coming out of the main entrance and I waited till he was back on the main road and then took him on the flank. While I was speaking I was picking out a half-crown from my loose change.

"I wonder if you'd try and save me a lot of time," I said. "Does a Miss Marsham have one of the flats?"

"Marsham?" he said. "Not that I know of. There's a Miss Masters. I've just left something for her now."

I gave him the half-crown.

"My client's a Miss Marsham," I said. "But this Miss Masters: she isn't a lady doctor, is she?"

"Not her," he said. "They tell me she's on the films."

"That settles it then," I said, and smiled and thanked him and moved off. And it did seem to settle it. I didn't see a film actress involved in the death of Godfrey Prial.

I told the driver to take me to The Cenotaph, and as we moved off I wondered what I could do. The best thing seemed to be to try 1008, and I ought to do that from my flat. But in the meanwhile those finger-prints might tell me something. Or couldn't I ring the number and see what happened? And that's what I did. As soon as I'd paid off my driver I found a telephone kiosk. There *was* a Cunningham 1008, and a woman's voice answered me.

"This is Lucille," she said.

"Excuse me," I said, "but Lucille what?"

"Lucille: Milliners and Costumiers," she told me just a bit tartly.

"Of course," I said. "And what is your address?"

"Seventeen to nineteen Abbot Street," she said, and I promptly rang off.

I noted name and address and began wondering again. It certainly sounded more promising. One of their mannequins or show-girls seemed a likely acquaintance for Laver. But it could wait. If nothing happened at the Shireton end, then I'd turn Hallows on to Lucille. A brunette of theirs might have left. Or that blonde that had been seen once with Laver at the dog track.

I walked through to the Yard and found a trusting soul to take those two prints. I spun the same yarn to this particular acquaintance, that in the course of a job I'd come up against two people in whom I thought the Yard might be interested. If the prints proved it, then there were things I'd pass on.

I had only twenty minutes to wait and I knew what had happened when I saw that Sergeant's face. The Yard weren't interested, and that was that. I ought to have asked him something else, but maybe I was too disappointed.

It was well after four o'clock and I'd promised to be home, so I hurried back to the flat. A friend was in and after I'd put that snuff-box well at the back of a drawer of my desk, I joined in for tea. Bernice suddenly thought of a show that began at six o'clock, so I rang for seats and the three of us went to it and Bernice and I had a meal out afterwards. It was quite late by then and I didn't do any more thinking about the Case. That was a pity. If we hadn't gone to that Hippodrome show and I'd spent the evening at home with Bernice, I'd had saved the devil's own heap of time. I don't say I'd have solved the Case—and certainly not that evening—but I'd have had a few of the answers.

In the morning I took the nine o'clock from Liverpool Street and on the way to Shireton I had an idea. It arose out of the fact that whichever way Hallows and I turned, we nearly always came up against that brunette. But surely we'd been barking up the wrong tree in confining our enquiries to a brunette. It was true that we had based those enquiries on the theory that that brunette and Laver had parted company, and the theory was founded solely on the fact that Laver had not for some time been seen with a brunette, whereas he had been seen with a blonde. *But why shouldn't that brunette and that blonde be one and the same person?*

Somehow I liked the idea. Penelope Stangate would naturally have taken the blonde she saw at the dog track for quite a different person from the brunette she'd seen occasionally before. That change of hair, with one or two little unobtrusive additions, would make the devil of a difference to a woman's appearance, and I was trying to think what Bernice would be like if she suddenly became a blonde. And I shuddered. All I could think of was barmaids, which must have been my sub-conscious creeping up on me from a misspent youth.

CHAPTER 12
HERE AND THERE

HALLOWS WAS having a pint in the smoking room so I ordered one for myself. He'd put in a goodish bit of time on Comfort, he said, and he gave his dry smile when he added that if ever that vicar became a bishop and entitled to an official life, he wouldn't make too bad a hand of writing it.

Mrs. Comfort was splendidly spoken of in Stadmore. She had been something of an invalid since the birth of her youngest boy. She wasn't ill exactly, Hallows said, but just not strong, and she was often confined to the house. She had been a Miss Voles, and that Chaplain I'd seen with the Comforts at St. James the Less, was her brother. Comfort had kicked off, as Hallows put it, by being curate at that same church.

In Stadmore, Comfort definitely wasn't liked by the men though reasonably thought of by the women. The men didn't like him because he had to have a finger in every village pie, and he was pig-headed beyond all bearing. The women liked him better because he was undoubtedly devoted to his wife, and, when she had one of her sick spells, he was known to have done both housework and cooking himself if the daily woman wasn't there. He was also devoted to his children, and was finding time to act as private tutor, though the daughter also went into Shireton once a week for dancing lessons at the special academy, and once for piano lessons. The children were liked in the village. They were friendly—not too much so—and gave themselves no airs, and that in spite of the fact that Comfort didn't like them associating with Stadmore children, other than those who might be considered somewhat of their own class.

In Hallows' opinion Comfort was undoubtedly hard-up. He could make do, perhaps, and no more. One might have expected those children to go to some good-class preparatory school in the neighbourhood, but that was clearly beyond his means, even if they were day pupils. To go as boarders was unthinkable, with modern charges at preparatory schools as heavy as those of even the public schools. Comfort owed no money in the village but tradesmen often had to wait. That was about all Hallows had gathered from village talk, except that Comfort's nickname was Dreary.

He had called on him on the Friday afternoon and Comfort had left the study—used as a schoolroom—to see him. Hallows had asked to consult the parish register and Comfort had been most careful to ask his precise needs. Hallows had told him he was tracing a genealogy and with particular reference to some people called Samson who might have lived in Stadmore in the eighteenth century. Comfort went back to the study and a few minutes later came back with the assurance that no Samsons were mentioned in the register.

"Then he asked me if I was working on my own or for any Society or firm," Hallows said. "He had his eye right on me and it put me rather in queer street. I thought I'd take a chance, so I showed him I was working for the firm. I thought if he'd anything to hide, it'd bring him out in the open."

"And did it?"

"Not that I could see, sir. The Agency didn't ring any bell."

"A pity," I said. "And what did you think of him as a man?"

"Stuffy," Hallows said. "Decidedly stuffy. Never a smile. Courteous, of course, but always just a something that made you wonder if he weren't suspicious. Which reminds me. When he was seeing me off at the door he asked if he hadn't seen me somewhere in the village before. I said that was quite likely. I'd been once or twice before. I said I was making enquiries about Samsons everywhere in the district."

That was that. I said that as far as Comfort was concerned, he was teetering up and down on a seesaw. At one end was a man who'd acted remarkably suspiciously. At the other was a man full of good works: the man who'd stored Monaghan's things at his own expense and who'd been prepared to buy Monaghan's cottage at a reasonable price so that the old man might have a home in case of recovery. I said we'd leave him till the see-saw tilted a bit more at one end, and I began telling Hallows what I'd discovered in that snuff-box. I showed him the prints and that piece of paper. I was glad I'd taken a note of what I'd seen, for the mere pressing against the papers of my wallet had slightly flattened the marks, and they were far less clear than before.

He couldn't make head or tail of that extract about experts and fortnights, and his private idea was that it had nothing to do with the Case. He thought the paper came from a tear-off note-book, the kind we call a flimsy: some old note-book that Godfrey had had with him.

"It might have been in that snuff-box for heaven knows how long," he said. "Long before his holiday for all we know."

"You're wrong," I said. "That snuff-box was Godfrey's pass-port to a certain kind of society. The simplest way for him to have made friends in Shireton was to have shown the tricks of that box."

He still had his own opinion. Take that Lucille business, he said. Some girl of theirs was one he'd picked up at some local place and she'd given her telephone number.

You know old Hudibras Butler?

> *A man convinced against his will*
> *Is of his own opinion still.*

That still holds good, so once more I left it. I told him about the brunette and how she and the blonde might be one and the same person. That was more attractive, though he wasn't enthusiastic. I couldn't expect him to be. After all it was his idea to base things on something the other way about. And when he asked me how it helped, I was rather flummoxed. All I could say was that we ought to get out of our heads the idea that we had to make enquiries about nothing but brunettes. Since the date of Godfrey's first letter, there'd been ample time for her to bloom out into a blonde. I said I didn't know for a certainty how long the process took, but I offered to bet him a couple of drinks that it could be done in a morning.

"Funny in a way," he said, and he hadn't taken the bet. "A brunette in the morning and the same afternoon your own friends might pass you in the street."

"Funny's the word," I said. "You and I must try it some time."

And that was when Hallows was called to the telephone. It was about time for the gong to go for lunch and I was most devilishly hungry, so I went upstairs and had a quick polish. When I came down Hallows was waiting at the foot of the stairs. He drew me aside.

"That was Mr. Norris," he said. "I'll bet you can't guess what about."

I was too hungry to be flippant.

"Comfort!" he said. "He rang the office last night after Mr. Norris had left. Mr. Norris got the message this morning and thought he'd better ring me up. Comfort wanted to know if I was genuine, and Mr. Norris says God forgive him but he's just telephoned Comfort that I was."

I said that was fine. The see-saw had teetered down at one end. Hallows asked at which end and the funny thing was that I was damned if I could say. And we couldn't argue the point because I was due at the cafe to meet that attendant from the Mental Home.

I had no clothes but those on me, but it couldn't be helped if I was looking far too smart when I turned up at the Kosy Kaff. I was a minute or two early but my man got off a bus at the Odeon. There was nothing lean and furtive and conspiratorial about him. He was well-built and on the plump side; and the look he gave me was just a bit nervous, and no more. He told me his name was Wilming.

"And what's this place like?" I asked him as we neared the Kosy Kaff.

"We'll be all right in there, sir," he told me. "My brother-in-law keeps it."

The door opened into a long narrow room with a couple of steaming urns and piles of crockery. Sandwiches and highly coloured cakes were under glass containers. There was a smell of fried liver with a touch of onion. The shirt-sleeved man who'd been talking to the one customer moved behind the counter towards us.

"How're you, Charlie?" Wilming said.

"Not so bad," Charlie said. "How's yourself, Ted?"

"Can't grumble," Ted said. "How's Mabel?"

Mabel was fine and the kids fine. Ted said he was going to see the Town, which meant, I was gathering, Shireton Town playing at home. Charlie said there was no hurry. They didn't kick off till a quarter past three.

"What'll you have, sir?" Ted asked me.

I didn't want anything, but coffee wouldn't kill me.

"Two coffees, Charlie," Ted said, and drew back for me to go through the curtained doorway.

We were in a smallish room that held about twelve tables. There had been a lorry parked outside and its driver and his mate were the only occupants. We found a table at the other corner and Charlie came in with the coffee. He wiped the American cloth with a damp rag, gave me a quick look and went through to his counter again.

"Charlie's all right," Ted assured me, and I said I didn't doubt it. There was nothing alarming about the place. Frowsty and a bit fly-blown, perhaps, and the tables just a bit forlorn with their cruets and sauce bottles stacked on the mantel-piece.

"Look here, Ted," I said. "I want you to know that I'm up to nothing that's likely to get you or me into trouble. I'm interested in Monaghan. I don't think that's his real name. I want to get a line on what his real name was."

I expanded a bit speciously and even hinted at a connection with the police. To get down to brass tacks, I wanted to know all he could tell me. He couldn't tell me anything, and I had to prompt him.

"He's always been what I might call one of your patients?"

"Well, more or less," he said. "When I'm on duty, he is."

"Ever hear him say anything? Any word or words you could recognise?"

"Not him, sir. Never says a word. Just like you saw him them two times."

"Nothing ever rouses him or stirs him?"

Nothing ever did, he said, and then corrected himself. There was that time when another loonie snatched that rosary out of his hands. It was almost as soon as Monaghan arrived at the Asylum and a fine sunny day. He had been walking in that enclosure I'd seen, fingering his rosary as usual, and it caught the eye of another patient who snatched it from Monaghan's fingers.

"Forward, his name is," Ted said. "Thinks he's a medical student."

"And what happened?"

"Well, I wasn't there at the time, sir, but Monaghan went for him and there'd have been a bit of a dust up if someone hadn't been right on the spot. Monaghan got it back all right, but that's why it's sewn on his waistcoat. No one can snatch it—see?"

I said I saw. But I wanted to know how Monaghan had indicated that he wanted it sewn on his waistcoat. He said it was by signs, and showed me how it was done.

"When he goes out now, he doesn't walk about," Ted said. "He sits on one of the seats. Never gives no trouble. Just like an old sheep, he is."

"Right," I said. "What I want to know now is, who comes to see him?"

He said that after he first arrived, a clergyman used to come and see him. I described Comfort and he said that was the one. And Comfort apparently used to sit quite near Monaghan and talk to him in a soothing voice.

"The last time he came he looked a bit riled," Ted said. "Reckon he'd got a bit fed up coming all the way there and doing nothing but sit and talk to a mummy. He didn't come again, not that I know of."

"And no one else came?"

"Yes," he said, and he said it slowly. "There was a lady came, I think she was young—well, somewhere about my age. Couldn't see much of her face though. She was wearing a sort of veil. Monaghan didn't like her."

"What do you mean?"

"Well, he sort of cringed away as soon as she sat down. He made some noises. Sort of whimpering noises."

He shut his lips and made squeaky noises through his nose. It was almost frightening when you thought of Monaghan, cowering away and making noises like that.

"What happened?" I said. "Did she go on trying to talk to him?"

"No go, sir," he said. "Monaghan just wouldn't have it."

He had hesitated. There was something he was wondering about.

"Yes?" I said. "This is strictly confidential, by the way. I'm trusting you and you're trusting me."

"Well, sir, there's strict orders against taking money or tips. Some of the visitors try to slip us money to spend on the patients, but you haven't to take it. But this here woman asked me to keep my mouth shut about Monaghan, and him not letting her near him. She slipped me a tip. A quid, it was."

I nodded.

"And what would you call her? Fair, or dark?"

He didn't know, but he thought she was dark. Not too dark but just not fair.

"She wasn't one of these platinum blondes?"

She wasn't, he said. He'd have spotted that at once, if only because his own wife was a blonde. That visitor had definitely been on the dark side and, now he came to remember it, her hair hadn't been down on her shoulders but drawn up, so to speak, under her hat. She was what he called smartly dressed, and a lady.

"No possible chance of discovering what reasons she gave for visiting Monaghan?" I asked him.

"Never a hope," he told me emphatically, and it was clear that between him and the office there was a great gulf fixed. So I asked him about the difficulties there might be in seeing a patient.

It wasn't difficult on visiting days, he said, if you were a relative or had a good reason. But it depended. There were times when a patient couldn't be seen at all, according, I gathered, to his sanity, or was it insanity. But with a man like Monaghan there'd be few restrictions. He was absolutely harmless and trustworthy, and visits never upset him.

"Except that one visit," I said, and was showing him those photographs of Godfrey Prial. He gave me a quick look.

"You've probably seen one of them before," I said. "In the local newspaper."

That was it, and he was suddenly looking a bit more nervous. Not because of himself, but because it must have been clear that I really was connected with the police.

"That's right," I said. "He's the man who was killed at the George. Murdered, if you like. Not that you need worry about that. All I want to know is, did this chap ever visit the asylum?"

He had a look. He frowned before he shook his head.

"You think you've seen him some place before?"

He didn't know. So I tried pencilling in a moustache, and suggesting glasses; even dark glasses.

"I've seen him," he said. "But I don't know if he saw Monaghan. He may have done when I wasn't actually on duty. But I'm sure I've seen him."

I gave him time to think back and he thought he'd seen him in that waiting-room annexe sort of place by the Superintendent's office. I didn't press the point. Godfrey had been to the Asylum and that was good enough for me.

There seemed nothing else to say so I gave him Hallow's name and private address. If Monaghan had any more visitors he was to write immediately. No name, no address, no date: merely the statement that X had had another visitor and giving as good as possible a description of that visitor.

His free days were alternate Sundays, and alternate Wednesday and Saturday afternoons, so I took down his Puckford address and said that if I wanted him urgently I'd drop him a similar message with no name, address or date. Then I gave him five more pound notes and that was that. We went out and he had another cheery word with Charlie, then once outside he went one way and I another.

As I watched him go down a side street that probably led to the football ground, I was doubtful if I'd ever clap eyes on him again. Not that he was a twister or likely to try a double-cross or even string me along for the sake of easy money. After all, he might suspect that he had something on me, but he knew I had far more on him. But he hadn't shown signs of that. In a sheepish, hesitating sort of way he'd been frank enough, so it wasn't that that worried me. What I was guessing was that he'd have no more to tell. Comfort had persevered with Monaghan till at last he had lost hope and patience. As for the lady—once more our elusive brunette—Monaghan had somehow recognised her or reacted instinctively to her mere presence. If she was really his grand-daughter, that wasn't surprising, but it seemed a certainty that she would never dare the risk of seeing him again.

And who else would be likely to see him? Not Laver or Alf. That brunette had been Laver's associate. She had gone to see Monaghan because Laver himself didn't dare risk a visit. If Monaghan reacted badly to the mere presence of the brunette, what would he be like with the man who—as we thought—had stunned him and been in the act of torturing him?

That was why I told myself that I doubted if Ted Wilming would ever write us a word. And I was to be right. As for seeing him again— well, I was right and I wasn't, and the best way to leave it is like that. As for the value of what I'd learned that afternoon in the Kosy Kaff, that remained to be seen. Hallows, when I talked it over with him, thought there had merely been a dotting of i's and a crossing of t's.

We knew, in fact, what we had known before: that Godfrey had been working on those diamonds through the Monaghan clue; that the brunette had put him on to that clue, and that Comfort had been a highly interested party. As to where he went from there, frankly I didn't know. But I was sure there was much more to be unearthed at the Shireton end, and I'd stay on over the weekend. I'd like to go to a service at Stadmore Church, I said, but Hallows needn't waste a Sunday. He might as well get away for a day at home and come back on the Sunday night. Maybe a change of scenery would bring ideas.

So Hallows left and I had tea by myself. Then I went round to police headquarters.

I was lucky. Jewle, an old colleague and now a Chief-Inspector, was handling the Prial Case and as soon as I went through the doors

I saw him coming down the stairs. I nipped back and ran into him casually on the outside pavement.

I said, "Good lord!" and he said, "Good God!" and we were shaking hands. I had Hallows' car on the opposite side of the road and I made him get in and we went to the Suffolk. He told me about the Prial Case and how he'd seen Norris and how things weren't going too well. I said I had business in the district and was staying on till the Monday—maybe a day or two more.

He hadn't had tea so I ate another one with him. I told him about Godfrey, the kind of chap he was both privately and on a job, and he seemed grateful. Then I put something in his way. I'd let him see clearly that Loame had been a difficult chap with whom to co-operate.

"It's different with you, Mike," I said. "Besides, the idea only occurred to me a day or so ago, and I'd thought of passing it on to you, only I've been rather busy. There may be nothing in it and the devil of it is I've destroyed the postcard."

I'm not blushing. In the cause of what one calls justice, I'm a fluent liar, which is something you've had no need to guess. In the early days when I was first teamed with George Wharton a lie would never—as the Victorians had it—have sullied my lips. But I soon got out of that. When the other side starts telling nothing but the truth, that will be the day when the law becomes virtuous. *Que messieurs les assassins commencent.*

I'd had a picture postcard from Godfrey, I said. I believed it was of Shireton Town Hall or something equally gruesome, and he'd said he was having a good time, and there'd been something I very vaguely remembered about business and pleasure. Then there'd been something cryptic about was I in the market for diamonds.

"Diamonds?" Jewle said. "What was the idea?"

"Don't ask me," I said. "I've told you the kind of chap he was. He'd meet all sorts and sizes, as they say. Maybe he'd met someone who wanted to part with some diamonds."

"You mean the old diamond trick and the switch?"

"I doubt it," I said. "Godfrey'd have been far too fly for that. He wouldn't have parted with a cent unless he knew he had the right thing. I don't say he'd have been too particular about where it came from."

That didn't ring a bell. Diamonds conveyed little to Michael Jewle. They didn't tie up with the Prial Case.

But he did want to know about something else. What about that mention of business and pleasure? Did I know about that make-up box Prial had had?

"Loame tried to pull a fast one over that," I told him. "Said we'd said Godfrey was on holiday, so what about that box. He didn't get away with it. But my idea's this. Godfrey got wind of some missing diamonds and thought he might as well try his luck at recovery. He was on a holiday. Business and pleasure. It's far-fetched, but there it is. If you know of any missing diamonds in this locality—well. . . ." And I shrugged my shoulders for the rest.

There were questions enough but I had to keep telling him he knew as much as myself. He had to show a certain gratitude but it didn't come easily. That diamond story was too fantastic, as I'd said. So we switched to old times and this and that and it was six o'clock when he said he'd have to go. He was at the George, and he'd ask me there for a meal, he said, but he never knew just when he'd be there.

I went up for a bath and change and I was wondering if I'd done right to tell Jewle what I had. Then I knew I had. Sooner or later I'd have to have him on our side. And it was handy to have someone from whom to learn in the course of a chat something that we could learn nowhere for ourselves. Even in that matter of the diamonds there were things which he could unearth. And what did it matter if I shamelessly picked, or tried to pick, Jewle's brains provided we arrived at the same end. He wanted to know who killed Prial. So did we. But that killer was our special meat. He'd be working for us, not the Yard. Specious perhaps, and illogical, but it made sense enough to me.

And a funny thing happened, at least from my point of view. I was in the bar having a pre-prandial pint when I was called to the telephone.

"That you, Mr. Travers?"

"Speaking."

"Jewle here. About that tip you gave me. Most grateful. Good-bye."

That's all. Almost as quick as you've read it. Jewle hadn't wasted time. He was on to the Mallett Case. Which was all to the good. Or had Mark Antony put it better?

> *. . . Mischief, thou art afoot*
> *Take thou what course thou wilt.*

But it made me change my mind about Hallows. That night I rang him and said I'd run up against Jewle and both of us hadn't better be in Shireton. So would Hallows get to work on the Monday at the Lucille end, and try to unearth anything about a brunette or a blonde, or a brunette who'd turned into a blonde. I said that Mrs. Travers would probably lend a hand if Hallows thought fit.

On the Sunday morning I drove Hallows' car to Stadmore and timed things so that the final bell was tolling as I went in. Even while I stood the indecisive moment on the step I could count the congregation, for when I joined it there'd be exactly a dozen of us. So there wasn't any need to worry about a pew. I took the books the sidesman gave me and went well up front, and moved along my pew till I was in line with the pulpit.

To my left I saw Mrs. Comfort and with her the younger boy. The other boy, whom I remembered from that matter of a lost dog, was in the choir, and a girl whom I took to be his sister. There were ten children in that choir, two youngish women and an older one, and three men, one of whom turned out to be a remarkably shrill tenor. The other two sang a not too audible bass.

The service was low church; the kind of thing in which I'd been brought up. The hymns weren't too familiar and there was only one tune that I knew, and the choir outnumbered us in any case and did most of the singing. Comfort's sermon lasted exactly eleven minutes by my watch. I don't know if he recognised me. I think he did, even if I was a someone whom he'd somewhere met. But he couldn't avoid the sight of me, for I was clean beneath his eyes. The text was something out of Paul's Epistle to the Romans.

The word is nigh thee, even in thy mouth.

There seemed something apposite about it, though I couldn't quite see what. As for the sermon, it justified the village wit who'd bestowed the nickname of Dreary. Its matter was boring and the delivery monotonous. Every word was read from the ill-concealed script and had it been a warm morning of summer I should have dropped off to sleep.

The last hymn was sung: the sidesmen came round with the bag, the benediction was pronounced and matins were over. I took my time about leaving. Most of the worshippers had left the churchyard but Mrs. Comfort was talking to an elderly woman who'd chirped a thin treble just behind me. I liked Mrs. Comfort's face, and her manner and her kindly smile. The daughter was with her, and I thought her the very image of her mother.

I went out to the car. The two Comfort boys were looking at it. I spoke before they could veer off.

"A bit old, isn't she?"

"She is, rather," Martin told me. "Better than a lot of the new ones, though."

"So I'm told," I said. "And by the way, did you ever find your dog?"

He looked surprised. Then he remembered me, and smiled.

"Oh, yes," he said. "He's always going off. We haven't seen him this morning—not since breakfast."

"It's the Smiths' dog," Paul said. I said why didn't they ask the Smiths' dog to breakfast, and he laughed at that.

They gave me a smile as I moved the car on. They were nice boys, I thought, and I was suddenly thinking that I wouldn't mind if they were my own.

And it was thinking that that gave me an idea.

CHAPTER 13
THUNDERBOLT

AFTER LUNCH that Sunday afternoon I wrote a couple of letters. One was to Bernice, telling her that Hallows might possibly want some help, and if so she was to use her own judgment in the matter. I also said I should probably be home on the Wednesday, and the reason why I made that calculation was that something might arise which might make necessary a further interview with Ted Wilming on that free Wednesday afternoon.

The other letter was to Myra Cowle. A report mightn't be due but it seemed good policy to let her know we were up and doing, and to keep the facile optimisms from her mind. And I thought it best to make it a personal letter.

> DEAR MISS COWLE,
>
> While I must insist that you should not place any great hopes on what has been so far done, I think you should know that we have been a long way from idle in that matter of the recovery of your lost property.
>
> Thanks to enquiries previously made in this district on another case, we have picked up a useful lead which may bring results. Already we are pretty sure what happened to the property on a certain night and we have more than an idea of the identity of those concerned. Further we cannot at the moment go.
>
> All good wishes,
>
> Yours sincerely,
>
> L. TRAVERS.

That done, I settled down to crosswords. For what I still call the Torquemada I hadn't a Chambers's dictionary, so I found it heavy going, and that was why I forgot to post my letters till it was almost too late. When I slipped along to the main post-office so as to take no chances, I found we were in for the first fog of the autumn. It was the sort of thing one could expect after the abnormally fine weather: not that I could call it an old-time fog. The night was just damp and almost drizzling, and there was a thick mist so that one could see across a street and very little more.

While I was having my usual at the bar I was told that the wireless had mentioned wide-spread mist and fog. It was the autumnal type apparently, that cleared in the morning and reappeared in the late afternoons, except perhaps in industrial areas. You've heard it enough to know the way it goes. But so long as the days were clear I wasn't worrying. As I saw things, I needn't even leave the hotel. My policy was to wait till I heard something new from Jewle.

In the morning I went to the public library and consulted Crockford. It wasn't a new edition but it was good enough, for it told me the only thing I wanted to know—that Comfort had been at a famous public-school, and from there had gone to Oxford, though that latter I had known from the red of his hood when I had seen him in Stadmore Church at that morning service. He'd be a younger son, it seemed to me, or else he should have inherited some money. But that was sheer surmise. His parents must be still alive. They might be victims of the Cripps millstones. And if Comfort had any brothers, they hadn't entered the Church.

After lunch I drove round the back way to Copley's Corner, but I didn't stop. I just let the car go easy round the sharp angle of the fork and I could see that the men were at work, and I noticed too that the concrete above the well had been covered in. Three big electricity vans were drawn up at the roadside as I neared the village and I could see that Copley's Corner, with the rest of Stadmore, would soon be having light and power. If a good job was being made of the interior, Laver mightn't be so much of an optimist in asking fifteen hundred for the place.

1 gave Hallows' car a quick clean and went in to tea. Jewle was on the telephone before I'd taken my first mouthful.

"Busy, Mr. Travers?"

"Not too busy," I said. "Why?"

"Could you spare me and Younger a few minutes? Say in a quarter of an hour? We'll come to you."

I said I'd be delighted. He said he was lucky to find me still at the Suffolk. I asked if he and Younger would like tea and he doubted if they'd have the time. I finished my own tea in any case and the two turned up ahead of time. I took them into the small lounge and switched on the electric fire.

Jewle was a huge chap with a back like the end of a barn. His sergeant, Younger, was the lean sort, and a bit on the mournful side. What his capabilities were I didn't learn for he said hardly a word.

Jewle was all over me. I had only the vaguest idea what my Yard reputation was, but he was talking about just the kind of thing that was expected of me. That long-shot about diamonds, he meant, and how, as soon as he'd made his first enquiries, he'd learned about the Mallett Case. Since then he'd been to the Yard and gone through the local records, and he and Younger hadn't had half a night's sleep between them.

Naturally I had to pretend some knowledge of the Mallett Case, though the diamonds were a surprise. Jewle had certainly been putting two and two together. I heard about Mallett's wife and daughter whom the Yard were now trying to trace.

"You think it was to them that Mallett wrote that letter-card?" I asked him naively.

"Who else?" he said. "The Mallett business was open and shut, so Shireton didn't call us in, but we did lend a hand trying to trace the diamonds. Tried to find Mallett's wife and daughter too, but it wasn't any go. This time we may be luckier."

"Won't it be a colder scent?"

He didn't think it'd make all that difference. One thing had been found already—that Mallett didn't post that card himself. He had given it to a girl to post—a girl who was on her way to school—and the reason might have been that he didn't want to be seen in the open himself. He'd kept in the cover of the Forest and only popped out to thumb that second lift.

It was curious that that should give me another idea about Comfort, even if at the moment he didn't seem of first importance. But what I was asking Jewle was what he now proposed to do.

"We thought you might have some ideas yourself," he told me hopefully.

"I'm not in harness," I told him regretfully.

"But Prial was one of your men. I thought you'd feel a special interest."

"And butt in on an official Yard enquiry? My dear Mike, what would you have thought of me!"

Jewle said he didn't give a damn for officialdom. All he'd be was grateful for any ideas.

"Well," I said, "I might as well own up that purely unofficially I have been doing a bit of thinking. I *am* interested in Prial. He was one of our men and he was a friend of mine, as I told you. That's why I pass something else on, if it's any use to you. What I've remembered is that that postcard he sent me had Stadmore as its postmark. If you know anything about me at all, you'll know I'm most damnably curious. I like to know the whys and wherefores, and that's why I wondered where this Stadmore place was. So I looked it up and found it was near Shireton. I've been there myself once or twice, since. But I still didn't see why he should buy a post-card of Shireton town-hall and post it at Stadmore. You can buy postcards of Stadmore at the local post-office. There's a particularly fine one of the vicarage which I might commend to you."

It was just a bit involved, and deliberately so. Jewle frowned for a minute. Younger spoke for the first time.

"What you mean, sir, is that Prial was spending his holiday having a crack at those diamonds, and something brought him to Stadmore."

"That's about it," I said. "That's how it looks to me—now. It may be nonsense. I don't know. I do know that there's dam-all in Stadmore to attract anybody except that fine old timbered vicarage."

"Sounds interesting," Jewle said, and was suddenly giving me a perky sort of look. "You wouldn't feel like going along there with us tomorrow, sir?"

"Can't be done," I said. "I'm on business and the poor have to live."

Jewle grinned. Myself and poverty seemed incongruous.

"Not only that," I said, "but you don't know yet if there *is* anything at Stadmore."

"I don't know, sir," Jewle said as he got to his feet. "A tip from you is as good as from the horse's mouth."

"Even horses don't always speak the truth," I told him with an easing of conscience. "Sure you won't have a drink before you go?"

He was too busy, he said. And he didn't mind telling me that he and Younger would be off to Stadmore straight away. I wished them good luck as I saw them off. I didn't envy them that trip to Stadmore. It wasn't drizzling but it was a raw, misty night. As for what they would come up against in Stadmore, I didn't know, though I had some shrewd ideas, and some that made me just a bit apprehensive, even if I'd partly covered myself by casually remarking that I too had been to Stadmore once or twice.

The morning brought a surprise, and in a letter from Hallows. With regard to Lucille, he had toiled all day, as it were, and caught nothing, and he didn't think it worth a further try. He'd nobbled a man who worked in their delivery yard and stock room, and nothing had been unearthed. But he had found something else.

"I was thinking about that blonde and brunette business, and I happened to be passing what looked like a high-class shop, so I walked in and asked to see the proprietor. I said I was an author and wanted to verify something I had to put in a book. He was a nice pleasant sort of man and took me into his private room and gave me the complete low-down. What I'd wanted to know was if any dark-haired person could be turned into a blonde. I write down just what he told me. It seems to be routine, and I wouldn't mind betting that all the establishments work on the same lines. Here it is. I'd like you to note it carefully.

"Anybody can be made into a blonde. The time necessary will vary according to what pigment in the original hair has to be broken down, but anything from 1½ to 4 hours will see it done with. The proprietor or manageress asks the customer what kind of a blonde she wants to be, and there seem to be four kinds. *Ash blonde*—lightish brown, with no what they call fire in the hair. *Pure blonde. Platinum blonde*—the hair bleached and then given a bluish tinge by the application of a blue wash. *Golden blonde.* But listen to how the actual bleaching's done.

"The bleachers are bought from wholesale firms already made up in various strengths. The usual application is of what's called 20 vols. peroxide of ammonia, plus the addition of 880 ammonia. The numbers refer to strengths. That bleaches the hair but the customer has to have it retouched every fortnight, otherwise the original hair would show where it's begun to grow again, particularly at the parting. I asked if a man in the street like myself could tell a synthetic blonde from a natural one—he called the synthetic blonde a bottle-blonde—and he said that if the job had been done by any reputable firm, only an expert could tell.

"Now, sir, put all that up against those marks on that sheet of paper and see where it gets you. It shows beyond all doubt, at least in my view, that Godfrey had made similar enquiries, and that he was aware that his original brunette had become a blonde. That's the only way I can read it. . . ."

Hallows was dead plumb right. Godfrey had been interested and he had taken notes. But where? And when?

At least I could find out where he hadn't been, and that was in the best establishments in Shireton. But I was wrong. I asked the lady-receptionist to tell me the best two places in the town but all she could tell me was the very best. I went there and tried the same approach that had worked in the case of Hallows. It was the manageress whom I saw and I had a bit of a shock.

"You're the second author who's asked me about that in the last month or so," she said. "There must be quite a lot of books being written about blondes."

I showed her Godfrey's photographs. She too was giving me a queer look.

"That's right," I said, just as I had said to Wilming. "That's the man who was shot at the George. If you've guessed who I really am—well, just keep it to yourself. The thing is, was that the man who came here asking about blondes?"

She said if it had been, she'd have notified the police. So I showed her another photograph with moustache and glasses. That shook her. She'd seen that man before though she wouldn't swear that he was the one who'd been in the shop. I asked if he'd taken quick notes on a small pad, and she said he had. That was good enough but I didn't tell her so. What I did tell her was that it was a matter of importance—even if she did later on think the man of the photograph was the man I was asking about—that nothing should be said to a soul.

I went back to the Suffolk, got myself a drink and took it to a quiet corner. I had been thinking for more than a minute when I was called to the phone. It was Jewle.

"You're a bit of an optimist, aren't you Mike?" I said. "Expecting to find me here on tap?"

"Just hoped for the best," he said. "Wanted to thank you for that tip. I think we're on to something here. That man of yours was at the local pub. Called himself Trevor. Spent his time nosing around, from what we gather."

"Extraordinary!" I said. "What was he interested in?"

"I think we're on to that too. If anything comes of it, I'll let you know later. But there's a complication. Another chap's been here too. We've got his description. Called himself Prial's brother."

"Good lord!" I said, and asked him to hold on for a minute while I tried to remember.

"I believe I was actually there and saw the man. He helped me do something to my car. I remember the landlady asking him about his brother."

"That's the one," he said, and gave a bit of a laugh. "We picked you up too."

"Once seen, never forgotten," I told him. "But you've made me all of a fever. When're you going to let me know what's happening?"

He thought it might take a day or two. Then just as he was sounding like ringing off, I thought of something.

"Just a moment," I said. "A little thing you might do for me, just as a matter of interest. I rather gathered from Loame when I had that little talk with him, that Prial hadn't slept at the Royal one night. What night was it?"

He said it was the Thursday night: the Thursday before the Saturday when he was shot. It looked as if he'd been away and found something, because as soon as he got back to Shireton on the Friday, he'd left the Royal and gone to the George. I didn't want to seem too interested, so I said that sounded likely. Then I thanked him and he thanked me, and that was that.

But it was of Jewle that I was thinking when I went back to my pint. He was on to Monaghan. That would lead him to the Asylum, and to me. He was on to Hallows, whom he didn't know, but who he had every reason to suppose was the one who'd shot Godfrey Prial. I'd already told him that Prial had no relatives whatever, so that deduction was reasonably obvious. It looked therefore that in practising to deceive I'd spun the poet's tangled web. At almost any minute Jewle might be demanding of me just what sort of a game I was playing. It looked, in fact, as if the sooner I left Shireton, the better, and the deeper the oblivion into which I vanished, the better too. And yet I wanted to learn just a bit more, and I told myself that I'd hang on till the next day. If Jewle had suspicions of me, then I'd somehow contrive to string him along. And something was telling me that things were about to happen. I had no reasons beyond a few ideas, so maybe it was a kind of instinct.

But I could at least dismiss Jewle sufficiently to get back to Godfrey and his enquiries into the origins of blondes. What it all meant I couldn't fathom, unless it was that his brunette, as Hallows had suggested, had suddenly and mysteriously become a blonde. But was that tied up with his absence that night from the Shireton hotel? London seemed the place where he'd most likely been, and making enquiries about that brunette-blonde, and what he'd learned had made him go into hiding, though still at Shireton. Surmise again, and nothing but—and where did it get me. The answer was, exactly nowhere. And yet, as I tantalisingly knew, the answer must be staring me in the face. Godfrey hadn't intended it, but maybe he'd left a trail like a tree dragged through brushwood. Maybe it was too plain a trail. To make the metaphor as woolly as my thoughts, maybe I couldn't see the wood for the trees.

But something was to happen to give me a nasty jolt. You know how it is when you're jogging along complacently, and all at once something crops up clean out of the blue. That happened to me just after lunch. It made me go hot and cold all over.

I was drifting along, as it were, past the open door of the saloon bar. It was fairly crowded but I caught sight of a somebody whom I ought to know. Something made me stop in my tracks. I was almost at that nervous trick of polishing my glasses as I went back to the opposite door. Something told me I had to know who it was that was talking so confidentially to the barmaid, so I gently eased the door open and had a quick look. I didn't need another. It was Alf!

As I said, I went hot and cold, and for the life of me I didn't know why. I didn't want to be seen by Alf, but I had nothing to fear from him. Or had I? I didn't know, but I suddenly got my hat and overcoat and went out the back way to the car. I drew it out of the yard and halted it on the opposite kerb with the bar door of the Suffolk in view. I thought I should have some time to wait, but I didn't. It must have been inside five minutes when Alf came out, and he didn't halt outside or show an indecision, but set off towards the centre of the town. I moved the car on behind him. The traffic lights halted me at Bruce Street but I was lucky. He crossed the road and entered the main post-office, not fifty yards on.

I moved over with the lights and drew up just beyond. I sat there for a quarter of an hour and then a policeman moved me on. So I circled round and came back to the High Street again, and outside the post-office on the opposite side. Just as I saw another policeman making for me, I saw the sign which mentioned parking on alternate days, so I moved the car hastily on, and back to the garage of the Suffolk.

It was after closing time, but Minnie, the barmaid, was still giving the place a quick clean. There was an unusual look on her face as if she was glad to see me.

"That chap with the thick ear, Minnie, who was talking to you about half-an-hour ago. He didn't mention me by any chance?"

That's just what he had done, she said. She hadn't liked the look of him. He was common.

"What'd he want to know?"

"Well, he described what you were like and asked if you were staying here. I knew who he meant but I wasn't telling *him*. Then he wanted to know if anyone of the name of Travers was staying here and I said there wasn't. I didn't like the look of him. Looked like a dolled-up burglar to me." Her eyes popped. "Oh, and I must tell you this. He slipped me a ten-bob note and I'm to let him know if you happen to come in. Good, isn't it!"

"Dam-good," I said. "I didn't know you had it in you, Minnie."

I slipped her a ten-bob note of my own. "Put this to it and buy yourself a perm."

She laughed.

"Doing well, aren't I. But honestly, Mr. Travers, you can't have Nosey Parkers like that coming in and asking about the residents. Besides, he was as common as dirt."

"Where've you got to let him know if I come in?"

"The Royal," she said. "Posh, isn't he. Ask for Mr. Jones and if he isn't in, leave a message. Jones, my foot!" The duster stopped in mid-air. "Who was he, Mr. Travers? Did you know him?"

"Yes," I said. "I rather fancy he's on the run."

"From the police?" she said, and her eyes popped.

"Maybe," I said.

"But you aren't connected with the police?"

I could see the doubt in her mind. I said she'd been dam-smart and I wanted her to go on being smart. If Jones came in again she was to go on stringing him along. Better still, tell him I'd been in and asking about someone like himself. That'd scare him.

I left Minnie with that and went to the desk. The lady there was just finishing lunch but she came out. No one had asked her about me and no one had asked to see the register.

But it was disconcerting. Alf at the Royal and asking about me. Alf going the round of the hotels. Alf ringing someone—and most likely Laver—to say he hadn't yet got wind of me. I didn't like it. I'm no ruddy hero even if I did get a medal in the first world war. Death sounded too much of a finality to me, whichever way it came. I didn't want a bullet like Godfrey and I didn't want a knife in my ribs if Alf met me that night in a misty street. I didn't even want a rough and tumble. Some people fight to the last drop of blood: I'm limited to the lenses in the tortoiseshell rims. Break my glasses and I'm as blind as a bat. And whereas all that may sound pretty sensational to you, it wasn't so to me. Laver and Alf were covering up Prial's murder, and if I knew too much, that'd be the end of me.

Then when I had a brain-wave, Minnie had gone out for the afternoon. But I caught her just before the bar opened. I got her to telephone the Royal and gave her the message written down. The gentleman Mr. Jones wanted had been in soon after Mr. Jones left. He had let fall that he was just going back to London.

Minnie did the job well, and it had been Alf himself to whom she had spoken. I gave her another note and told her to have a better perm.

A letter from Hallows in the morning said he was getting nowhere with the Lucille business, so he would await my instructions at home. I sat tight in the Suffolk and waited for Jewle to ring me. Lunch-time came and nothing had happened, and I was feeling uncommonly bored. So in the early afternoon I thought it wouldn't look too obvious if the mountain went to Mahomet.

I didn't take the back lane but drove straight to Stadmore Ram. No car was in the back garage but the landlord's, so I went across to the church, even if I hardly knew why, unless it was because of the stress I'd laid on the beauties of Stadmore vicarage. There again was something I'd thought that Jewle might notice. Maybe he had, if he'd heard about Comfort and Start and that night at Copley's Corner, but he wasn't in the church and when I craned up over the vicarage wall, there was never a soul in the garden. So I took a chance and drove past Copley's Corner, and there was no car parked there and never a sign of anyone but the workmen. So I reversed the car at that gateway by the pond and drove back to the lane to Shireton again, and it was tea-time when I got there.

It had all been rather conspiratorial with a touch of melodrama for luck. No call had come for me, and all sorts of thoughts went through my head. Maybe Jewle and Younger had been at the Asylum, which would mean that they'd know that I'd been there too. Or mightn't it. I didn't know, but I did know that Shireton wasn't any longer the ideal spot for me, and as soon as I'd finished my tea I told myself I'd get back to town. I was almost on the point of going to the telephone to tell Hallows to expect me, when a call did come for me. I knew it was Jewle, and the cold perspiration was on my forehead as I picked up the receiver. "Hallo? Travers speaking?"

It was Hallows, and saying something had happened.

"A stroke of luck, sir, or we mightn't have heard of it for days. It's about that client, Miss Cowle."

"What about her?"

"She had an accident. She's dead."

CHAPTER 14
THE NAME

IT WAS A horrible drive, especially when I reached the outer suburbs. There the mist of the country became a fog, with just enough visibility to enable one to crawl from traffic hold-up to traffic hold-up. It was five o'clock when I left Shireton and a quarter to nine when I got to Hallows' place. And was I glad of that hot coffee his wife had ready for me!

Hallows said once more that but for a stroke of luck we mightn't have known a thing. I might have sent in a final report and merely thought it part of that secrecy understanding when I received no answer. We might, in fact, never have known that Myra Cowle was dead. Hallows had tried a new approach—which hadn't worked—at Chez Lucille, and had thought somewhat idly of having a look at Oak Avenue, since he was so near. He'd seen it only by night and he thought he'd like to see it by day. So he walked the half-mile or so, and when he got to the Avenue, he saw that something was going on at Myra Cowle's flat. A middle-aged couple were coming out of it, and the woman was crying. Someone who looked like a plain-clothes man was with the couple, and the car outside was definitely a police car.

Hallows waited till the three had gone, then made enquiries on the opposite side of the road. There he learned that Myra Cowle had been knocked down on the Tuesday morning by a car which hadn't stopped.

"I knew the spot," Hallows told me. "It's where you cross the road from Old Church Street. It's pretty wide and there isn't an island. About a quarter-past eight when it happened. That'd be when she was on the way to business."

He'd rung me at once. I'd told him to find out who was handling matters, and now he told me it was the local Division, and their Inspector Kolper.

"I know Kolper," I said. "Wonder why he hasn't got in touch with me."

Hallows didn't see it.

"If they went through her things," I said, "they'd find that contract with my name on it. And the letter I wrote her on Sunday. Kolper knows me. He'd have wondered what it was all about."

Hallows wasn't so sure. There'd been an inquest that morning and an accident verdict. Except for trying to find the car responsible, the matter was over as far as Kolper was concerned.

I didn't like it. I used Hallows' phone and rang Divisional Headquarters. Kolper wasn't in, so I told the sergeant to try to get him at his private address and tell him to ring Hallows' number. I said it was urgent.

"You don't think it was an accident?" Hallows asked me.

"Two chances," I said. "It was or it wasn't. If it was, we've lost a client and that's all there is to it. If it wasn't, then we're in it up to the neck. But listen to this."

I told him about Alf and his Shireton enquiries. Funny, I said, that Alf should have come straightaway to Shireton on the day Myra Cowle died.

"Look at it this way," I said. "Godfrey was murdered, and because of those diamonds. Myra Cowle decided to do something about those diamonds, and now she's dead. I was the one, according to the contract, who was working for her, so Alf came to Shireton. I might have been dead. It may be melodramatic," I said, "but it's logical. If you're going to be had for a murder, what's it matter about a second, or third, provided they clear you of the first?"

"Yes," he said. "But everything was so secret. She wasn't supposed to tell a soul what she was doing."

"But she did," I said. "It's incontrovertible that she did. My letter told her that I knew what happened to the diamonds the night when Mallett bolted. That meant Copley's Corner. That meant danger to Laver, and something had to be done about it."

"But who could she have told?"

"That's what we've got to find out. I'll see Kolper and hear all about the accident. He may let something fall. I'll go to the Salon and find out who her friends were. There's her secretary, for one thing. She may have said something to her. There's the question of the will and who gets the property."

The telephone went. Kolper was on the line.

"Hello, Kolper," I said. "This is Ludovic Travers."

"Good God, sir! Fancy hearing you!"

"Quite a time since I saw you," I said. "How are you?"

"Pretty well, sir. And you?"

"Can't grumble," I said. "And by the way, you've been handling that Myra Cowle accident business, haven't you?"

"Yes."

"You knew I'd taken over Bill Ellice's Agency and Norris was in charge?"

"Yes, sir. We'd heard about that."

"Well, Myra Cowle was a client of ours. That's in confidence, of course. I'd like a word with you in the morning, if there's a chance."

"Any time you like, sir."

"Fine," I said. "This fog may be a bit awkward so shall we say half-past ten at her flat?"

"Suit me fine, sir. Can you give me any idea what you want to talk about?"

"I don't altogether know that myself yet," I told him. "See you in the morning, then."

I told Hallows it might be as well if he was there too, even if I'd have to do all the talking. At the moment there was nothing else we could do, and it was pretty late and so I left. Hallows showed me the way to the Tube station, and we stopped for a moment or two at the spot where the accident had been. The road was pretty wide at that crossing and a car could have loomed up out of the fog with a sudden acceleration.

"What's the fog been like here?" I wanted to know.

"Not a real pea-souper," he said. "Like it is now. Never any worse."

That meant a visibility of thirty yards. Being able to see comfortably across a wide road, and little more. Not that it was worth while discussing all that. In the morning I should hear about it from Kolper.

It was midnight when I got home and Bernice was asleep. I didn't have too good a night's rest but I was sound asleep at half-past seven when she woke me. I was glad of the hot cup of tea, and while I was drinking it I told her what had brought me back to town in all that fog. I didn't think she'd be so distressed to hear about Myra Cowle.

There are occasional times when I've known that Bernice hates my job: times when she has looked at me as if I were in some way responsible for horrible things that happen, instead of being merely one who has to find out why they've happened. There was something of that look when I told her about Myra Cowle, and when she began telling me, almost accusingly, what a charming girl she'd been, and how lovely, and how dreadful to think that she was dead, I said it was a bad business, but even the best of us were subject to accidents, and then before that point could be taken up, I sidled off to the bathroom.

I wasn't too happy myself, for if Myra Cowle had been killed, then it was partly through myself. It was that letter I had written which had killed her, and though I could assure myself that I was in no way to blame, yet there had to be doubts. And another curious thing was that, try as I might, I could feel no sense of personal loss at her death. Put it bluntly like this, that for me she'd had no appeal of sex or anything else. I hadn't felt a warming of the heart and a wish to number her among my friends. I had thought her good-looking and there had been moments when I had found her attractive, but that was all. Bernice had seen far more in her than that, and so, in some faint way, had Hallows. So all I could tell myself was that it took all sorts to make a world, and if everyone was equally attractive to everyone else, there'd be a remarkable promiscuity in court-ship and marriage.

The weather report just before eight o'clock said that the fog would be gone that day and a period of cloudy, rainy weather was on the way. It was just beginning to rain when I set off to see Kolper. When I got to Swiss Cottage there was little more than a mist in the air and I could see the whole length of Oak Avenue. I was a bit early but Hallows was waiting outside the flat. Kolper drove up dead on time.

We went up to the flat to which he had a key. It had two bedrooms, only one of which was furnished; a bathroom-lavatory, a smallish lounge and a kitchenette. Everywhere was spotlessly clean and everything showed taste.

It was rather chilly and Kolper switched on the electric stove, and I told him at once that we'd been looking for some property that had been stolen from Myra Cowle. Before he could ask for details I spiked his guns by saying that was nobody's business but mine and the executor's. All I had wondered was why he hadn't found the Agency contract and the one interim report she'd received, and so have seen my name and asked me what it all meant.

He didn't remember either. The previous afternoon, after the inquest, he'd been at the flat with a Colonel and Mrs. Pengold to whom everything had been left, and they'd gone through the papers and so on.

"Are they relatives—the Pengolds?" I said, remembering that Myra Cowle had been an only child and Bertram Cowle had never married.

"Not really," he said. "But she was engaged to their son who was killed just before the end of the war. He was in the Tanks. A fine chap, so I gathered. At any rate, the Pengolds thought of her as if she'd married him."

"Where's the body?"

"At the undertaker's. The funeral's on Friday. At Chislehurst. That's where the Pengolds live. Very nice people, they are. No swank or anything. Real gentry, if you know what I mean."

"And as far as you're concerned, it was an accident?"

He shrugged his shoulders but he gave me a quick look.

"Everything open and shut. She was knocked down by a car that didn't stop. Someone at a house on the corner heard the actual car go shooting by only a minute or two before her body was seen. The dirty bastard took a chance and slipped away into the fog. Into Old Church Street and then left."

"I'm not questioning it," I told him. "All I'm puzzled about is your not finding that contract and letter. They weren't in her bag?"

"They certainly weren't," he said. "It was a couple of men who saw the body only a few seconds after she was knocked down. She actually passed out while one was telephoning the police. The other one stayed by the body and picked up her bag. He wasn't the sort of man who'd pilfer from a dead woman's bag. And how should that contract interest a man like him? He's a bank cashier in the City."

"Mind if we have another look?" I said.

There was a very nice early Georgian walnut bureau which, so Kolper said, held all her private papers, and we went over it methodically together. I managed to slip a couple of envelopes into my pocket, but neither the contract nor the letter was there.

"Probably at the Salon," Kolper said. "Why don't you try there, sir?"

"If you've no objections, I think I will," I told him.

"Just what's the importance of it? That contract, I mean."

"Only this," I said. "She was our client and we were trying to trace something she'd lost. The heirs might wish us to carry on. They might want to read that contract and see its terms. We might—I don't say we shall—put in a claim against the estate for work done."

That satisfied him. I don't say it would have done if I'd been a stranger, but there it was. He had only one last thing to say before we left.

"As I told you, sir, it was an accident, and that's that. But if you *should* run up against anything—well, anything fishy, you'll give me the tip?"

"I don't expect to," I told him. "I'm prepared to accept it as an accident. Why shouldn't I? All the same, as you say, you never can tell. Anything suspicious I'll pass on at once. If you don't hear from me you'll know I've nothing to tell."

He left in his car and we walked to the end of the Avenue. When we were dead sure he'd really gone, we turned back. I went the whole way and knocked at the door of the lower flat. I asked the woman if she could spare me a moment.

She asked me to come in, and I found her as nice as Hallows had said. I was from the insurance people, making just a few final enquiries into Myra Cowle's death.

She told me what she had told Hallows, that she was a charming girl and an excellent neighbour. She didn't often have visitors, and there was never any noise from above except the faint sound of the wireless, and that was never on after ten o'clock. I asked her if Miss Cowle had come in at the same time as usual on the Monday evening, but she couldn't tell me that. What she did know was that she had certainly come in because she had gone out at half-past seven, or about. Her husband had slipped out to post a letter and at the gate he had met Myra going out, and had had a word with her about the fog. And that was why she knew she had come home just before eleven o'clock. She and her husband were in bed and he had been wondering how Myra had got on in the fog, and then they had heard her in the room above.

An hour later we were at the Salon where everything seemed to be functioning much the same as before, at least the secretary said they were busy. Hallows and I squeezed into her cubby-hole of an office and we had to do our talking in the middle of interruptions. But that secretary was a nice, helpful soul. Her name was Mrs. Holster, a war widow. She had been an employee there before her marriage, and she had come back as secretary-receptionist. She had known Myra Cowle ever since Myra had been connected with the business, and said she was as much a friend as an employer.

"A happy ship, was it?" I said.

"Very happy," she told me. "I oughtn't to say it, perhaps, but we were well paid and Myra was always most considerate. She could afford to pick her girls, and they always stayed."

"Till they got married."

She smiled at that and said I knew what she meant. I'd told her that I and Hallows were there on account of business, and then I opened out a bit. She was looking most puzzled and intrigued when I made her give a pledge of secrecy.

"Did she ever tell you about her uncle?"

"Oh that!" she said, and smiled. "I knew all about that. I was the only one who did know."

I questioned her very warily and she knew nothing about any missing diamonds.

"It'll surprise you to learn," I said, "that she had asked me to undertake certain enquiries about her uncle's death. It was all highly confidential and has to remain so. I wrote her a letter about it and she should have received it on Monday morning. It had *Personal* on the envelope."

"I remember it," she said. "I gave it to her when she came in. She slipped it into her bag."

"She gave you no hint what it was?"

"But no. Why should she?"

I shrugged my shoulders. All I could say was that if she was as much friend as employer, then she might have given a hint. She said she didn't mean it like that. She'd meant that Myra was a friend because she'd known her such a long time, and she was always so friendly and thoughtful, and so on.

"What other friends had she?"

She couldn't say. It was all highly involved. Some old clients could be called friends.

"Did you ever go to her flat?"

"Sometimes," she said. "When we had quarterly accounts to make up we'd do it there instead of here. It was much more comfortable. Sometimes I'd spend the evening there. We'd have supper in, and a chat, and listen to the wireless. Not very often, though."

"Did you ever meet any other friend of hers there?"

"Only once," she said. "Once Colonel and Mrs. Pengold were spending the evening there, and Myra asked me to come along."

"Ever hear her mention anybody sufficiently friendly with her to be asked round to her flat?"

She frowned, shook her head, and remembered no one.

"To go off at a tangent, and still in a highly confidential way," I said, "did you ever turn a brunette into a blonde?"

She stared.

"You mean a client?"

"Yes. A client."

She laughed. That kind of thing was regularly happening. But she wasn't prepared to give me a list. I'd have to get Colonel Pengold's authority for that.

"I shan't need it," I said. "Tell me just this one thing. Did you ever handle—if that's the word—a slinky brunette? A tallish stream-lined brunette? And during the three weeks comprising the last fortnight in September and the first week in October."

She frowned some more, then had a look at the books. She said there'd been no client of the kind I'd mentioned.

"Ever hear her mention anyone named Laver?"

She hadn't.

"Ever see this man?" and I gave her Godfrey's photographs.

She moistened her lips and peered at them.

"Try this one," I said, and gave her the one with moustache and glasses. She frowned again.

"He's very like a man who came in and asked for Myra."

"The first week in October?"

She tried to think back but still couldn't say, though it wasn't all that long ago. It well might have been the first week in October.

"Tell me what happened, if you can remember."

All she could remember was that a man had asked to see Miss Cowle. She had said she was busy and had asked if it was urgent. He had said it was, so she had spoken to Myra who had happened to be with a client. There was a little waiting-room and he had stayed there, or she thought so, till Myra had found time to see him. She had seen Myra go to the door with him, and that might have been twenty minutes or so after he entered the Salon. Myra hadn't mentioned the matter afterwards.

That seemed to be about all. But I'd been waiting for her to ask me a question, and it came as she was showing us out, and in a roundabout way.

"The police have been here, you know," was what she said.

I told her we were nothing to do with the police. We were engaged on a private enquiry to do with the uncle's death, and everything she'd been asked had had some bearing, though she mightn't think it, on that enquiry. Then I was thanking her warmly for what she'd done. I even asked her if she'd have lunch with me, but she said she always had lunch in the office. But she seemed pleased at the offer. She was a nice girl, and I liked her. Far from handsome but extremely likeable. And a first-class business woman as I'd seen and heard from the way she'd handled the interrupting phone calls, and business information handed in by the staff. She'd even managed to smile at departing clients, and had slipped out for a word with two of them.

It was after my own lunch-time. I didn't see what Hallows could do, at least till after I'd seen the Pengolds, so we went our ways in Bond Street—he home and I to a quick meal at the club. There I rang Chislehurst and fixed an appointment for three o'clock that afternoon.

They were delightful people, the Pengolds. It was the Colonel whom I saw first, and in a room that told only too clearly where he had done most of his soldiering. He was about sixty-five; tall and lean and just a bit sallow, but fit enough and with a back far straighter than mine. He had charming manners and I liked him at once. That was why I was so frank.

1 had with me the contract that Myra Cowle had signed, and after I'd given him a brief personal history, I gave it to him. He read it through twice.

"Lost something, had she?"

I explained. He'd already agreed that our talk should be regarded as confidential.

"The diamonds, eh?" He shook his head. "I did a bit about them, you know, as soon as we heard they were gone. I'm a bit of an authority on that sort of thing, though you mightn't think it."

He'd been political adviser or something like that in one of the smaller Indian states where the ruler had the usual fabulous collection of gems.

"Quite an unofficial enquiry, of course," he told me. "I saw that Hatton Garden wallah who acted for poor Cowle, and nosed round in all sorts of places but I never got any further."

"I rather gathered there were nineteen stones," I said.

"That's about right," he said. "He was thinking of a necklace of twenty and he had one more stone to come."

"The nineteen must have been worth the very devil of a lot of money," I said. "What're four carat diamonds worth?"

"About two thousand five hundred apiece."

"Good lord," I said, and he smiled.

"His weren't that sort of stone. Diamonds, I grant you. But not the properly cut stones which one sees mounted in metal. What he was buying were the old Indian drilled stones. They're pretty old. You might call them antiques. That's why they're so rare. Why that Hatton Garden chap had difficulty in picking them up."

"And what'd they be worth?"

"Three hundred or so apiece."

I said it sounded almost sacrilegious to drill a diamond.

"I don't know," he said. "Customs vary, you know. I've seen some remarkably fine work with drilled stones. But you: you haven't got on the track of them?"

I said that I hadn't, though I had ideas. But I'd always known there was very little chance, and that's why the contract called for no charge except a small retainer. But I had had to see him about that contract. In the event of our pulling off the million to one chance, would he be interested? Did he wish to consider the contract void?

"Not on those terms," he told me. "You carry on my dear chap, and good luck to you. I'll be only too glad to hand over the fifteen per cent. Or shall we have to make a new contract?"

"Not in your case, sir," I said. "We'll call it a gentleman's agreement. I go on working for nothing and collect if I'm lucky."

He said that was remarkably handsome of me. That was when my face straightened and I told him about Godfrey Prial. He was interested. He was as interested as if I was telling him where the diamonds were.

"Someone else after them, eh? And you think that's why that man of yours was killed?"

I said that was what the Yard thought too. And then I gave him what he must have thought a very queer look.

"Do you mind if I put something up to you, sir? Strictly between ourselves? Just us two? In this room? It's this. My man was killed, and we think we know why. What about Miss Cowle?"

"My God, no!"

He got to his feet and I wondered if he were going to ask me to leave the house. But he was frowning away and his fingers were nervously twiddling.

"It's unlikely," I said. "But it's possible. She probably had a fatal accident but she could have been run down by design."

"You've nothing else to base it on but what you've told me?"

"All sorts of queer things," I said. "Things I couldn't explain because you're not familiar with the background. Things I shall almost certainly have to tell the Yard."

"My God then," he said, "not a word to my wife. She's pretty cut up as it is. Myra was like a daughter to us, you know."

"But you yourself would like to help?"

"Of course I'd like to help."

"Well, it's unofficial at the moment," I said. "A certain verdict's been brought in and I'm not disposed to quarrel with it till I'm sure of the facts. And that may be very soon. But assuming the worst. You've spotted, of course, that Myra must have told somebody what I was doing?"

"Yes," he said. "But it wasn't me. I'm the only one she should have told."

"Any friends of hers do you know?"

"Can't say I do. Not real friends. There was Jill Holster, of course. The secretary. You may have met her."

"I saw her today. But anyone else? Anyone she mentioned in letters? Or when you and your wife happened to be at her flat?"

He was frowning again. He seemed to remember a mention of someone called Eileen.

"I'll mention it to my wife," he said, and moved towards the door. Then he came back, "Can't do that, though. We can't have her brought into this."

I said if he didn't mind a harmless and pious subterfuge, there *was* a way to do it. He heard what I had to say, and gave a nod or two when I'd done. He went to the door again.

"Lucy! . . . You there, Lucy?"

I heard her call something and in a minute she was coming into the room.

"This is Mr. Travers, my dear. He knew Myra slightly, in the way of business."

She must have been a handsome woman in her young days. And always a charming one as I knew from her smile.

"Perhaps you'll explain to Mrs. Pengold," the Colonel told me, so I explained. Miss Cowle had mentioned a friend of hers to me—a close friend I'd gathered—and had recommended her with regard to a certain matter. I was anxious to trace that friend.

"She never seemed to have any real friends," she said. "She was so busy."

"Wasn't there someone called Eileen?" the Colonel prompted.

"Yes, of course. I remember her mentioning an Eileen. What was her other name? . . . I've forgotten. In any case I don't think she was more than an acquaintance."

"Miss Cowle didn't mention anything to you about any particular thing she herself was doing recently?"

"I don't think so," she said, and then was changing her mind. "What was that I was telling you, Frank?'

"Oh dear!" she said. "I forget things these days. But it was a week or so ago. I'm sure I mentioned it to you, Frank. Something about doing something exciting. Don't you remember I said it must be something to do with the Salon."

"If you did, I've forgotten," her husband said.

"Don't worry, Mrs. Pengold," I said. "I assure you it doesn't matter in the least. Certainly not worth your worry."

I held out my hand and said I had to be going. She asked me to stay to tea and regretfully I had to decline. The Colonel went with me to the gate and a little way along the road.

"You think that was what you wanted?" he asked me as soon as we were out of the house. "That Eileen business?"

"I think it may be," I said. "If anything turns up I'll give you a ring. But don't worry if you don't hear from me for a few days. These things take time."

At the telephone kiosk at the station I rang Cunningham 1003. Miss E. Masters. That was what I was trying out, and with the emphasis on the E.

"Chester Hall," came the voice.

"May I speak to Miss Masters?"

"I could put you through, but Miss Masters is not in. Will you call later?"

Just a moment, I said, and in the same gruff voice. "It's Miss *Eileen* Masters I want to speak to."

"Miss Eileen Masters is not in," she told me reprovingly, and it was I who rang off.

Chapter 15
END OF THE TRAIL

SOMETHING RELENTLESS was behind me: driving me, refusing time for thought, demanding action. I didn't wait till I got home: I rang Hallows from Charing Cross Station.

"We were right first time," I told him. "That Masters woman was a friend of Myra Cowle."

He didn't say anything. He didn't even ask why shouldn't she be.

"Too great a coincidence that her number should have been on that snuff-box paper," I went on. "You'll have to pick her up and tag her from now on. Till we can build up a case."

"But won't she recognise me if she's in all that deep? Won't Laver have passed the word on?"

"I know all that," I told him impatiently. "Cut your moustache off, grow a beard, do anything you dam-please, but do what I say. Why don't you drive your car in when it's dusk? There's a car park all round the front. Just sit in the warm and watch."

I looked up Benny Markstein's number and rang him. I didn't have a lot of hope and I knew he was out as soon as I heard Rachel's voice.

"He's at the Studio, Mr. Travers," she told me. "Was it something important?"

"Very much so," I said. "What time do you expect him home, Mrs. Markstein?"

"You know how it is," she said. "He says he'll be home at five, and then it's six, and seven. But you come down, Mr. Travers. I'll let him know."

I had a polish in the station lavatory and went to the garage for my car. There wasn't any mist and traffic was slackening, and it was only just after five o'clock when I got to Benny's house at Denham.

I'd known the Marksteins for years. I'd backed Benny in those distant days when I'd money to burn and Benny was operating from a flea-trap cinema in Aldgate. He'd moved up since then, but it hadn't spoiled him. His kind can be the salt of the earth.

Rachel was glad to see me, and there wasn't any affectation of politeness about that. She made me have tea, though I didn't need much urging. Before I was through with it, Benny arrived. The way he greeted me you'd have thought I owed him money. He laughed when I told him so. He even reminded me of the time when things were the other way round.

He went into his office and he was asking what was on my mind. I told him everything was strictly confidential, and I didn't say it was business unconnected with the Yard. What I said was that it had to do with two cases: one definitely murder and the other tied up with it and very likely so. We had had a lead and it brought us to a girl who was something in films: what, I didn't exactly know. Nor was he to assume that this girl was directly implicated. We wanted the complete low-down on her because we were sure she could lead us to someone else—the man we did want. The girl's name was Eileen Masters.

"I know," he said. "I know the name, but she's not working for me."

"You could find out where she *is* working?"

Benny said in his mild way that he thought so. It might take a few minutes.

"You go ahead," I said. "It's taken me best part of three weeks to get as far as this office. Another hour or two won't count."

I didn't have to wait an hour. I left him telephoning and went out to talk to Rachel. She was asking about Bernice, and I wanted to know about Sammy, who was in Hollywood, and we'd just got settled to a real nice gossip when Benny called me.

Eileen Masters, he told me, was working for a new set-up which called itself Peacock Films Limited and specialised in second features. The studio was near Elstree. The people on their pay-roll were either just past it or on the way up—perhaps. Benny said they'd done one or two quite passable things: *The Weasel Didn't Pop* was one. Eileen Masters had had a small part in that, and she now had a slightly better part in a film they were shooting. *Who Cares About Love?* was the provisional title.

"Is she a blonde or a brunette?" I wanted to know.

Benny hadn't an idea, but he could find out. And he might find out who was backing Peacock Films.

"This is most damnably secret, Benny," I said, "but find out if a man called Laver—Harry Laver—has any money in it."

Benny said he'd try.

"And while you're at it, find out if this *Weasel Didn't Pop* picture is showing anywhere in town. Or the suburbs."

He said he could tell me that almost at once. In fact it took under five minutes and he ran the film to earth at one of the small circuits. The Paliceum at Golders Green seemed the handiest for me, and there it was the second feature to *Call Riverside 777*.

"Look Benny," I said. "I won't stay on here being a nuisance. You do that job for me and ring me at my flat at, say, half-past nine tonight. You tell me what you know and I'll tell you how it fits in. And the more you can get on Eileen Masters, the better. It won't even worry me to know she's got ladders in her nylons."

At Northolt I cut through to the North Circular Road and came out at the Edgware Road north of Golders Green. I found the Paliceum and drove my car into the park at the back, and bought myself a ticket for the two-and-nines. It was just after half-past six.

I was in luck, and I wasn't. I'd wanted to see *Call Riverside 777*, and now was my chance, even if it had just begun. But the fact that it had just begun meant that I'd have a longish wait before I saw Eileen Masters. But that main feature was so absorbing that I actually forgot all about her, except now and then, and when it did end, it was so abruptly that I hardly realised it. Maybe it was logical to end that way, but I'd have liked to know whether the Wanda woman had been made to talk and just what she'd said. But it was a good film. I kept going back to it during the News and the flashes of the next week's shows.

And so to *The Weasel Didn't Pop*. I guessed it was a catch title but that didn't worry me when I saw the name of Eileen Masters half-way down the cast list.

Coralie Vangel . . . . Eileen Masters.

There it was, and I wriggled a bit nervously on my seat when at last the first scene flashed. But I had to wait half-an-hour for Coralie, and it was pretty tough waiting. The plot was that of a returned soldier—an officer who'd been, or so I gathered, doing pretty well out of black-market operations in Germany. He was now trying to marry a sweet English girl who happened to have pots of money, and the Chief Commissioner at Scotland Yard as an uncle. The officer—Gerald Trench in the film—had ingratiated himself with the Yard and had been called in to help with one of the home black-market rackets. I know it sounds pretty silly, but it had plenty of verisimilitude as a film. Some of the shots were good and the story certainly had pace.

And then at last I saw Coralie. Trench had actually been given his own little room at the Yard—something that had never come my way—and he was working there when in popped a head.

"A lady to see you, sir?"

"What's her name, sergeant?"

"She wouldn't say, sir. She said you'd see her."

"Very well, sergeant: show her in."

In she came. Trench stared. He got to his feet while the lady regarded him with a cynical amusement. "Coralie! . . . What the devil *are* you doing here!" So there was Coralie. *There was Eileen Masters*. The story didn't matter. Words, tense or trivial, didn't matter. It was she who mattered: the slinkiness of her hips, the sheen of the brownish hair, the curl of her lips when she handed him a paper from her bag. I watched her and I wasn't aware of words. To me she was a single, spotlighted figure moving in some unnecessary sound. Then all at once I got to my feet and made my way out. I'd seen enough. All I wanted was to get home and hear the ring of the telephone, and Benny's voice at the Denham end. And I hadn't too much time to do it.

Bernice seemed relieved to see me, and I didn't know why unless it was that I'd been out all day with never a word. Hallows had rung, she told me, and had only said there was nothing to report. I told her something had broken and in a couple of days everything might be over. I said I might want her help, and then before I could tell her any more, the telephone went. It was Benny.

"Sorry I've been so long, Mr. Travers," he said, "but I think I've got what you want."

He had. Laver seemed to be the principal shareholder in Peacock Films, Limited. Eileen Masters was now a blonde. She'd been a brunette.

"Funny, isn't it, Benny?" I said. "Sort of changing horses while crossing the stream?"

"I don't know," he told me mildly. "The film may have needed a blonde. Besides, she's just a nobody. If she was someone with a name, that'd be different. Maybe the public wouldn't have stood for it. Maybe she thinks she'll do better as a blonde. Don't ask me."

"If our friend's backing her, it wouldn't matter. Isn't that so. The director would just have to fit her in."

Benny said there was a lot in that. Then he told me that Eileen was reputed to have a wealthy boy friend. The clothes she wore and the smart coupé she drove weren't paid for out of what she earned with Peacock Films.

"That's fine, Benny," I said. "Everything just as we wanted it. But just one thing more, and it's the hardest thing I ever asked you to do. Tell me: is it possible for you, on any excuse whatever, to pay a visit to Peacock Films?"

I heard his grunt. I waited for what seemed minutes.

"Maybe I could," he said.

"Listen, Benny," I said. "I don't want to tell you how to work it, but you're Big Business. You could swallow an organisation like theirs and not have to gulp. They ought to be flattered if you sort of dropped in."

The same mild voice said he didn't know. But he'd manage it.

"Didn't you say they were shooting a new picture?"

"That's right," he said. "*Who Cares About Love?* These people certainly find the titles."

"You're right," I said. "But something else, Benny. You fix up to go to Elstree while they're shooting. Bernice is here listening to me, and I want her to go with you. She can be your secretary, niece by marriage—any dam-thing you please. She'll drive my car down and be at your place any time you say. I'll give her a note to explain the set-up. You can do that?"

He said that maybe he could.

"Good for you, Benny. You're a friend in need and I won't forget it. Soon as you've fixed up things in the morning, give me a ring, and we'll get busy at this end."

That was how it was left. Bernice was all questions and I was finding the answers when Hallows rang.

"Nothing doing, Mr. Travers. She came in just before six and she hasn't stirred."

"No one called?"

"Not that I could spot. No one I knew."

"Did you get a glimpse of her?"

Never a hope, he said. He'd merely been told she was in.

"You didn't run any risks?"

"I don't think so," he said. "My own mother wouldn't have known me."

"Well get along home," I said. "Something's turned up that I didn't expect. Unless you hear to the contrary, get back tomorrow night. Try and get a peek at her. If you do, give me a ring."

I was up early in the morning and as soon as the shops were open in the Strand, I bought an autograph album: quite a stylish one that cost me over a pound. Then I got to work on a few forgeries, some with the left hand and some with the right, and Bernice lent a hand too. You'd never believe what autographs we had in that book; scrawled at all angles across a dozen pages. Most of the Hollywood hierarchy was there, and on intermingling pages a good sprinkling of the English. It looked pretty impressive to me.

I wrote an explanatory note for Benny Markstein and a few minutes later he rang. He'd been thinking things out, he said, and since he was due at Elstree at mid-day, it might be handiest for Bernice to take the Edgware Road route direct and park her car at the Royal George at the Stanmore crossroads, and he'd pick her up there. I said I knew where he meant. Bernice wasn't so happy about the change till after we'd looked at a large-scale map.

She left at half-past ten and there was I with the day on my hands, or so I thought till I remembered Comfort. And he sent me round to the Yard. George Wharton was the last person I wanted to see, and it was a relief to know that he'd been in Germany for the last three weeks, though I did think he might have sent us a postcard.

What I did first was to look up a Year Book. It told me that the Governor of Shireton Jail was a certain Major V. Mount. That rang no bell, so I nosed about a bit to try and find someone who might know Mount, but I had no luck. So I went back home again and did my telephoning from there.

I got Shireton Jail and asked to speak to Major Mount. I was told he wasn't there but I might speak to his Deputy. I waited a bit and then a brusque, military voice was asking my business.

"This is Canon Crewe," I said. "May I speak to your Chaplain?"

I think my canonical tones must have impressed. The voice that told me that Mr. Voles wasn't available was quite respectful.

"Oh dear!" I said mournfully. "I came to Shireton especially to see him in the Spring. Some time in May, I believe it was, and I was told he was away."

"That's right, Canon," he said. "He was on holiday. But he's not here. He just doesn't happen to be in. Can I give him any message?"

I said that was very good of him. Would he just say that Canon Crewe had enquired about him and hoped to see him early the following week. Then I babbled some thanks, and, just not too hurriedly, rang off.

What Voles would think I didn't know, nor did it matter if he racked his wits for a week and failed to recall a Canon Crewe. What I knew, or thought I knew, was that Comfort was just where I wanted him. And I didn't mean a precise locality, though Stadmore Vicarage would be where it was and so would Copley's Corner. And then as I was having lunch I began to doubt, though the doubts were not about Comfort but a certain side of my various-sided self.

But thinking of Comfort made me wonder about Monaghan, and then I thought I'd let the whole thing stand easy, so I treated myself to a walk in the Park. The frost and fog had made a sad mess of what, only a week before, had been a grand show of dahlias, and on that cloudy afternoon with its threat of rain I was not nearly so cheerful as I should have been. But I did watch some men at work on the flower beds and that took my mind off things. Then Monaghan come back again for I met a couple of nuns. What Society they belonged to I didn't know—their linen caps were an unknown shape to me—but I couldn't help noticing the rosary that one was fingering as they walked so stolidly along. So I cut back to the road and hopped a bus that took me near my club. I had tea and looked at this and that, and then I treated myself to a taxi home.

I gave a squint round as I had done whenever I'd come or gone— since I'd got back from Shireton, that is. But there wasn't a sign of Alf on the watch for me, and I let myself into the flat. I hoped to heaven that Bernice wouldn't be long. And she wasn't. It was just striking five when she came in.

"Any luck?" I was asking her.

"Perfect," she said. "A lovely day too. Most interesting."

I wanted that autograph album. It was perfect, as she said. Eileen Masters had a page to herself, and on two other pages were some nine or ten autographs. I dusted Eileen's page and a beautiful thumb-print came up. I looked at those two that Godfrey had hidden, and there she was! There wasn't a doubt of it. Eileen Masters had been his brunette.

"What was she like?" I asked Bernice.

She'd had make-up on which made her not too attractive at close range.

"A rather staggering blonde, that's what I'd call her," Bernice said. "Queer about the eyes and not so sophisticated as she tried to be. I didn't like her. She did her best to be gracious but—well, I just didn't like her. There was something a bit hard about her. You'd probably call it calculating."

"Everything went smoothly? No one had a suspicion?"

"Perfectly," she said. "Benny was simply wonderful. Everyone was most kind. I was all dewy-eyed, of course, which seemed to help quite a lot. And the things I had to invent about Hollywood!"

I said I'd get word to the Recording Angel to transfer it to my account. But what about the alibi?

There was a note from Benny about that. There'd been nothing for Eileen Masters at Elstree from the middle of August till work started on *Who Cares About Love?* and that was about ten days ago. In other words, she'd been free to run around with Godfrey Prial. Not that that was necessary when her evenings were her own. What I wanted to know was if she had an alibi for that Shireton Saturday, and I didn't mean the one that Laver and Alf would have cooked.

I rang the Salon and found Mrs. Holster there. I asked her to hang on till I could see her. I told Bernice I might be back pretty late, then I grabbed my hat and coat. Bernice had left the car outside and in ten minutes I was at the Salon.

I had to take a chance and let something out—that the police were working on the idea that Myra Cowle's death needn't necessarily have been an accident. That brought me back to the question of friends and I wanted to know if she'd be prepared to try to identify a woman who might have been both friend and customer. She was willing enough, even when it meant inconvenience. I should be at her Streatham house at seven in the morning, for instance, and I wanted her to fix herself a hat with a veil. The rest I'd tell her in the morning.

It was dusk when I got round to Chester Hall but parked in the shadow I thought I saw Hallows' car. I backed mine in alongside it, and Hallows spotted me. I wouldn't have known him. He was wearing a chauffeur's cap and coat, and though he hadn't sacrificed his moustache, he had trimmed it in the middle and twisted out the ends till they looked like needles. I slid into the seat beside him.

"Is she in yet?"

"Yes," he said. "She came in just after five. Good job I got here early."

"You've never seen her before in your life?"

"Never," he said. "She's a new one on me."

I told him what the day had brought forth and you'd have thought from the way he spoke that there was nothing to do but make an arrest. I said it wasn't so easy. We might think we knew but Jewle would have to be certain.

"How did she get here?" I said. "In her car?"

"She didn't have a car. She came in a taxi."

That was interesting, though I didn't tell him so. The time had been slipping by and it had long been dark. A great arc of light came from the lights above the main entrance, and now and again a car would draw up or a taxi. It was the hour of dinner and the theatre and people were going out and in.

"I'll have a look at her flat," I said. "We've got to take some risk. We might have to nip up there pretty quickly some time."

I went through the door to a spacious tiled hall and before I took off my glasses I saw a kind of bureau away back to my right. I made my way to the stairs on my left and hooked the glasses on as I went up. Two people were coming down and I bent my head and blew my nose till they were by. On the first landing I saw that her flat was to the left. I walked by it and round a corner to the right. A woman was coming towards me, so I went on. When she had gone I turned. At the door of the Masters' flat I stopped for a couple of seconds and listened, but there was never a sound from inside. With an eye always warily ahead, I went down the stairs again, located the door, hooked off my glasses, blew my nose as I crossed the hall, and made my way out.

I got in beside Hallows and told him how to locate that flat. Then we worked out a plan of campaign for the morning and where, still in that chauffeur's get-up, he was to join my car. It was then after eight o'clock. He had a Thermos of coffee, so I had a hot drink. While I was drinking it, his hand suddenly gripped my knee.

I couldn't see a thing but his eyes were more used to the dark. A car was backing just beyond us and in the shadow farthest from the main entrance. It was on Hallows' side and he was motionless and holding his breath. There was a sound of a door and a shadow passed in front of our car and moved on till in the arc of light it became a man.

"Laver!" Hallows said. "But it wasn't his car."

I slid out and told him to watch the main door. Though I could see little of that car and daren't flash a torch, I knew at least that it was a coupé, and a smart job at that: not a year old, probably, and the sort of job that wouldn't leave much change out of a thousand pounds. But I wished I could have inspected the lamps and the front bumpers.

"It's that car of hers," I told Hallows. "If it was she who was responsible for that accident, she drove it straight to Otway Mansions. Laver took it over and had the damage repaired. Now he's brought it back."

That meant more work and a longer delay. It was Friday night and we'd be lucky if we could get going by Monday.

"This is what we'll do," I said. "You park your car handy in the morning and keep an eye out for me in Devon Street. As soon as we've finished here, you get off to the neighbourhood of Otway Mansions and work the garages. If nothing turns up, try the neighbourhood of the dog track, and that Amusement Arcade and the Palais. Give me a ring from time to time at the flat."

I said he might as well get away at once and I'd stay on and keep an eye on Laver. He risked a flash of his torch to get the coupé number, and I got back in my own car. I moved it away from the coupé and out to the road. A minute or two later I came in again but on the other side of the main door.

I sat there for what seemed days. I smoked till I hated the taste of my pipe, but no Laver had appeared and that coupé was still there. Midnight came and I decided to call it a day.

CHAPTER 16
SHOW-DOWN

I'D LEARNED from Benny that Eileen Masters would have to be early on the set, and I'd tried to work out the timings, and what was worrying me as I drew near Chester Hall that raw October morning was whether I hadn't cut things far too fine. I caught sight of Hallows on the Devon Street corner and he took the wheel and I got out. I gave Jill Holster a pat on the arm and a smile and wished her good luck, and the car moved off again.

I know it was exactly twenty-six minutes later when the car drew up again, for I'd counted every minute of it. I had a word with Hallows before I got in.

"Laver with her?"

"No sign of him," he said.

"What about the coupé?"

"It wasn't there. She went off along Shepherd Street. Perhaps Laver garaged it there late last night."

I said he might have a look, and he got out and I took the wheel.

"How'd you get on, Mrs. Holster? Spot her all right?"

"I've seen her at the shop," she said. "I can swear to that."

"Miss Cowle used to be friendly with her?"

That's where the difficulties came in. She was practically always confined to her office, whereas Myra Cowle had been all over the place: serving in the shop, as it were; taking a look at clients in the cubicles; greeting arriving clients, and speeding the departing, and so on. Heaps of them might be called almost friends, and all that she could definitely remember of Eileen Masters was that she had first been in the Salon about three weeks before. She was sure there were no records of anything having been done to her hair, but she'd bought quite a lot of preparations. She remembered seeing her and Myra laughing together at the door, and the Masters girl had had several packages. But her name had never been mentioned.

I had to be satisfied with that. Like myself she had had a scratch breakfast but I insisted she should have another, and when we left the hotel I drove her to Rochway Street. I thanked her again and pledged her to strict secrecy—even with Colonel Pengold—and then drove back to my flat.

I did the usual things, if a bit restlessly, and it was surprisingly early when Hallows rang. He had the garage, he said; a little place just along Wigham Street, a turning off the east end of Holloway Road. Laver had brought the coupé in on the morning of the accident. The near headlamp was bent and its glass smashed, and the off wing had a nasty dent. Laver had said he had hit a lorry in the fog and the fault had been his own. He'd been prepared to pay for the job to be rushed, and he'd collected the coupé the previous evening at just before six o'clock and paid cash.

"What about Shepherd Street?" I asked him.

"Just what I thought," he said. "Just a few yards along. Not two hundred yards from the flats. Calls itself Blakey's Garage but a chap called Kemp has it now. That's where she garages the car."

"Good work, Bob," I told him. "Treat yourself to a weekend. I'm pretty sure I shan't want you again till Monday."

I rang the George and asked for Inspector Jewle, and was told that he'd left and wasn't expected back for a day or two. So I tried the Yard. Jewle, I was told, might be in at any minute, so I left an urgent message that he was to give me a ring. I was having lunch when his call came.

"Hallo, sir; you wanted me?"

"Pretty urgently," I said, and then he was cutting in. "As a matter of fact, sir, I was thinking of coming along and seeing *you*."

"I know," I said, and gave an ersatz chuckle. "Let bygones be bygones. Get along here as soon as you can. Bring Younger too, if he's available."

"Not another tip?"

"Better than that," I told him. "The nag's past the post. All you've got to do is collect your winnings."

I rang off and let him think that over. He must have thought mighty quick, and hard, for he and Younger were round in under half-an-hour.

Except for chit-chat I didn't say anything till I had them seated and each with his bottle of beer. We wished each other good health and then Jewle could contain himself no longer.

"Now, sir, what's this you've got for us?"

"Let me ask you something, Mike," I said. "Suppose Younger, here, stopped a bullet in the course of a job, and suppose, just suppose, mind you—that the French police wrote a sympathetic letter and asked if they could help, what'd you do about it?"

No wonder he stared. I told him I was serious.

"Well, I suppose they'd be thanked and all that?"

"And what'd be your private ideas?"

"Well, I'd probably think it was a bit of a nerve on their part."

"Good enough," I said. "That's how it was with Godfrey Prial. He was one of *my* men. I got the pig-headed idea it was my job to find out who'd killed him. That's a statement, not an apology, even if there is something on your mind: why I led you to Monaghan, perhaps, or why I went to Puckford Asylum. That's why I said let bygones be bygones."

"Yes?" Jewle said, and his eyes had narrowed.

"Now it's over," I said, "or I think so. I can take you straight to the one who killed Prial—perhaps. And the one who killed a girl called Myra Cowle—perhaps. That'll be for you to judge. All I ask you to do is listen to this."

I showed him and Younger that snuff-box and what had been in it. I showed them Godfrey's two letters and I told them everything I'd done, and knew or suspected. I gave them dates and addresses. There wasn't a thing I didn't give them—except one, and only when I'd absolutely finished did I want to know what Jewle thought.

"Sounds open and shut to me," he said. "And, if I may say so, Mr. Travers, you've made a dam-good hand of it. Not that I agree with—"

"Let bygones be bygones," I reminded him. "As for thanks or credit, I want neither. I want Laver and the Masters woman to get what's coming to them—just that and no more. Now you start telling *me* things. What are you going to do?"

"Looks like a Yard Conference," he told me.

"If so, I'm not going to be there," I said. "My name needn't come in. Have your conference and then get your witnesses taped. Later on I can give you a statement to include Hallows. Give me a ring when everything's set. My own idea is we ought to grab the Masters woman on Monday night. That's all. Unless you specifically ask me to do something else, I've finished. From now on everything's up to you."

We left it like that, though I had to warn him to go easy on shadowing. The couple had been scared. Another alarm and either or both might bolt. As it was, they and we were sitting pretty. Far better leave it like that.

There it was then, and I had nothing to do but wait. I didn't get a call till nine o'clock that Saturday night, and then it wasn't from Jewle himself, but a message to say that action would be taken. Nothing else came till about five o'clock on the Sunday, when Jewle asked if I was free. I told him to come along.

Younger was with him. Everything was ready, they said. Witnesses were lined up and they'd had a look at that coupé. An hour later we had things settled. Laver would be watched wherever he went and when the word went out, he'd be picked up. We would see Eileen Masters first, and he agreed to my stipulation that Hallows and I should be first in her room. I said, and he had to agree, that she'd brazen things out, but my way would be a short cut. I said I could make her implicate Laver.

We worked out timings and everything was set. When they left I rang Hallows and let him know that the balloon was due to go up. Unless he heard to the contrary, he was to meet me on the corner of Devon Street on the Monday night at seven o'clock sharp.

I don't know why it is, but whenever a zero hour gets near, my heart starts racing like a mad thing. I don't feel nervous, so maybe it's just because I get too many jumps ahead, and worry about counter-moves and the risks of a slip-up. But that was how my heart was that night when Jewle and Younger joined us.

"She's in all right," Jewle said. "Better get going. One at a time and rendezvous at the top of the landing."

We went in at intervals of a minute. I was the last and we moved together to the door of the flat. Jewle and Younger moved a little further on, and Hallows and I waited till someone had passed. I pushed the bell and that heart of mine was hammering against my ribs.

I held my breath and listened. There was a sound. The door opened and Eileen Masters was there. Her mouth gaped at the sight of me, and my foot was in the door. I pushed it open and in we went. Hallows made for a door across the room and his back was against it. It was done in a flash and the same stare was still on her face. She was trying to speak but the words wouldn't somehow come.

"Good evening," I said. "How nice to see you again, *Miss Cowle*."

* * * * *

Hallows must have started. I didn't look. My eyes were on her face and its sudden flush of red. Then she found her tongue.

"What're you doing here? I didn't ask you to come. You get out!"

"Oh no," I said. "We're going, but not yet. We're going to have a nice little talk."

She was furious. And there was fear.

"Oh no, you're not. You get out of here or I'll call the police."

"No need to call," I told her, and backed to the door. "Take a look outside. The police are here. I've just come as a friend. After all you were a client of mine. I'm just giving you the tip."

She didn't know what to make of it;

"Just the tip to come clean," I said. "If you don't believe me, take a look in the corridor. Inspector Jewle's there, of Scotland Yard. The one who's been at Shireton looking into the murder of Godfrey Prial. You know Godfrey. The man you shot in that room at the George."

"It's a lie!"

She stared frightenedly. Already there'd been something of an admission, and it was too late. Or wasn't it. As her lips trembled I could see her brain working.

"I don't know what you're talking about. I don't know anything about Shireton."

"Don't be a fool," I said. "Remember what you told me in my office. The next thing you'll tell me is that you never heard of Godfrey Prial."

"You know I never."

"Funny he should have sent me your finger-prints."

"It's a lie. You're trying to trap me into something."

"Oh no," I said. "There's no need to try and trap you. Laver's done that."

"That's right. And you never heard of Laver! The one who pays for this flat and bought you your car? The one who brought it back here on Friday night when the dents had all been smoothed nicely out?"

"If anyone told you that, he's a liar," she said. "I'm a film actress. I earn enough money to buy all I want."

"You're just a cheap-timer and Laver told us so. If it weren't for him you'd be back where he took you from."

"Get out of here. . . . Get out!"

She was coming for me like a wild-cat. My long arm went out and I caught her flat-handed across the face and she went back like a bullet to that settee. She crouched there, licking her lips and looking up at me.

"Get out," I said. "So that you can ring up Laver. But you can't ring Laver. We've just pulled him in at the Palais de Danse. He's just told us all about it. The way you killed Prial. And Myra Cowle."

"It's a lie!"

"Listen," I said. "Don't you know any other piece? You want me to prove it isn't a lie? You call yourself Eileen Masters. Who else but Laver knows what your real name is?"

She was listening, eyes narrowing.

"Laver knew," I said. "He's just given us your history. Says he did what he did just because he once had a bit of a crush on you and ever since then he's been trying to get you out of a mess. Laver told us who you were. Old Monaghan's your grandfather. Corkery's his real name. You're Mallett's daughter: Mallett, the man who murdered Cowle. Now do you believe that Laver's been talking?"

The last veneer went. She was on her feet.

"The dirty lying bastard! He's trying to save himself. That's what his game is. Can't you see it?"

I looked out and beckoned Jewle.

"Here she is," I said. "I think she'll make a statement."

"You bet I'll make a statement!" she told us. "I'll show that dirty double-crosser where he gets off!"

Her bag was on the mantel-piece. I fetched the hat and coat she had wanted to fetch for herself, and the coat was the velvet one she'd worn the first time I'd seen her. She put it on and squinted at herself in the mirror. Sheer bravado but it didn't impress me much. Younger took her out and I nodded to Hallows to go too.

Jewle made for the telephone. I went through to the bedroom and I heard Jewle saying something about picking up Laver at once.

"Looking for anything?" he asked me.

"Wondered why she wanted to get in here," I said. "We might do worse than have a quick look ourselves."

We had a look. In a locked drawer of the handsome mahogany chest and behind some oddments of clothing we found that contract, and my letter.

I went back to the flat. Things were as good as over but somehow I couldn't rest. I got out my old typewriter and long after Bernice was in bed I was drafting an official report, and even though I knew that what I might hear in the morning would make conjecture into certainty and the whole night's work merely a waste of time.

I began by quoting that first letter to establish contact between Godfrey and Eileen Masters. She and Laver had tried to find those diamonds and had failed. The search had been reluctantly abandoned and then Eileen had run across Godfrey. Imagine her report to Laver.

"I've run across a guy named Prial. He's a detective and, according to him, hot stuff. What about kidding him along and letting him have a try for the diamonds. He'll do it for love."

"How the devil can you?" Laver would say. "You haven't got a line of approach."

But they had. It was easy when they came to think of it. They knew all about Myra Cowle. All she had to do was tell Godfrey she was Myra Cowle. As simple as all that.

So he went to Shireton and there he had to be fed. A hint dropped, maybe, about Stadmore and so to the mysterious happenings at Copley's Corner. And then something went wrong. Something wasn't quite in keeping. Maybe they'd fed him just a bit too lavishly, and he got suspicious. He picked up Eileen in town, tailed her to the flat and found out she wasn't Myra Cowle. He looked up the real Myra Cowle—perhaps he got her address from the solicitors—and got her fingerprints, and he went back to Shireton a mighty suspicious man.

And the infuriating thing was that he'd told me all about it. I'd wondered why he hadn't given me a straight tip about that brunette. But he had. It was the postscript to that second letter.

On second thoughts, not the M.C. Something very different.

There it was. Most of what he'd called cryptic had been rightly interpreted, but not that. And it had said that Myra Cowle was not Myra Cowle but quite a different person.

How he was traced to the George and by whom I didn't know. Maybe Alf had been watching him for Laver. But both she and Laver must have been pretty nervy when Loame dragged things out. She must have been very near the breaking point, if it was she who had killed Godfrey. And she'd have been worrying if he had let anything drop to the agency and in spite of his pledges of secrecy. Even if Laver had killed him, then her name might have come out and her connection with Mallett. When a murder verdict was brought in and the Yard took over, she must have been frantic. *She just had to know.*

Who thought of the scheme? Laver or she? I didn't know, but once more it was simple. She became a blonde, though that would have been a natural precaution against being recognised by a possible witness at Shireton. Then she made friends with Myra Cowle, dropping in at the Salon and spending money. There would follow an invitation to Chester Hall, perhaps, and: "I hate to be personal but are you the Myra Cowle whose uncle was murdered? I've got friends at Shireton and they told me all about it." And so to: "Did you ever recover those diamonds the paper spoke about?"

Then at last would come the suggestion.

"I know an Agency which they say is awfully good. Why don't you let them try to find the diamonds? It wouldn't cost much. I'll go in with you if you like. And suppose they found them!" And when Myra hardly liked the idea: "Why shouldn't I do it for you? I can say I'm you and they'd never know."

That was the idea for which Myra fell. That was her awfully big adventure. But Eileen wasn't worrying about diamonds. She wanted to get into the Agency and find out if we knew anything about a certain brunette who'd been a friend of Godfrey Prial. And I fell for her, hook, line and sinker. I thought she was shy. I could sympathise with how she wanted secrecy.

But, and it was the essential *but*, Eileen Masters never intended that we should take up any case. Once she was reasonably sure that we knew nothing about herself—and obviously we didn't—then she was telling Myra that we weren't all we'd been described and the scheme ought to be abandoned. And then I said something about reports.

That was it. *Reports* that would say what we were doing, and tell her and Laver what we knew. And after that, as Laver would insist, she had to go on. If she had given Myra a bad account of us, then she had had to change her tune. But there was the insistence on absolute secrecy. No calling at the Salon and no telephoning. Nothing but reports marked *Personal*. So Eileen was shown the contract and Myra signed it and the cheque.

That would have been at Chester Hall, and it was there that Myra took that first report on the Monday evening. And once I'd said that I knew about Copley's Corner, Myra signed her death warrant. She knew too much. And that scheme had to be dropped. Eileen Masters had to disappear.

That roughly was what had happened, and some of it I should have known. There were questions I should have asked myself. Why had everyone spoken of Myra as delightful and charming, when I had seen her as nothing of the kind? I had complacently thought my own judgment correct. I was the only man in the battalion who was not out of step. And there were plenty of other things. That morbid wish for secrecy, for instance. How, now I came to think of it, could being the heiress to a murdered man be a likely cause of disaster to a flourishing business?

As soon as I saw her I should have known she was not a genuine blonde: even that she was naturally a brunette. Blondes don't have brown eyes. Their eyes are a blue or a steely grey. And there was something even more obvious that should at the very least have made me suspicious. Hadn't Hallows and I been telling ourselves that our baiting of Laver would force him to take some sort of action? Yet when that action came and the self-called Myra Cowle turned up at the very precise moment in my office, I took it as merely a stroke of luck.

But there it was and there I left it. It had begun as a report and it ended with recrimination, and, as I said, a telephone call might give me all the answers. But of at least one thing I was sure—that whatever I heard from Jewle, most of what I had written was absolutely true.

CHAPTER 17
AFTERMATH

I HATE TO BE pestered with other people's dreams, and that's why I won't bore you with mine. But you may guess I didn't sleep any too well that night, and when I did doze off I kept dreaming about that poor devil Monaghan. Maybe the subconscious was at work for when I woke up I had an idea. But I daren't leave the house to test it out for at any moment I was expecting to hear from Jewle. He didn't ring but he turned up unexpectedly at about midday. He couldn't stay more than a minute, he said, but he just had to thank me.

"You needn't thank me," I said, "Godfrey Prial's the one to thank."

He didn't see it.

"What he hid in that snuff-box," I said. "I don't mean the two finger-prints. I mean that telephone number. I might have searched all England and never come up against that Masters woman."

"Yes," he said. "Funny how things turn out. You might say he acted as his own hangman, if you know what I mean. He's the one who got Laver and Masters hanged."

"Never a doubt," he said. "Both accusing each other. Giving everything away. Alf's been picked up too. Both of them swear he did the Myra Cowle job. Remanded in custody, all three of them, this morning."

"Well, that's that then," I said. "I'm out of it and all you've got to do is marshal your facts. That shouldn't be any trouble."

"No," he said. "Just something I *would* like, though. I'd like to have those diamonds. Talk about sensation in court! The most damning piece of evidence we'd have."

"A lot of people'd like them," I told him. "They wouldn't do me any harm for one. I expect Colonel Pengold wouldn't mind either."

"Well, you can't have everything," he said, and held out his hand and said he'd have to be off.

"Any chance of reaching you this afternoon?" I said. "Say round about tea-time?"

He said I could leave a message.

"Likely to be busy tomorrow?"

He said he'd probably be up to the eyes.

"Even if I wanted you to go and have a look for those diamonds?"

He stared.

"You know something?"

"Can't say," I said. "But what about meeting me at Shireton George tomorrow morning? At about ten."

He gave me another quick look and shook his head. Not because he wouldn't be able to make it, but for the queerness of Ludovic Travers.

"All right, sir," he said. "I'll be there. All I hope is you'll have something good."

I had lunch and then went out to a little shop in Soho. I had a talk with the proprietor and from that shop I rang Colonel Pengold. I asked him if he could meet me at Shireton George at ten the next morning. He was a bit puzzled even when I said I didn't think he'd be wasting his time. I told him a train to take and he said he'd be there.

I went to the flat and broke the news to Bernice that I'd be away for the night, and for the last time, I hoped, for a good long while. Then I took a bus for Liverpool Street and got a train to Shireton. I booked for the night at the Suffolk and then hired a car to take me to Puckford.

I asked to see Dr. Goodrow and was glad to hear he was back. I guessed he was at his tea for I had a long wait. When I did see him I had to tell him frankly that I was there on behalf of Chief-Inspector Jewle of Scotland Yard. He didn't ask to see my warrant card; he was far too interested for that. Then I had to eat a few of my own words, and when I came to what I wanted him to do, he was almost horrified. I said I'd rather have his willing co-operation than have to get an order, and that changed his tune. And I'd brought something with me that might help things, and finally he agreed to co-operate. I said that Jewle and I would be along at about a quarter-past ten in the morning.

It was too late for tea but I had my pint in the bar and a chat with Minnie. She was delighted when I told her our thick-eared friend might soon be taking the long drop, though that, I admit, was wishful thinking. I was in the bar again after dinner. In fact I had quite a few drinks that night. I thought I'd need them if I was going to get a good night's rest. As it happened, I was asleep as soon as my head warmed the pillow, and it was after my usual time when I woke.

Jewle had met Colonel Pengold in the course of that week-end check-up. And Jewle had been to Puckford as I'd guessed, so I didn't have to show him the way, and on that short drive in the police car he and Pengold were trying to worm out of me what I expected to find, and how. Jewle thought I'd hit on some method of making Monaghan talk, and I was giving nothing away. After all, I had nothing to go on but what might have been a highly delusive recollection.

For the first time at the Mental Home there wasn't long to wait. I introduced the Colonel. Goodrow and Jewle had met before. I couldn't help noticing what was on the desk.

"No trouble to get it, Doctor?"

"Just a mild sedative," he said, "then we sewed the one you brought on his waistcoat instead. He doesn't seem aware of the difference; at any rate he was fingering it quite happily just now."

"Excuse me," said Jewle, "but isn't that that rosary of old Monaghan's? I seem to remember him fiddling with it when I saw him there."

"This is it," I said. "Notice the different sizes of the beads?"

You may have guessed for quite a time where those diamonds were. They knew when I picked up the rosary. The bottle of methylated was ready and I half filled the beaker. I rubbed those larger beads with my fingers and the methylated was brown. It took three rubbings before those diamonds were reasonably clean.

Goodrow merely raised amused eyebrows. Jewle was staring, and Pengold peering.

"Drilled Indian stones," he told us. "See how yellow they are? And not too well cut?"

We poured out some more methylated and rubbed them again and got them dry. There they were, nineteen of them.

"Right under my nose all the time," Jewle told us indignantly. "I was so near to that Monaghan I could have had them out of his hand. How'd you come to rumble it, Mr. Travers?"

"Various things," I said. "I thought I knew all about rosaries, but I didn't. I thought it might be quite common to have different sized beads to mark the Our Fathers, for instance. Or a whole ten of Hail Marys like this bottom row. But I was wrong. I was in St. James's Park the other day and I passed quite close to a nun and I happened to notice that all the beads of her rosary were the same size. Then the Colonel had told me about these Indian drilled stones and—well there we were."

Jewle still seemed to think that fate had played him a dirty trick. He even had a grievance against that poor devil, Monaghan.

"What made him do it?" he wanted to know.

I said it was pretty logical, at least to me. I wasn't going to risk a second ticking off in that room by analysing states of mind, but everybody in Stadmore had regarded Monaghan as feeble-minded. I preferred to call it childishly simple. Mallett had roused him that night to give him the diamonds, and had told him to hand them over to no one but the grand-daughter. Maybe Monaghan hadn't liked that grand-daughter. He'd shown the aversion when she visited him in the Home. And he'd been attracted by the flash of the stones; attracted as a jackdaw might be. So he refashioned his original rosary, darkening the stones with Brunswick black or something similar that dried hard and matched the black of the smaller beads. That's all there was to it, unless the Doctor wanted to add a rider.

Goodrow smiled dryly and said that all he needed was a receipt. Jewle gave him one, and there was the usual handshaking and out we went. The Colonel said we ought to have a drink to celebrate, so after a few minutes at the Suffolk we set off back to town in Jewle's car. Pengold wondered if it would be too much trouble to come in by Regent Street, where there was a friend of his at the Goldsmiths and Silversmiths who'd probably give us a rough idea of the value of those nineteen stones. Jewle thought it a good idea.

So we saw the Colonel's friend and he had another expert in, and the two of them thought the stones were worth about five thousand pounds.

"Five thousand," Jewle was later to say. "Two murders for a lousy five thousand!"

"Oh no," Pengold told him. "They wouldn't know they were Indian drilled stones. Ordinary four-carat stones would have meant nearer fifty thousand than five."

"The diamonds were the beginning," I said, "not the end. Prial was almost certainly killed because of what he turned up about Laver and Masters. If he could have proved that Laver, for instance, had attacked Monaghan that night, it might have meant anything up to ten years for Laver."

Poor Jewle would have had apoplexy if he'd known that I was hoping to collect seven hundred and fifty. But he was full of gratitude as he set us down at Piccadilly, and as he tapped his breast pocket he told me that what was there was so many nails in I-knew-who's coffins.

I took the Colonel to my club. He rang his wife from there and then we had lunch. When I left him he was still delighted at—as he put it—the fact that he was going to pay me quite a slab of money. He wasn't a wealthy man but I could see he had a hankering to keep those stones himself. As for the seven-fifty, I'd already spent it in my mind. I'd recoup myself for expenses, give Hallows a bonus of a hundred, and add the rest to that trust fund that Godfrey had initiated. Somehow I couldn't make money out of Godfrey Prial.

I met Hallows that afternoon and brought him bang up to date. I risked giving him his bonus, and it was queer that he too didn't want to make money out of Godfrey. I told him he was being quixotic and at last made him change his mind.

But there was something he said to me.

"Funny thing about that parson chap at Stadmore, Mr. Travers? I could have sworn he knew something about those diamonds, especially after what he did when they were deepening that well."

"Just shows how you can be deceived," I said. "A suspicion here and another there and before you know where you are you're building up a case against a man."

"Just a Nosey Parker, that's all he was," Hallows said. "Everyone said he couldn't keep his nose out of anything that went on. He puzzled me, Mr. Travers, and that's a fact."

So there it was. My father was always telling me in my youth that only the fools never made mistakes, and by that paradox he meant, I now know, that a wise man owns to a mistake but never makes the same one twice.

I would add my own rider to that—that only a fool is afraid of losing face.

Why should I be ashamed of admitting to Hallows that I too had been wrong about Comfort? A white lie, but what did it matter? And who was I in any case to judge Comfort? Who was I to go to Stadmore Vicarage and tell Comfort just what I knew? Maybe it was a case of there but for the grace of God goes John Bradford. Should I have been a better man than Comfort if I had been in his place?

Consider the circumstances. Voles was going on holiday and he put money in his brother-in-law's way by making him—subject to the Governor's approval—his deputy while he was away. Comfort would have spoken to Mallett. Mallett, while he wouldn't reveal where those missing diamonds were, was worrying if his daughter had received that letter-card, and whether that girl had posted it. He confided in Comfort, and the confidences would be regarded as the secrets of the confessional.

And so to the temptation when Mallett was dead. Comfort desperately needed money. There was an ailing wife and constant doctor's bills. Above all there were those children of his, and especially that eldest boy. Was he to be denied a public school? Would he, and Comfort as well, have to lose face by having to attend some local school, with its lack of everything that, according to Comfort's valuations, could fashion and make a gentleman? There was the girl too, and the younger boy to follow on, and I could tell myself that Comfort had certainly been tempted.

That was why he had called on Monaghan. He had been going to see him that night when Laver was there. That explained the storing of the furniture, the visits to the Mental Home, the searches at night at Copley's Corner, and the last hope that those diamonds might have been thrown into the well.

But, as I said, who was I to judge or condemn. What Comfort had done would recoil upon himself when he read how those diamonds had been found and how the things for which he had sacrificed more than mere principles had been over and again within his very grasp; and when I thought of that there was even a furtive pity. And then as I strolled along towards the flat, and was thinking of everything that had happened, I suddenly realised something else. Bernice had had a part in things. Maybe she ought to have something of a bonus. Maybe I'd disposed of that seven-fifty a bit too speedily, and all at once I found myself polishing my glasses as I pondered the nicely calculated less and more, and I shuddered as I remembered that more than once recently she had hinted at a car of her own. Then even in that there was a small mercy. Thank heaven she had never seen that four-figure coupé that had been parked one night at Chester Hall.

THE END